NIAGARA FALLS PUBLIC LIBRARY

Y0-CPC-181

# MURDER
# AMONG
# GENTLEMEN

394.8 Hal

Murder among gentlemen.
Halliday, H.


PRICE: $15.47 ( ONF/an/v)

# TO THE PUBLIC.

HAVING been grossly and wantonly insulted yesterday, in the Streets of Bytown, by Edward V. Cortlandt, and having promptly demanded from that individual (through a friend) the usual satisfaction, which that cowardly miscreant, without assigning any reason, refused to grant.

I have no other course left to me, but to proclaim to the world, and I now do so, that *Edward Van Cortlandt, Surgeon,* of this place, is a mean and contemptible liar. slanderer, and ruffian ; a miserable, drivelling, cowardly scoundrel, a pitiful poltroon, and utterly unworthy of the notice of any one having pretensions to the character of a gentleman.

## R. HERVEY, Jr.

Bytown, Saturday Morning,
19th August, 1848.

"Posting" your grievances against the other party and demanding satisfaction was often part of the sequence of events leading to a duel. (Bytown Museum)

# MURDER AMONG GENTLEMEN

---

## A HISTORY OF DUELLING IN CANADA

---

HUGH A. HALLIDAY

⤳

ROBIN BRASS STUDIO
*Toronto*

Copyright © Hugh A. Halliday 1999

All rights reserved. No part of this publication may be stored in a
retrieval system, translated or reproduced in any form or by any
means, photocopying, electronic or mechanical, without written
permission of the publisher.

Published 1999 by Robin Brass Studio
10 Blantyre Avenue, Toronto, Ontario M1N 2R4, Canada
Fax: 416-698 2120
e-mail: rbrass@total.net
www.total.net/~rbrass

Printed and bound in Canada


**Canadian Cataloguing in Publication Data**

Halliday, Hugh A., 1940–
    Murder among gentlemen : a history of duelling in Canada

Includes bibliographical references and index.
ISBN 1-896941-09-5

1. Dueling – Canada – History. I. Title.

CR4595.C2H34 1999    394'.8    C00-932423-3

NIAGARA FALLS PUBLIC LIBRARY

JAN 2 9 2001

# Contents

From a 19th-century French print. (Toronto Reference Library)

✿

# Preface

Duelling is not a subject that many Canadians associate with their history. This is scarcely surprising; such incidents were infrequent in the nation's past, and with few exceptions were confined to the central and Atlantic regions. Moreover, they were relatively insignificant in their impact on social developments; the Warde–Sweeney duel of 1838 may have been more spectacular (or at least more melodramatic) than Lord Durham's mission that year, but there is no question which was more important, the former being a murderous row between two historical nonentities while the latter markedly advanced Canadian constitutional development. Indeed, far from influencing events, duels more often reflected current social or political situations. The rash of duels in Lower Canada in the 1830s was the outcome, not the cause, of prevailing tensions.

Here and there particular duels have attracted local attention. The Jarvis–Ridout tragedy of 1817, climaxing a bitter family feud, has been mentioned in histories of Toronto, and in Newfoundland Joseph R. Smallwood has done much to publicize the Rudkin–Philpot duel of 1826. Perhaps the best known encounter is the Wilson–Lyon duel of 1833, which has become a part of Ottawa Valley folklore, celebrated in song by Stompin' Tom Connors[1] and in a regionally produced play.[2] That combat has been described by many, notably the tourism boosters of Perth, Ontario, as "the last fatal duel in this country," which it was not. Since 1982, when this writer brought the Warde–Sweeney duel to Perth's attention, spokesmen for that town have endeavoured to sweep it under the rug with the dubious argument that the incident of 1838 did not constitute a proper duel. At the same time, Perth has continued to trumpet a false claim. Civic pride demands that a dubious honour be upheld, and damn the facts of history.[3]

The Perth duel has been the most frequently described in Canada, but in fact there is a considerable body of literature dealing with these events. Some of the best articles have appeared in scholarly or legal publications. The only general overview of the subject, Aegidius Fauteux's *Le Duel au Canada*,[4] has neither been reprinted nor published in English translation since its appearance in 1934. Nevertheless, the bibliography at the end of this book demonstrates that the subject has been well covered by earlier writers. Canadians who complain that "nobody teaches these things" simply have not been paying attention.

Duelling as a subject lends itself to romantic myth-making. Any serious study must lead to the conclusion that duels were actually vicious, immature violations of the public peace, tantamount to conspiracies to murder in which the victim had not yet been chosen, but with the field of candidates narrowed down to two. They were also manifestations of class snobbery; self-styled "gentlemen" reserved to themselves the right to violate the law, and other "gentlemen" (judges, jurors, Crown counsel) covered up for them by either not pressing criminal charges or arranging acquittals that flew in the face of the law. The fatal duel was indeed "murder among gentlemen," and to that murder there were often many accessories.

In preparing this work, I have received assistance from several persons and institutions. The chapter dealing with Atlantic Canada owes much to Robert S. Elliot, formerly of the New Brunswick Museum, who was generous with his own research notes on duels in that region. Robert J. Burns of Parks Canada pointed out some additional encounters in central Canada. Contributions from Britain's National Army Museum, the Detroit Public Library and the Windsor Public Library were also most valuable in rounding out accounts of various duels. Tim Dubé of the National Archives of Canada suggested valuable sources on the Warde–Sweeney duel and was helpful with numerous details.

Historical works are seldom definitive; I am aware that, even after many years of research and revising, several parts of this book are incomplete. Exactly what provoked the Gilbert–Wilson duel of 1836? Who were the principals in the vaguely reported March Township duel? Precisely when did Lieutenant John Evans kill Lieutenant John Ogilvy? What other duels have escaped notice?

Yet eventually one must put an end to private research and revision if there is to be a public sharing of findings. Perhaps readers will be able to supply some of the answers to the questions raised in this volume.

Duelling has been widely used as a metaphor for politics. In this cartoon by Henri Julien in the *Canadian Illustrated News*, June 12, 1875, Charles-Eugène de Boucherville (left), premier of Quebec, is challenged by the leader of the opposition, Henri-Gustav Joly de Lotbinière. (National Archives of Canada C-62731)

# Chapter 1

# The Deadly Ritual

Duelling has attracted considerable literary attention over the past 400 years, although today it is principally a metaphor for single combat or direct conflict involving limited parties. Modern political cartoons have employed the duelling image. Books and films on military topics occasionally feature allusions to events being duels, be they of wits or weapons. Books on duelling itself have appeared, from "how to" manuals (chiefly in the use of swords and rapiers) to sociological studies.

Early writers, seeking to explain duelling, sought examples in Biblical as well as Classical works; David and Goliath were trotted out as proto-duellists, along with Hector against Achilles. Gladiatorial contests and medieval "trial by battle" were also cited as precedents. Apart from their dubious historiography, these authors confused different types of combat. The gladiator forced to battle to the death with a stranger could hardly be compared to a duellist who exercised some choice in whether to offer or accept a challenge.

Trial by combat was a judicial procedure (linked with trial by ordeal) in which the proceedings were watched and refereed by a court official (sometimes the king himself). Eventually churchmen recognized (though scarcely admitted) that God did not regularly intervene in legal contests, and feared (rightly) that such encounters merely perpetuated blood feuds, particularly in countries such as Scotland and Ireland where clan allegiances frequently overshadowed dynastic or national loyalties. Monarchs viewed such deadly arbitrations with mixed feelings. Early Norman kings of England tried to discourage them, lest the conquerors do so much mutual damage as to weaken their class vis-à-vis a hostile Saxon populace. The development of circuit courts, trial by jury, professional lawyers and expert judges further undermined "trial by battle," which faded away before the Renaissance – about the time that the modern duel began to emerge in European society.

Duelling was rooted in class consciousness, and the most curious thing about the practice was its growth among aristocracies even as those groups began losing power to autocratic kings, national assemblies, professional bureaucrats and merchants. It was particularly prominent where moribund upper classes continued to lord their self-perceived superiority over groups whom they wished either to humiliate or intimidate. This was most marked in its period of decline, when duelling was particularly common among slave-holders – the West Indies and the American south being the most notorious instances. V.G. Kiernan, in his analysis of the practice, described it as "a vestigial survival of the early feudal right of private warfare" and ascribed it to aristocracies that were becoming increasing irrelevant. They fought precisely because the practice was against the law, and thus asserted their claim to some superiority above the common herd. As upper-class fortunes waned, sensitivities seemed to increase; Kiernan explains the propensity of Frederick the Great's army officers to duel as the outcome of many being landowners "with more ancestors than acres."[1]

Kiernan's thesis is particularly striking when he compares European attitudes towards the duel with those elsewhere in the world. Islam preached egalitarianism and discouraged the practice. Wrestling and competitions of physical endurance were the norm in settling disputes. In 1547 the Turkish ambassador to the French court expressed amazement that such methods were even tolerated by the king.[2]

The futility of duelling was most apparent as it began to evolve. There was little to distinguish between brawls and duels. Men hacking at one another with swords were apt to inflict terrible wounds, leaving even a survivor scarred and crippled. When seconds joined the fray, mayhem increased exponentially. A French duel in 1578 involved two principals and four seconds; when it was over, one of the main parties was dead, the other wounded and on the run, and three of the four seconds were dead as well. The bloodbath had been witnessed only by three or four "poor persons, wretched witnesses of the valour of these worthy men"; the duellists may have been particularly ferocious, knowing that they had a peasant audience to impress. An Italian duellist, having killed his opponent, was confronted by three successive challengers, each bent on avenging their friend, and all of whom were despatched.[3]

In recognition of these excesses, courts of honour attempted to deter challenges made for frivolous reasons. These courts were particularly common in the 16th century and were most useful when the higher nobility was involved. Monarchs – Elizabeth I most notably – kept a close eye on their courtiers and intervened to prevent the loss of valued advisors. But lesser aristocrats and those with patrician pretensions either duelled impetuously or ignored the existing avenues of mediation.

Gradually a number of duelling codes evolved to mitigate the worst features of the practice. Hasty meetings were discouraged; a few hours between challenge and confrontation allowed time for tempers to cool and compromises to be discussed. If a meeting could not be avoided, the presence of seconds was essential, for without witnesses there would be no way to prove that an encounter had been anything other than ambush or murder. At the same time, the survival of the witnesses dictated that they should not become directly involved. Duellists stripped down to their shirts, not only to have maximum freedom of movement but also to prove that they sought no advantage from concealed body armour. The codes varied in detail with time and place; by 1840 the French followed a set of rules with eighty-four clauses covering pistols, sabres and rapiers, explaining what constituted "duellable" offences, when reconciliations could be negotiated, and the roles of seconds. It stipulated that swords had to be of equal length with points only (no sharp or notched edges), that the minimum distance with pistols should be fifteen paces, and that a wounded man was allowed one minute to return fire upon his opponent – unless he had fallen to the ground, in which case he was allowed two minutes.

The combat itself became a ritual based upon necessity. Weapons associated with lower classes – longbows, pikes, cudgels and clubs – were shunned. Military duellists resorting to swordplay were assumed to be more or less equal; when pistols appeared they found favour because they were deemed to place civilians on about the same footing as an officer adversary. Opponents in pistol duels regularly stood roughly sideways to one another, presenting the smallest possible target to the enemy. The firing arm was raised straight out; this also offered slight protection. Shooting at close quarters was necessitated by the inaccuracy of early firearms (the same situation that compelled armies for 200 years to march upon one another in straight lines and open fire at close to point-blank range).

Monarchs tried halfheartedly to suppress duelling. James VI of Scotland was particularly annoyed that upon his ascension to the English throne (as James I), Scottish courtiers following him to London battled frequently with their southern counterparts. Local governors and military commanders had varying success in controlling the practice. One of the more ingenious was a French general occupying Turin between 1545 and 1550. Duellists had been meeting publicly on a bridge; he compelled them to fight on the parapet, a supplementary order stating that any combatant who lost his balance should not be rescued but be left to drown.[4] Gustavus Adolphus of Sweden and Peter the Great of Russia both threatened to hang the surviving party of any fatal duel. Indeed, royal efforts to suppress duelling altogether may have encouraged the drafting of codes that mitigated its worst excesses.

The evolution of duelling coincided with the development of the modern theatre. Not surprisingly, events in the streets were mirrored on the stage. Tybalt's encounter, first with Mercutio, then with Romeo, was as chaotic as it was tragic (the impromptu challenge was one of the real vices of early confrontations). Falstaff as duellist was a figure to be ridiculed. Sir Toby Belch was equally ludicrous in teaching a friend how to write an intimidating challenge. Christopher Marlowe warned against hasty quarrels, only to die in a tavern brawl. Many other writers followed, introducing duels into their works as incidents of drama as well as comedy. Their depictions ranged from Lewis Carroll's ridiculous sparring match between Tweedledum and Tweedledee to Tennyson's tragic duel in *Maud*, where a young man tries to sever the relationship between his sister and her preferred lover. Brother and lover exchange fire; the brother dies; the guilt-ridden lover joins the army.

England, France and Spain exported to their colonies their habits of governance and society; local conditions and custom soon modified these practices. The hard-nosed Puritanism of the New England colonies discouraged duels just as surely as Oliver Cromwell's Roundheads managed, briefly, to snuff them out in England between 1649 and 1658. Colonial garrisons included many bored officers whose only diversions were drink and gambling – both sure to inflame tempers and lead to challenges. This was especially true in British India and was almost as bad in the post-Revolutionary American army.

The most conspicuous duellists in British North America were lawyers and merchants who, having acquired a veneer of culture and a claim to be a local aristocracy, seized upon any device to assert their primacy. "Respectability" was measured in terms of land owned, income earned, public offices held (or handed on to friends and family) and even the number of servants employed. In 1793 the Militia Law enacted for Upper Canada stated that a man had to own at least

400 acres before he could be considered eligible to hold the rank of colonel or lieutenant colonel, 300 acres to be a major or captain, and 200 acres to hold a junior commission. These rules were not incorporated in the revised Militia Law of 1800, but there can be little doubt that colonial societies were riven by class distinctions deliberately created by individuals anxious to set themselves off from their neighbours. There were few so proud as those who had just managed to get one rung up on what was really a very short societal ladder. Most Canadian duellists would have been regarded as country bumpkins by the patrician classes in England, and only a rare colonial duel (notably the Bowie–Uniacke encounter) was even noticed by British reporters or authors. In the international realm of duelling, Canadians were small fry, and their encounters decidedly *déclassé*.

A DISGRACEFUL DUEL IMMINENT.

Another example of politics compared to duelling. In this case, an early version of Uncle Sam prepares to square off against Sir John A. Macdonald in a tariff war. This cartoon by J.W. Bengough appeared in *Grip* on September 15, 1888. (National Archives of Canada, C-6452)

# Chapter 2

# New
# France

Seventeenth-century France was notorious for its quarrelsome nobility whose members so frequently sought the satisfaction of their
honour by resorting to duels. It was remarked, only half in jest, that
no gentleman could marry until he had killed at least one opponent
in single combat. The practice had become especially pernicious during the reign of Henry IV; it was estimated that between 1589 and
1607 some 4,000 nobles, gentry, and wealthy bourgeois had been
killed in single combat. The king had issued several edicts against
duels, but they were riddled with loopholes and Henry himself had
preferred to pardon duellists rather than enforce his own laws. The
ensuing reign of Louis XIII witnessed a similarly confused attitude
towards duels.

Louis XIV was anxious to stamp out the practice. During his reign
he issued at least ten edicts aimed at discouraging or outlawing duels. The first, published in 1643, ordered all potential combatants to
refer their disputes to court marshals for arbitration; disobedience
would bring banishment for three years, official disgrace and forfeiture of one-half of one's property, regardless of the outcome of the
fight. A person who killed an opponent was to be executed; the victim would also be subject to criminal punishments involving loss of
honours and consignment of his body to a rubbish heap.

The fact that the king issued ten edits is itself a fair indication that they were widely ignored, even though penalties were increased and broadened. The *Édit des duels* of 1679, the most famous of Louis' pronouncements on the subject, made virtually any party subject to punishments, including witnesses and those who carried messages for the principals. The law, however, was enforced indifferently; great figures duelled without being prosecuted, and only rarely was a duellist hanged to make an example. There was no system to the application of the law. The Royal Will was known, but it was also scorned. Not surprisingly, New France saw ambivalent enforcement of those laws that sought to suppress duels.

Duels during the French régime were all conducted with swords; it was not until the period of English rule that pistols became the accepted weapon on the "field of honour." Documentation of duels was incomplete in this era. The printing press and newspaper were unknown in New France; legal records would be the historian's principal source of information, coupled with sketchy, often incomplete, official and ecclesiastical correspondence. Indeed, when writing of this time, the term "duel" must be loosely applied, for it is uncertain whether some incidents were conducted under formal rules or were simply spontaneous fights.

The first two Canadian duels are mentioned by Father Jérome Lallement in the *Jesuit Relations*. Writing in May 1646, he reported that two men employed in Quebec by the Ursulines had insulted each other and had then crossed swords; their names, the cause of their quarrel and the outcome were all omitted. At Trois Rivières two soldiers named La Groye and Lafontaine had fought a duel in which the former had been twice wounded. La Groye was probably the innocent party – Father Lallement described him as having "behaved discreetly, like a Christian" – and this was confirmed by evidence from the Indians. Lafontaine was punished by imprisonment in a pit.[1]

The Sovereign Council of New France took a harder line against duelling than the Common Law courts introduced into the colony after 1760. (National Archives of Canada C-13950)

Already we see the official attitude revealed; duelling under French law would be treated more seriously than by succeeding English administrations. This was made clear in 1669. About April 28 or 29 a soldier named François Blanche dit Langivan, of the garrison at Trois Rivières, killed a fellow soldier, Daniel Lemaire dit Desrochers. The victim was the first known fatality of a Canadian duel. Judicial proceedings were set in motion at once. They were climaxed on July 8 when the Sovereign Council[2] of the colony, meeting in Quebec, sentenced the victor to death by hanging and forfeiture of possessions. The penalty was exacted that afternoon, after which the body was exposed at Cape Diamond. Langivan's property went to the support of the newly founded Quebec Hospital.[3]

Two years later, in the spring of 1671, Montreal was shocked by a savage affray. Lieutenant Phillipe de Carion du Fresoy had conceived a violent hatred for an Ensign Roch Thoery de Lormeau. On May 19 the latter was walking home with his wife after Mass when de Carion, backed by two friends, confronted de Lormeau, bent on provoking a fight. Hot words were exchanged and the two men sprang at each other, swords at the ready. After several blows in which de Lormeau was thrice wounded, in the head and arm, they briefly wrestled. De Carion tried to stab his opponent in the stomach, and when that failed he used the handle of his sword to strike de Lormeau repeatedly on the head.

The duel (if such a term can be applied) might have had a fatal outcome but for the intervention of two priests and three civilians who rushed up and separated the combatants at considerable risk to themselves. One of the priests, Father Dollier de Casson, was a former cavalry officer and a great bull of a man, famed as much for his courage as for his intellect; his efforts probably were crucial in halting the fight. The little outpost town, only 1,200 souls, was scandalized by the brutality of the assault and the fact that it had occurred in the presence of Madame de Lormeau.

Montreal quickly became a brawling, unruly place, quite out of character with the religious ideals of its founders. On August 23, 1676, twenty-two-year-old Pierre Robineau de Bécancour was deep in his cups. The proud son of a knight in the Order of Saint Michael, he accused a local merchant, Claude Porlier, of having been disrespectful of that warrior saint. The merchant's denial seemed only to provoke the youth more, but Porlier declined to accept any challenge, pointing out that duels and secret meetings were forbidden by law.

That incident came to naught, but on June 27, 1678, a complaint was sworn out against several Montreal soldiers for having wounded a citizen with their swords. Twenty-five months later, on July 27,

1680, two officials were making an evening inspection of the town. Among other things, they were checking after-hours wine sales. In a tavern run by one Charles Testard de Folleville they observed several men drinking, including a prominent doctor and a servant of the local governor. The revellers emerged long enough to hurl stones at the officials and pursue them with drawn swords. Denis Marceau, who served also as Montreal's gaoler, was wounded in both hands and one arm. The tavern appears to have been a particularly notorious watering hole, for it was finally closed down by indignant authorities.[4]

François-Marie Perrot (1644-91), Governor of Montreal for fifteen years (1669-84), was both brave and corrupt; his wholesale involvement in the fur trade while holding office was as profitable as it was illegal. About June 24, 1684, he fought a duel with Jacques Le Moyne de Sainte-Hélène (1659-90), a belligerent member of a fighting family. The origin of their quarrel is obscure, nor is much known about their combat other than that it was in a public place and that each man was wounded slightly. The Governor of New France, Joseph-Antoine Le Febvre de la Barre, did not move against Perrot, knowing that the older man was about to be dismissed from his position, but orders went out that Le Moyne be arrested. The young man left Montreal until the affair had blown over. Six years later he died of infection from a bullet wound sustained during the Phips expedition against Quebec.

Hitherto, duels had been infrequent, but the population of New France was expanding. Moreover, the number of troops increased, a response to continuing Iroquois threats and the prospect of war with the English colonies to the south. Idle soldiers were given to drink and disputation. Duels and outright murders became more numerous. Of the former, at least four such incidents occurred between 1687 and 1691. The official response was contradictory. Duelling was denounced, but the law was unevenly applied, with officers escaping the worst consequences while common soldiers bore the brunt of legal displeasure.

The patchwork nature of the law was due in part to circumstances prevailing in North America. A person wishing to escape punishment could flee to the woods, to the English colonies, or even to another French colony; the edicts of a court in New France were not enforceable in Acadia or Guadeloupe, unless they dealt with horrendous state crimes. Then, too, in an atmosphere of real or apprehended war, authorities were reluctant to hound promising officers out of the colony, even when public order was disturbed.

An incident on September 8, 1687, illustrated the hazards when excessive drink went down the throat of a bored soldier. Jean Hubou de Longchamps dit Tourville had spent twelve hours in a Montreal tavern. He turned upon one of his companions and inflicted a wound with his sword; whether the victim was able to defend himself before others broke up the fight is uncertain. The aggressor had to pay a heavy fine, which was divided among the wounded man, the notary who heard the case and the doctor who had attended the victim.[5]

Whether this was a duel or a brawl is unclear, but there is less doubt about the next incident. Raymond Blais des Bergères de Rigauville (1655-1711), an officer of some distinction from Indian warfare, was ordered in 1689 to assume command of Fort St. Louis (modern Chambly). The post was already held by Captain François Lefebvre, Sieur Duplessis, who initially refused to step aside. The two men became enemies, and on July 15 they fought a duel in which des Bergères was wounded. Both combatants were imprisoned while the authorities investigated the incident. Eventually, in November 1689, the case was reviewed by the Sovereign Council of New France. Each duellist claimed that the other had started the fight, but witnesses testified that Lefebvre had been the aggressor; he was ordered to pay court costs and a heavy fine of 600 livres to des Bergères. Both men had to pay modest sums to colonial charities. Curiously, the formal charge of having duelled was dismissed.

Raymond Blais des Bergères de Rigauville kept the command of Fort St. Louis until 1696; later he was given charge of Fort Frontenac

(Kingston) and after that he took over Fort St. Louis again. In spite of his adventurous life, he preferred quiet ease, which he at last gained with an administrative post in Trois Rivières.

A more serious affair in October 1690 saw two officers of the Montreal garrison duelling. Captain Bosson or du Bosson (not further identified) was apparently attacked for no good reason by Ensign Joseph du Bocage. Bosson, a veteran campaigner, was wounded in one leg but was able to slay his adversary. Governor Frontenac ordered an investigation but referred the case to Paris for final disposal, noting that he considered Bosson to have been the victim of an unprovoked assault. Details are lacking, but in April 1692 the royal court wrote Frontenac, advising him that Bosson had been acquitted and would be resuming his duties in Canada. This apparently did not happen, for in June of that year he appeared in Guadeloupe, still holding commissioned rank. Metropolitan officials in France were particularly zealous at that time in suppressing duels; the fact that Bosson escaped severe punishment indicates that others agreed with Frontenac that the successful duellist had been an innocent party who had killed in self defence.

Yet another duel, this one in Quebec, occurred on the night of February 17, 1691. Captain Guillaume de Lorimier de la Rivière (1655-1709) and Pierre Payen de Noyan (1663-1707), both captains, were at a gathering of officers in the Lower Town when they quarrelled over the winnings of a gambling game. They hacked at each other fiercely until the former was wounded in the back and the latter in the hand. The duellists were ordered to keep to their quarters during investigations. In the case of de Lorimier there was no choice; his injuries were so severe that late in March the Sovereign Council acceded to his request that he be excused from travelling to the Upper Town to testify. Instead, evidence was taken at the house where he was confined. Both men were fined 50 livres, payable to charity, and were briefly deprived of their commissions. The two were counted as good officers and saw subsequent honourable service. De Lorimier, however, had a penchant for getting into trouble; in 1707 he was fined for slandering a Montreal butcher, then beating the man with the flat of his sword.

The authorities were alarmed at what seemed to have become a duelling epidemic. Immediately after the trial of de Lorimier and de Noyan, the Sovereign Council ordered that the royal *Édit des duels* of 1679 be publicized in the colonial towns. For a time it seemed to have the desired effect. On January 7, 1698, however, the body of Sergeant Henri Begard dit Lafleur was found on a Quebec street. A brief investigation revealed that he had been killed in a duel with a Sergeant Dubé (first name not cited) who had already fled to the wilderness. The killer would be tried *in absentia* and outlawed.

Authorities vented their anger on Lafleur's corpse. It was placed on trial, complete with witnesses, surgeon's reports, defence counsel and formal indictments. The body was convicted of "having fought and been killed in a duel." Punishment was harsh. Begard's memory was declared forever shamed, his possessions were forfeited to the Crown, and his corpse was dragged face down through the streets before being tossed onto a rubbish heap. No such treatment had been accorded any previous victim of a Canadian duel – it was certainly worse than that accorded Joseph du Bocage, who had been given an honourable Christian burial in 1690 – and it is evident that Begard's modest rank had been held against him. Duelling by common soldiers was not merely criminal – it was vulgar!

The point was emphasized again eight years later. On the night of October 23, 1706, Sergeant Emmanuel Fouré dit Ladvocat fatally wounded Private Charles Legris dit David in Quebec. The latter died the following day. Fouré went into hiding and was never taken. In April 1707, six months after the duel, the Sovereign Council tried and convicted both soldiers. The treatment accorded Begard (shamed memory, forfeiture of goods, desecration of the body) was to be meted out to Legris, but the corpse had already been buried, so the punishment of dragging through the streets was inflicted on an effigy. The victor was to be hanged and garrotted publicly, but as he was not in custody this sentence was also carried out in effigy. The process was reported to Louis XIV, who personally commended the authorities for setting an example that would, it was felt, discourage duelling.

The need for such disincentives was evident. In another case tried in 1706 the Sovereign Council had acquitted two officers (Jacques-Charles Renaud sieur Dubuisson and Jean-Joseph Foucault sieur Mouzens) of duelling charges – then had warned them to keep the peace lest the ordinances be applied against them. Such a hypocritical disposal of the issue would not inspire others to obey the law, and on November 1, 1708, Quebec experienced yet another bloody cut-and-thrust affair, this one involving common soldiers, one Chateauneuf (not further identified) and a Claude Dufay. The former was wounded in the chest and died two days later. Dufay was arrested and taken to the General Hospital for treatment of a wound; he contrived to escape and thus avoided direct punishment. Once again, trials were ordered for both duellists – *post mortem* for one, *in absentia* for the other. The council's final rulings are not known.

One of the most curious tales of duelling illustrates how the law might be evaded, or at least how it was softened to meet conditions. Jacques Maleray de Noiré de la Mollerie (1657-1704) killed a fellow officer in a duel in France (1685). He fled to New France, where he served with great distinction in the frontier wars; at the same time he was beyond the reach of metropolitan courts that had condemned him to death and disgrace. In 1693, with royal assent, he was allowed to return to France. Supported by numerous officials including Governor Frontenac, Maleray petitioned for a pardon, which was granted in 1695.

Jacques Maleray died at sea, apparently during an action with English ships, in 1704. Two of his sons were subsequently involved in duelling incidents of their own. On December 16, 1714, Louis-Hector

Maleray died in Montreal from wounds suffered the previous day. Jean d'Ailleboust, chevalier d'Argenteuil, had heard reports that Maleray had insulted and ridiculed him behind his back. The confrontation that followed led to words, blows and swordplay. The victor fled to New England and then to Martinique, where he appealed for a royal pardon. Back in New France he was outlawed and beheaded in effigy, but in 1719 the desired pardon was granted. In September 1716 Jacques Maleray, the younger brother of Louis-Hector, killed Charles Fusel, a merchant, in a Quebec tavern. He too fled into exile, was executed in effigy and secured a royal pardon in 1720.

Another duellist who saved himself by flight was François Mangeant.[6] Variously described as a doctor and a clerk, he was employed chiefly as a trader and ship owner in the lower St. Lawrence. In the summer of 1726 he killed Joseph-Alphonse Lestage, the master of a ship owned by Mangeant, while it was near Gaspé. The victor fled to Annapolis Royal, the former Acadian capital that was now under English rule. He swore a deposition claiming that he had killed Lestage in a duel after having been grossly insulted and provoked; the fugitive placed himself under the protection of the British crown. Although granted a royal pardon by the French court in 1732, Mangeant remained in Nova Scotia until his death. He was not an easy subject, for he quarrelled bitterly with some officials and was unpopular with Acadian settlers. However, he appears to have avoided swordplay during his voluntary exile.

Louis-Jacques-Charles Renaud Dubuisson (1709-65), son of the 1706 duellist, and Charles Hertel de Chambly were Canadian-born and were military cadets on the verge of being commissioned. On January 12, 1736, at Trois Rivières, they fell into a drunken brawl during which Hertel challenged his comrade to battle. He received a wound in the lower abdomen and succumbed two days later. On February 17 a court martial denounced the memory of Hertel and sentenced Dubuisson to death by firing squad.

The penalty could not be exacted, for the successful duellist had fled to Albany, New York. He was imprisoned there for eleven months on suspicion of spying. Once he had been freed, he went to Martinique, from where he maintained a steady flow of appeals to Paris and Quebec, pleading for a pardon. Louis XV declined to act until the colonial courts, notably the Superior Council, had rendered their judgement. The wheels of justice turned slowly in New France. In part this was because the investigating officer was embarrassed through being related to both duellists! Moreover, a protracted search for reliable witnesses was unsuccessful. With the legal process stalemated in New France, the metropolitan court finally granted a pardon. Dubuisson returned to his native land, where local authorities ratified the royal decision; the Superior Council formally cleared him of all charges relating to duelling in September 1740. He resumed his military career and fought bravely in the campaigns of 1759-60, but retired to France after the capitulation. The former exile was awarded the Cross of St. Louis in 1762; ultimately he chose to die under French colours.

The distinction between duel and brawl was not particularly apparent on January 10, 1738. Timothy Sullivan (1690-1749), an Irish-born doctor living in Montreal, had invented a colourful pedigree to suit his vanity. His marriage to Marie-Renée Gaultier de Varennes had linked him to a powerful colonial family. Nevertheless, he beat his wife repeatedly, and on this day he was confronted by Madame Sullivan's brother and nephew, who were intent on removing her from Sullivan's rages. The doctor held them off with a sword and poker, beat his wife once more and shouted at all of them. He paused to dress the nephew's finger, which had been cut during the affray, then resumed the quarrel. The domestic dispute ended up in the courts, with Sullivan attempting to prosecute the two other men for assault. While hearings were in process, he attacked a court usher, wounded the man, treated the cuts and forced the victim to drink with him. Madame Sullivan, having petitioned at one time for a separation, forgave her erratic husband and supported him in succeeding disputes.

Formal duels, as distinct from impromptu incidents such as the Sullivan affair, seemed to go out of fashion for a time. Fauteux suggests that authorities simply ignored such contests if no fatalities occurred.[7] On January 27, 1748, however, two merchants writing to a client described some recent incidents which, though newsworthy, did not appear to interest those charged with keeping the peace:

> We have learned of recent swordplay in Montreal, first between Mssrs de Pensence and de Lery, and secondly involving Mssrs de Jumonville and de la Bourdonnais. Two are reported as being hospitalized. These gentlemen with their miserable affairs! They should save their courage to fight our enemies.[8]

However much the law officers tried to ignore duels, three such incidents in 1751 attracted enough attention to merit court proceedings. The first, which occurred on January 26, 1751, had an unusually romantic outcome. Two soldiers of the Quebec garrison, in their cups, exchanged insults in a tavern before adjourning to a suburb to duel. The pair clashed swords for a few minutes, paused, then renewed the fight. One, a man named Coffre, was nicked in a finger. Blood had been spilled, honour redeemed, and the two returned to the tavern to resume their imbibing.

The affair aroused official ire, probably because once more mere soldiers had dared to dabble in gentlemanly combat. Warrants were sent out for the arrest of the principals. Coffre fled, but Jean Corolère was sentenced to a year in prison, and as further investigations were being conducted, he faced the prospect of even more drastic punishment after that.

A young woman, Françoise Laurent,[9] was in the adjacent cell, awaiting execution for having stolen from her employer. The sentence could not be carried out immediately because the post of official hangman was vacant. Once an appointment was made, her fate would be sealed. The lady knew, however, that her life would be spared *if she were married to the executioner.* She turned her charms upon the impressionable young Corolère (he was no more than twenty) and was successful. On August 17 he petitioned the Superior Council to be appointed hangman, a post considered odious in the colony. The request was granted and Corolère was released immediately. The next day he petitioned the authorities for permission to marry Françoise Laurent. That too was granted, and the wedding took place on August 19.

In March 1751 Etienne Beaudry and Joseph Deguire, respectively fife player and drummer in the Quebec garrison, clashed so violently that the former was hospitalized and the latter immediately left New France. Beaudry, once he had partially recovered from his wounds, also escaped to friendlier soil. Both men were tried *in absentia*, convicted of illegal duelling, and sentenced to be hanged and garrotted. In the absence of the proper parties, these penalties were inflicted on effigies.

In May 1751 two sergeants named Delmas and Deville spent a day touring Montreal by carriage, visiting numerous taverns along the way. They fell into a bloody, drunken brawl, barely a duel at all. Deville was killed on the spot. Delmas evaded arrest and disappeared.

Yet another duel that year took place in the sister colony of Île Royale (Cape Breton Island). Two junior officers at Louisbourg argued over a game of billiards and vented their anger in swordplay. Ensign Pierre-Jacques Druillon de Macé, who had been lightly wounded, was transferred to New France, where he pursued a distinguished military career. Ensign de la Cousinière, deemed to have provoked the fight, was sent to France and posted in turn to Louisiana, where he was involved in another duel in 1759.

Louisbourg witnessed a further encounter in 1757 – again as much a brawl as a duel. One Lieutenant de Bellefosse, having taken a violent dislike to Captain Garsement de Fontaine, insulted the latter in public. De Fontaine asked for time to fetch his sword, but de Bellefosse was unwilling to wait. In the unequal struggle that followed, de Fontaine managed to wound his enemy in the hand, either with a knife or with de Bellefosse's own weapon. The lieutenant was posted back to France. Captain de Fontaine, a popular officer, remained in the garrison but was killed in action the following year during the second siege of the fortress.

The closing years of New France saw the colony reinforced by regular line regiments from Europe, led by aristocrats who held exaggerated ideas of their honour and importance. Affairs of honour were reported to be fairly frequent, yet little information has been found about them. This apparently stemmed from General Montcalm's attitude that duels among his officers were legitimate means of relieving tensions and maintaining military élan – hence a refusal to discipline duellists and a lack of supporting documentation. Compared to their metropolitan kinsmen, the *canadiens* were less insolent and swaggering, although their leaders included several hotheads.

Montcalm's ambivalent attitude to honour and order was demonstrated in February 1758 when he clearly condoned a duel between two officers named Heré and Liébaux who had fallen out over a woman. Indeed, other officers in their regiment virtually demanded that the pair fight. The French general was astonished when, in May 1759, a colonial officer carried before him a complaint against a fellow officer rather than seeking personal satisfaction.

In August 1758 Pierre-Antoine de la Colombière declared himself ready to fight a young officer named Clapier for having struck the veteran Canadian campaigner. In July 1759, thirty-six-year-old Captain Michel Chartier de Lotbinière, a colonial officer and military engineer stationed at Quebec, quarrelled with Lieutenant Francide Caire of the metropolitan forces; the *canadien* was wounded in the shoulder.

Thereafter the battles of 1759-60 took precedence over private disputes. When, in September 1760, General François Lévis ordered the regimental colours burned before his formal surrender to British troops in Montreal, the curtain was rung down on the French régime. There would be many changes, not only to duelling. Coming events cast their shadows before: in July 1759 two officers in Wolfe's army exchanged fire; Captain David Ochterlony, 60th Foot (an American regiment) was wounded slightly by a Captain Wetterspoon; the next day Ochterlony was killed in action.[10]

# Chapter 3

ᔓ

# The New Régime

The transfer of sovereignty from France to Britain brought a basic change to Canadian duelling. Pistols replaced swords as the weapons with which to defend one's honour. Aegidius Fauteux suggests that this reflected fundamental differences in national temperaments:

> Gallic ardour was best suited to the sword, which enabled the duellist to slash, parry, and beat the air, exercising his entire being. Conversely, the phlegmatic British found more satisfaction in pistol duels in which two adversaries were placed face to face, at a distance, in an attitude as cold as it was correct, the advantage being that one could be killed without having one's uniform or attire even rumpled.[1]

Interesting as this theory may be, a more likely reason for the change in weapons was the evolution of contemporary dress. The late 18th century witnessed the abandonment of swords as part of normal walking-out dress; they were thus less ready to hand should tempers flare and challenges be issued. Officers continued to carry swords, particularly on formal occasions, but they were also under orders to equip themselves with pistols at their own expense. Thus, as principals and as seconds, officers were able to produce firearms when duels were organized. Equally important was the fact that non-military professions, notably the law, took to duelling. The men involved would not have been trained in wielding edged weapons but would have found pistols easy to use.

Pistols were normally sold in pairs, but not every matched set was designed for duelling. Gunsmiths and vendors advertised and sold different types of weapons. True duelling pistols tended to be large in bore (a half-inch), long-barrelled (ten to twelve inches) and very sensitive on the trigger. However, most Canadian duels were probably fought with whatever hand guns were readily available.[2]

While the choice of weapons had changed, the law itself was altered little from the French to the English régime, although enforcement differed markedly. England, of course, had received the medieval trial by combat with the Norman conquest, and by 1100 A.D. it had spread to Scotland and Ireland. This was a recognized legal procedure; opponents in judicial cases fought before judges, sometimes with the king himself present, in the belief that God would award victory to the party whose cause was just – that right made might. By the 13th century it was recognized by all responsible parties, the Church included, that the Almighty did not necessarily intervene in mortal disputes, and trial by combat virtually disappeared. However, no law was formally passed to abolish it until 1819. Two years earlier a man charged with murder had demanded trial by battle with his accuser, the victim's brother. When the latter declined to fight, the case was dismissed. Parliament quickly moved to enact a statute that closed the anachronistic loophole.

Nevertheless, trial by combat differed radically from duelling. The former was a legal device carried out in open court; the latter was a private encounter, conducted outside the law and away from official eyes. The laws of Scotland, Ireland and England were unanimous in declaring duels to be violations of the public peace; killing an opponent was tantamount to murder. The Scottish Parliament, meeting in 1694, made this particularly clear. In England, the Honourable William Blackstone declared in 1769:

Express malice is when one, with a sedate deliberate mind and formed design, doth kill another; which formed design is evidenced by external circumstances discovering that inward intention; as lying in wait, antecedent menaces, former grudges, and concerted schemes to do him some bodily harm. This takes in the case of deliberate duelling, where both parties meet avowedly with an intent to murder; thinking it their duty, as gentlemen, and claiming it as their right, to wanton with their own lives and those of their fellow creatures, without any warrant or authority from any power either divine or human, but in direct contradiction to the laws both of God and man; and therefore the law has justly fixed the crime and punishment of murder, on them and on their seconds also.[3]

Notwithstanding his forceful condemnation of duelling, Blackstone recognized that the practice was widely accepted by "polite society" and that convictions in court would be rare. This was due not to any fault in the law but to popular refusal to enforce it. The French régime had inflicted occasional punishments on duellists in Canada, but from 1761 to 1888 *only one person was ever convicted by a British North American court for having killed an opponent in a duel; this one case may have been the only convicted duellist to have been penalized for his crime; not a single duellist was ever executed for having killed an adversary.* The custom was suppressed by means less drastic than legal proscriptions, and it may be argued that to a great extent social mores, having tolerated duelling for decades, finally turned against the practice.

Yet so long as duelling persisted, there were those who attempted to give it dignity and a code of behaviour. This was particularly so in Ireland, where the process was deeply rooted though unlawful; one writer reported 227 duels involving judges and public officials in roughly half a century (1770-1820). Much witty folklore was attached to these encounters; men chuckled at the tale of the duellist who stated that he was ill and wished to lean against a milepost; his opponent consented, provided that he be allowed to lean against the *next* milepost. Reportedly, when a wealthy young Irishman sought to marry, his prospective inlaws asked first, "Of what family is he?" and then, "Did he ever blaze?" All the same, the landed gentry feared that duels were becoming too frequent, with many combats being fought over clearly trivial causes and between grossly mismatched parties. Concerned that their preciously polite form of anarchy might attract public scorn, they adopted a set of rules subsequently called the Irish *code duello*, described as having been "adopted at the Clonmell Summer Assizes, 1777, for the government of duellists, by the Gentlemen of Tipperary, Galway, Mayo, Sligo, and Roscommon."[4]

The rules were not the first laid down for duellists, nor would they be the last. They did gain fame and general acceptance in the grey underworld of duelling. The Irish code reflected the highly ritualistic form that duelling had assumed. Combats for minor causes were discouraged, but the principle was laid down that if honour could be redeemed only by combat, then the meeting must be conducted in a serious manner, befitting a life-and-death encounter. For example, firing in the air was frowned upon as mocking the dignity of the affair.

The duelling code was interesting for many reasons. One was that the role of the seconds was described thoroughly. They were to do more than merely hold the coats of the principals; they were to load the pistols (usually in sight of each other), regulate the means of firing, serve as witnesses to the proper conduct of the duel, and above all they were to attempt negotiations aimed at preventing or terminating a duel before fatalities occurred.

Since in the absence of seconds a duel would be nothing but a vulgar gunfight, proceeding without seconds was unthinkable. This was demonstrated in Montreal in 1834. One S. Neill of that city had a dispute with an M. Tompkins of New York and wrote a letter inviting him to come north and give satisfaction. Once Tompkins had reached Montreal, he was visited by Robert Sweeney, acting as Neill's second, seeking either a retraction of Tompkins' objectionable statements (whatever they may have been) or agreement on the time and place to duel. Tompkins declared that he could give no immediate answer, as he had only just arrived and had not yet secured a second.

It is difficult to say how earnestly he went about getting one, although he had certainly travelled far enough to meet Neill. A local merchant agreed to carry messages to Sweeney on Tompkins' behalf but refused to be a second (which would have meant going to the battleground). Sweeney refused to deal with any but a formal second. Tompkins claimed that several Montreal friends whom he had expected to be available were out of town, and through his merchant spokesman he asked for more time. Sweeney, adamant in sticking to the rules, declared that Tompkins must find a second within twelve hours or lose his standing as a gentleman. The deadline passed, the second was not recruited and Tompkins returned to New York. He argued that by coming to Montreal he had demonstrated his good faith. Sweeney took a more hostile view; he believed that Tompkins had not made a serious effort to find a second and had used this as a means of avoiding an encounter.[5]

If Robert Sweeney understood the rules so thoroughly, not all his contemporaries did. A Niagara newspaper, the *Gleaner*, published an item on September 20, 1823, which indicates that the term "duel" could be open to fairly broad interpretation in British North America:

> The King vs. John Norton – Tried for murder – found guilty of manslaughter only, and fined £25, which was instantly paid, and he discharged. His conduct in the affair (a duel with another Chief) was truly honourable, and he would no doubt have been acquitted altogether, if he had not from feelings of delicacy withheld his best defence. Counsel for prisoner Hagerman, Beardsley & McAulay.

Other than that it occurred in July 1823, the precise date of this "duel" is uncertain. The defendant was John Norton ( ? –1826), an English-born Indian agent with a distinguished record in leading the Grand River Mohawks during the War of 1812. His victim, Big Arrow (alias Joe Crawford), had served with him in that conflict. Their encounter became part of Haldimand County folklore, with different versions of the story describing the conduct of Norton and his wife (herself a Mohawk) in contrary ways. The only direct, contemporary account is that given by Norton himself in a letter to his former commander, Colonel John Harvey.

By John Norton's self-serving account, Mrs. Norton had been indiscreet in her relations with Big Arrow, and her husband had ordered them both off his farm near Brantford, though neither obeyed. The woman complained bitterly to Norton that Big Arrow had insulted and taken advantage of her. The Indian veteran came to their house, confronted Norton and dared him to fight. They took up pistols, advanced towards each other and fired at close range. Norton's scalp was grazed while Big Arrow was shot through the thigh. The two men grappled until Big Arrow collapsed. Either the wound inflicted was more serious than described or complications set in, causing the death of the unfortunate Indian.[6]

The affair was certainly conducted in a manner far removed from that recommended in the duelling codes. There had been witnesses but no seconds; the opponents had communicated directly and had acted in the heat of the moment, and from exchanging bullets they had gone to trading blows. In spite of these departures from the formal procedures, the press still described it as a "duel." Those more concerned with the niceties might have labelled it a brutal brawl.

However widely the Irish code was known and followed, it remained an illegal list of rules for an unlawful custom; the fact that upper class scofflaws carried it on did not make it otherwise. The description of the code as having been established at the "Clonmell Summer Assizes, 1777" is actually misleading, for there is not a scrap of evidence to suggest that any judicial body, be it high court, coroner's inquest or grand jury, ever deliberated upon the subject. D.O. Luanaigh of the National Library of Ireland offers one theory as to how the code came to be associated with a legal occasion:

Duelling was in fact illegal in 1775, but paradoxically, was frequently resorted to by lawyers. The meeting of the Clonmell Assizes would thus have been a suitable occasion for drafting the Code Duello in that it brought together a large number of people of a legal bent and with an interest in duelling. The drafting of the code would have formed no part of the official work of the Assizes.[7]

Sir Jonah Barrington, a judge whose memoirs include two lengthy chapters on the topic, gives the closest thing to a first-hand account of the code's origins that we are likely to have. He relates that the frequency of duels had so increased in Ireland that even the most intemperate "fire eaters" thought it prudent to restrict them. In the forefront of this movement was a private group called the Knights of Tara who met regularly in a Dublin theatre to conduct fencing lessons and public demonstrations. Barrington's description of their organization relates:

> The Knights of Tara also had a select committee to decide on all actual questions of honour referred to them – to reconcile differences, if possible; if not, to adjust the terms and continuance of single combat. Doubtful points were solved generally on the peaceable side, provided women were not insulted or defamed; but when that was the case, the Knights were obdurate, and blood must be seen. They were constituted by ballot, something in the manner of the Jockey Club, but without the possibility of being dishonourable or the opportunity of cheating each other.[8]

It was, then, either a committee of a private organization or an informal conference of lawyers – but not a legally recognized body – which apparently drew up the rules that became so widely known. Further proof of their extra-legal nature is indicated by two additional items. In the first instance, the code was signed by men using titles ("president," "secretary") not employed in the courts. The second was the manner in which it was distributed. The Irish code was never put on a printing press; instead it was repeatedly copied by hand, to be kept in gentlemen's pistol cases "so that ignorance might never be pleaded." A legal document would never have had to exist in such a furtive way.

To those who persisted in maintaining the practice, it mattered little how their sport stood in the eyes of the law. In Canada the king's new subjects readily adopted the methods and customs of duelling brought with the occupying armies. The *Canadiens* quietly resisted assimilation with the newcomers, but in this matter they gave themselves over wholeheartedly to British ways.

The first recorded duel under the new regime took place on March 30, 1767. It was staged on the Plains of Abraham between an officer and a lawyer. Neither was identified in the accounts of the day; the affair ended without bloodshed after one exchange of fire. Another incident occurred in the last week of October 1782. An artillery officer, Kenelm Connor Chandler, was principally responsible for the ordnance stores at Quebec. His work brought him into an unspecified dispute with Alexander Davison, a merchant in that city. The quarrel broadened to include Davison's partner, John Lees. Following a confrontation in a local coffee house, they met on the Plains of Abraham, where Chandler traded shots with Davison and then with Lees. Again, no one was hit, honour was satisfied and the dispute terminated.

Two unnamed French-Canadians fought a duel at Boucherville on or about August 17, 1789. A friend tried to persuade them to desist, but they went on, exchanging shots at only eight paces (about twenty-five feet). Incredibly, considering the short distance, neither was hit. They agreed to continue the duel the following day, but by the time another dawn came around they had been reconciled.

Although soldiers were reputed to be notorious duellists, the British army (in Canada at least) strove to prevent such incidents. On November 29, 1788, Captain Alexander MacDonald sent a challenge

The Plains of Abraham – The former battlefield just outside Quebec City offered accessibility and privacy and was a favourite duelling spot for 18th- and 19th-century officers and politicians. (National Archives of Canada C-11893)

to Captain John Parr. The two were members of the 60th Regiment, then in garrison at Montreal. MacDonald claimed that his brother officer had insulted him at a dinner party three days earlier, supposedly saying that MacDonald "governed the major" and the he "wiped his arse with his hand." Parr, through intermediaries, declared that he had no recollection of saying these things and that he wished no harm to MacDonald. Three other officers who had been present at the party also refuted MacDonald's assertions; he in turn argued that they had been drunk and were not credible witnesses. He pressed over two weeks for a duel with Parr. On December 17, the officers of the 60th Regiment resolved that they would no longer associate with MacDonald. He was subsequently court-martialled for sending a challenge and sentenced to be cashiered. The sentence was reviewed in London and MacDonald was allowed to retire at half-pay instead.[9]

Sir James Lemoine, a chronicler of fact and folklore, wrote of a peculiar incident that may or may not have happened. By his account, sometime in the 1780s, an officer named Broadstreet, 24th Regiment of Foot, stated his belief that a Mr. Nesbit was actually a woman masquerading as a man. Nesbit, hearing of this, challenged Broadstreet to a duel. One Captain Doyle, designated as Broadstreet's second, was certain that the original allegation was true and went to the Governor, Lord Dorchester. He in turn suggested that Nesbit submit to an examination by the garrison doctor. Nesbit refused and threatened to complain to friends in England, but finally admitted that the accusation was correct – "Mr. Nesbit" was actually a Miss Nevile, who left the colony at the first opportunity. The story was a romantic one – but Lemoine was often inaccurate, and the story has not been substantiated elsewhere; it may be more fantasy than fact.[10]

The first known fatal duel in Lower Canada was the Shoedde–Holland affair of March 24, 1795. It involved Lieutenant Samuel Lester Holland and Captain Lewis Thomas Shoedde, both of the 60th Regiment, stationed in Montreal. The origins of their quarrel are not known with certainty; it may have begun over a card game, but traditional accounts give a more dramatic version. Holland, who was only nineteen years old, committed some indiscretion with respect to Mrs. Shoedde during a formal ball – possibly a mild attempt to flirt. Captain Shoedde issued a challenge.

The facts of the duel and its aftermath are fairly well accepted. The protagonists and their seconds met at Point-au-Moulin-à-Vent (Windmill Point), St. Charles suburb, where an unusual procedure was adopted. The men were placed ten paces apart, and one was to fire first. A coin was tossed, Shoedde won, and he shot Holland through the trunk, the bullet entering just under the ribs. Holland staggered but managed to fire his own weapon, shattering his opponent's right arm. Then he collapsed and was carried away to a nearby coffee house. Shoedde fled to the United States.

The body of Lieutenant Samuel Lester Holland was taken to Quebec City, where it was buried on his father's estate under a lone fir tree. Six years later the father died and was interred under the same tree. The property changed hands in subsequent years and the graves became overgrown. They were rediscovered and marked in 1957, but soon afterwards the old Holland estate was built over by developers and the Holland remains were likely moved to a Protestant cemetery. Visitors to Quebec City may visit the former estate near de Callières Street, roughly halfway between Holland Avenue and Ernest Gagnon Avenue, where a plaque describes the original owners but not the family tragedy.

The McCord Museum in Montreal has a brace of pistols with an inscription on the barrels: "The Gift of General James Wolfe to Captain Samuel Holland, 1759." The recipient, of course, was Samuel Jan Holland, later Surveyor-General of Lower Canada and father of the unfortunate Samuel Lester Holland. These pistols were reputedly used in the duel, and there is an interesting story centred on them. However, the tale has been perpetuated by tradition, and there is no original documentary evidence to either substantiate or demolish it.

According to legend, Lieutenant Holland hesitated before accepting Shoedde's grim invitation. The young man sought counsel from

The pistols used in the Shoedde–Holland duel. Fine workmanship is evident not only in the weapons but in the case that housed them. (McCord Museum, Montreal)

his father. Major Holland (as he then was) refused to give direct advice, but presented the youth with his own weapons, saying as he did, "Samuel, my son, here are the pistols that my late friend, General Wolfe, presented to me on the day he died. I hope you know how to use them in such a way as to preserve the honoured family name from being stained."

At the meeting itself, Shoedde reportedly boasted that his pistols were distinguished for having been used in a duel involving an English lord. Lieutenant Holland replied, "Mine are better, for they served General Wolfe." At the suggestion of the seconds, the opponents exchanged weapons, and thus young Holland was killed by one of his father's pistols! The tale goes one step further. It is related that, on viewing Samuel Lester's corpse, Major Holland wept bitterly and declared, "My son, when General Wolfe presented me with those superb pistols, I never thought that they would bring you to a dishonourable death."

There may be some truth to this story, but there is probably embellishment as well. If Wolfe did indeed present the pistols to the elder Holland (a captain in 1759, and one to whom Wolfe had not normally been friendly), it is unlikely that he did so "on the day he died"; the general, after all, was busy preparing for and fighting the Battle of the Plains of Abraham and would not have had time to concern himself with private gifts. The meeting between father and son on the eve of the duel is dramatic – but was Major Holland in Quebec or Montreal at the time? If the former, then the conference is clearly fictional. Finally, there is a curious contradiction between his exhortation to use the pistols in upholding the family honour and his sorrowful reference to Samuel Lester Holland suffering a "dishonourable death." If duelling was honourable, then to die in a duel would be no disgrace. The father's reported statements were inconsistent.[11]

Another fatal duel was fought about June 1797 but the exact date is uncertain. The facts were set out in a British publication, the *Monthly Magazine*, and reprinted in the Quebec *Mercury* of

December 15, 1812 – fifteen years after the duel itself. The principal character was Lieutenant John Evans, 24th Regiment of Foot, an Irish-born classical scholar who had abandoned his studies for the British army. He had joined his regiment in Montreal and in 1797 had gone with it to Quebec. The garrison was overcrowded; the blockhouse where he was quartered accommodated some officers of the 26th Regiment of Foot, including a Lieutenant John Ogilvy.

One night, after Evans had retired to bed, Ogilvy entered the room and struck up a conversation. The two men compared regimental messes, and the talk was amicable until Evans remarked that the quality of spruce beer was about equal in the two messes. Ogilvy suddenly protested that it was much superior in that of the 26th Regiment. Surprised at the sudden heat in their discussion, Evans declared, "If you talk in that way, you must mean to insinuate that I lie." His guest took it one step further: "I do," he shouted, "and you are a damned lying scoundrel."

At that point, Evans asked a third man present to shut the door, and the argument ended. Next day, however, Evans asked the witness to the quarrel to speak with Ogilvy, pointing out the impropriety of his remarks and suggesting that an apology was in order. The hotheaded young officer refused to do so; instead he declared to others that Evans was no gentleman, that he should have demanded satisfaction, and that if it came to a duel, he (Ogilvy) trusted both his pistols and his aim. The *Mercury* went on to describe the affair tersely:

> Thus repeatedly insulted and provoked, a duel was no longer to be avoided; they met; and after an exchange of shots, an accommodation was again proposed by Mr. Evans and indignantly rejected by the other; another case of pistols was fired, the same accommodation proposed and again rejected; this was no longer to be borne – Mr. Evans took aim and his opponent perished.

The Court of King's Bench was about to sit, and in three or four days Lieutenant Evans surrendered to, and was instantly tried by, the laws of his country; when, after a most impartial investigation and able charge from Chief Justice Osgoode, the Jury, without hesitation, gave a verdict of acquittal.

This unfortunate affair, however unavoidable, cast ... an occasional gloom over the future days of Lieutenant Evans, for never was a duel named but his countenance fell, and his spirits instantaneously fled.

The date of the duel was clearly in June 1797 – the 24th and 26th regiments were both in Quebec between then and 1799 – but no contemporary account of the fight or of the subsequent trial was published; Fauteux missed it in his study, and even the spelling of the victim's name has varied – it could have been Ogilby. The account given in 1812 was detailed in several matters, including the year that Evans was commissioned (1796), the fact that he was promoted to captain at a later date, and his death in the Battle of Talavera, Spain, on July 28, 1809 (all confirmed by the National Army Museum, London). However, a Lieutenant Ogilby, 26th Regiment, with no initials given, remained on the British Army List until 1802![12]

Very late in 1798 or early in 1799 two ensigns of the Royal Canadian Volunteers apparently duelled, although the date, reasons and meeting itself are shrouded with uncertainty. The opponents were Antoine-Ovide de Lanaudière and Hippolyte de Hertel. The latter was brought before a court martial where charges were dismissed; de Hertel subsequently resigned his commission and left Canada.[13]

Not all duelling incidents went so far. In September 1810 a Quebec notary, F.-X. Chevalier, sent a challenge to another of his profession, Martin Martineau. The latter went to the authorities. Chevalier was summoned into court, fined ten pounds, and ordered to post a bond of 100 louis (about 150 pounds) as insurance that he would keep the peace for five years. A similar incident occurred late in 1817. François Baby, aged twenty-two, son and namesake of a prominent official, had a dispute with one Jacques Oliva. The latter apparently sent a challenge, and when Baby did not respond, the irate party had posters distributed in Quebec and Montreal publicly accusing Baby of being unworthy to be called a gentleman, and further accusing him of being a coward and a poltroon. Baby wrote a letter, published in Montreal's *Spectateur canadien* of November 29, 1817, putting forward his side of the story.

According to Baby, he had on November 3 received a curt message from Oliva demanding satisfaction for some slight which Baby claimed to be purely imaginary. Baby stated that he accepted the challenge and went that same night to Trois Rivières. On arriving he sought out a friend to serve as second and together they waited in a hotel until 11 p.m. of the 4th. A bailiff suddenly appeared, and after a noisy alternation, which included the forcing of the door to his room, Baby was arrested. The authorities had been summoned by persons whom the young man described as "officious friends," but Oliva apparently evaded the bailiffs and fled the town. He had for several days previously announced his intention to challenge Baby, so the law officers had been amply warned.

Baby went before a magistrate, posted a bond and promised to keep the peace. Nevertheless, he waited another day, hoping to meet Oliva (so much for his assurances to the court!). Still the challenger failed to appear, so Baby returned home to St. Pierre-les-Becquets. When Oliva "posted" him for non-appearance, the indignant youth took to the papers. In doing so, he also suggested that, apart from specific warnings, the authorities had been alerted by Oliva's bombastic statements beforehand. In any case, Baby did not press for another rendezvous.

About May or June 1818 another duel involved members of the Quebec garrison. Doctor William Hackett (or Hacket) was wounded in an exchange of fire with Captain Theodore Power, 60th Regiment, on the Plains of Abraham. The exact date and cause of the quarrel are unknown.[14]

The next year Montreal was the scene of one of the most vicious "affairs of honour" in Canadian history. The dispute began with a Montreal delegation petitioning the Legislative Assembly of Lower Canada, sitting in Quebec. The group requested that a publicly funded Protestant hospital be established in Montreal. Hitherto the city had relied upon Catholic institutions for its medical services. The existing medical facilities were insufficient to satisfy a rapidly growing population which included many immigrants. Although the petition itself was worded in a dignified fashion, some supporters of the project were known to have expressed fears that Protestant patients were receiving less attention than Catholic ones in the Montreal hospital, and some had claimed that the nuns who acted as nurses were contaminating Protestant patients with Catholic dogmas.

Some Catholic legislators, aware of these lurking prejudices, attacked the petition. One of these was Michael O'Sullivan, the thirty-three-year-old lawyer and MLA for Huntingdon, who treated the petition as an affront to those currently serving Montreal's medical needs; he contrasted the selfless nuns with the "mercenary hirelings" that he claimed would staff the new institution. O'Sullivan went further, heaping ridicule and abuse on the proponents of a Protestant institution, and suggesting that the measure was being pushed for selfish reasons by doctors – and quacks at that. The petition had suggested that a new hospital might be useful in advancing medical knowledge. O'Sullivan sarcastically forecast that the proposed establishment would use patients for medical experiments. What should have been a rational discussion turned into a hot, bitter, sectarian debate. At length the Speaker moved to adjourn the Assembly. The petition was pigeonholed for several months.

On April 10, 1819, a Montreal newspaper, the *Canadian Courant*, published a letter signed merely "An active advocate of an Hospital." Most of the text was a reasoned, logical case for the proposed institution, but towards the end the writer allowed his anger and frustration to surface. He cast doubts on the personal courage of Michael

O'Sullivan, hinting that on a previous occasion the member for Huntingdon had ignored an insult which friends had thought so grave as to have merited a demand for satisfaction.

O'Sullivan was stung by this piece. A man of combative temperament, he was a veteran of the War of 1812, and his bravery had been singled out for praise after the Battle of Châteauguay. Moreover, he was a militia officer as well as a political figure. He sought out the editor of the *Canadian Courant* to find out who wrote the letter. It was Dr. William Caldwell (1782-1833), a distinguished surgeon and public personage who would later help found McGill University and the McGill School of Medicine. Caldwell too had a military background; between 1805 and 1814 he had served in Wellington's Peninsular armies. Unquestionably he loathed O'Sullivan.

Caldwell and O'Sullivan met near Windmill Point, the favoured duelling spot for Montreal society. It was 6:00 a.m. on April 11. No complete account of their confrontation has survived; we do not know the distance between them, the names of their seconds, or of any attempts to reconcile the principals. What is certain is that the opponents went through *five* exchanges of fire. At the conclusion of this deadly affair, Caldwell had suffered a broken arm while a bullet had lodged in his coat; a little more powder behind it might have proved fatal. O'Sullivan had been wounded in both heels, and Caldwell's fifth shot struck the lawyer down, lodging in his enemy's torso. Many duels had been terminated upon the least drawing of blood; in this instance it was clear that each participant had come to the field bent upon killing his adversary.

O'Sullivan lay close to death for several days. The doctors were uncertain about removing the bullet and finally left it in place. He gradually recovered, but for the rest of his life he suffered recurring pains and was in precarious health. Nevertheless, he continued in law and politics, rising to the post of Solicitor-General (April 1833) and finally to Chief Justice of the Court of Queen's Bench (October 1838). He was on the bench scarcely one term, for he died on March

Windmill Point was to Montreal duellists what the Plains of Abraham were to those in Quebec – a favourite spot to play a deadly game. (McCord Museum, Montreal)

7, 1839. An autopsy revealed Caldwell's last bullet resting against O'Sullivan's spine.

Nothing in these events ultimately stopped the intended project. The Montreal General Hospital was chartered late in 1819; it was the embryo from which developed McGill University's Faculty of Medicine. Doctor Caldwell continued to rise in the medical field; he was also a combative figure in sectarian disputes within the local Presbyterian Church. He died of typhus on January 25, 1833.[15]

There may have been another duel in Montreal in 1819. Lawyers Samuel Gale (1785-1865) and James Stuart (1780-1853), both destined to become judges, reportedly fell out while arguing a case in court and adjourned to exchange shots. By one account, neither was injured, but another report had it that Gale was seriously wounded.[16]

On March 8, 1821, one Louis-E. Archambault of Montreal wrote to F.B. Pilet, inviting the latter to duel on the following morning. Pilet had called Archambault a "blockhead," but whether they met is unrecorded. Fauteux speculates that Pilet may have been François-Benjamin Pillet, earlier a principal in one of the few duels staged in Western Canada.[17]

In mid-November 1827 a rising young lawyer, Robert-Shore-Milnes Bouchette, boarded the steamer *Chambly* in Montreal, bound for Quebec. He fell out with a James Bell, and on reaching their desti-

Robert-Shore-Milnes Bouchette was one of many men whose duels were pressed more vigorously in the newspapers than on the ground. (Artist unknown, Archives nationales du Québec)

nation they fought a duel. Bell's shot grazed Bouchette's chin, and the affair ended there. The trip must have been particularly boisterous, for on the same voyage two other gentlemen, G.W. Usborne of Quebec and Charles Morrison of Berthier, were prepared to duel as well, but intervention by the constables prevented this happening.[18]

The British military – either of Montreal or Kingston – figured in one further duel in this period. The Quebec *Star* of June 18, 1828 carried a New York despatch which was dated June 10. Two officers had gone to an American island near Ogdensburg. After three exchanges of fire, one man had been gravely wounded and was brought back to Canada. The successful duellist was arrested by local officials, but no subsequent trial was reported.[19]

*Chapter 4*

ℬ

# The Duel
# in Upper Canada

Upper Canada, created in 1791 by the Constitutional Act, existed as a separate colonial entity until 1841, when the Act of Union joined it to Lower Canada in a brief (1841-67) shotgun marriage. English criminal and civil law prevailed, modified slightly to match local conditions. The letter of the law stood opposed to duelling. Nevertheless, Upper Canada witnessed several such incidents, five of them fatal in outcome. There was much litigation, but only one person was convicted for participating in a duel. The legal profession was strongly represented; in the five duels involving death, nine of the ten combatants were law officers, lawyers or students-at-law. Of the five survivors, one became a cabinet minister and another was appointed to the bench.

Relatively little is known of the first such fatal encounter in the province – a reflection of the undeveloped state of Upper Canada at the time, with no newspapers to report events and the judicial system only then taking shape. It happened at Kingston in the late winter or early spring of 1793. The victim was Peter Clark, an English-born trader who had been appointed Clerk of the Legislative Council the previous September. His opponent apparently was Captain David Sutherland, 25th Regiment of Foot, then stationed in the area. Unfortunately, the precise date and the names of the seconds are unknown.

The affair grew out of Sutherland applying for Clark's job. That precipitated a quarrel which developed into a challenge and formal meeting. One exchange of fire resulted in no injuries. Sutherland was willing to negotiate an understanding, but Clark was determined to go on. The pistols were reloaded and on a second exchange the unfortunate Clerk of the Legislative Council was shot dead; his brother, James Clark, succeeded to the office on May 7.

Sutherland was detained, and on August 7 he was brought to trial on a charge of murder. Chief Justice William Osgoode presided, while the prosecution was handled by the provincial Attorney-General, John White. The judge sympathized with duelling, provided it was done in what he perceived to be a fair manner, and he virtually acted as defence counsel from the bench. However, Peter Clark had been a popular local figure, and several jurors resisted Osgoode's persuasive directions. The jury deliberated for three hours before returning a verdict. Sutherland was acquitted of the murder charge but was deemed to be guilty of manslaughter. Osgoode, relieved that he had not had to wear the black cap used when sentencing people to death, fined Sutherland thirteen shillings and fourpence, then set him free.[1]

Seven years would pass before another fatal duel rocked polite Upper Canadian society. There was a close call, however, in the spring of 1795. William Jarvis (1756-1817) was accused of having written a libelous lampoon of several prominent families and posting it in Newark (Niagara-on-the-Lake). He hotly denied the charge and challenged no fewer than four persons to duel. One apologized, two brought him to court, where he was ordered to keep the peace, and one he met over pistols – lawyer Richard Barnes Tickell, who emerged unscathed but who drowned a month after the incident.[2]

The two men who had avoided meeting Jarvis by seeking the protection of the law were John White (1761-1800, already met as Captain David Sutherland's prosecutor) and John Small (1746-1831). Having steered clear of an encounter with Jarvis, they subsequently

Chief Justice William Osgoode imposed
a fine of 13 shillings and 4 pence on a
man who had killed his opponent in a
1793 duel. (Toronto Reference Library,
J. Ross Robertson Collection T32112)

duelled with each other in Upper Canada's second fatal "affair of honour."

John White, an English-born barrister, was a member of the Legislative Assembly as well as being Upper Canada's first Attorney-General. He was a genial, gregarious man who mixed freely in the colony's upper crust, at least until 1797 when his wife finally joined him in York (modern Toronto), which had recently been made the capital. During his long tenure as a semi-bachelor, White had become especially friendly with Major John Small (another expatriate Englishman and Clerk of the Executive Council), and Mrs. Small. In a diary kept between 1791 and 1796, White recorded many occasions of visiting and dining back and forth between himself and the Smalls. Nevertheless, his entry of April 5, 1796, may have marked the beginning of a disastrous falling out; it read, "Dined at S's. A little coquetry! so came away immediately after tea."

White was industrious in his duties but was evidently prone to trouble. On July 12 and 13, 1799, an angry Captain William Fitzgerald, Queen's Rangers, wrote him two threatening letters and challenged him to duel. We do not know the reason for the altercation, but White

43

immediately sought protection in the Court of King's Bench, which ordered Fitzgerald to show cause for his behaviour, to post bonds totalling 1,000 pounds and to keep the peace for twelve months. The court's instructions were obeyed; by November 12, 1799, the judges were able to release Fitzgerald from these orders and refund his deposits. Attorney-General White was to have much less happy dealings with the Smalls.

York, the provincial capital, thrived on gossip and rumour within the tiny social elite; the smaller the pond, the more vicious the fish. The initial spark in the Small–White affair was women's quarrels. At a public gathering late in 1799 Mrs. Small pointedly insulted Mrs. White. Exasperated at this behaviour, John White passed on to a friend, D.W. Smith (acting Surveyor-General), some shocking remarks about Mrs. Small – that in England she had been the mistress of Lord Berkley, that Major Small had been bribed to marry her, and that he (White) had kept her for a time as his own mistress.[3] Smith in turn ran with these stories to Chief Justice John Elmsley, and from there they ran through York society. They soon reached the ears of Mrs. Small herself. She in turn demanded of her husband that he defend her honour and her reputation.

John Small first sought to get a reasonably clear statement of just what people were saying about his wife. He visited Chief Justice Elmsley (Smith, the initial scandalmonger being out of town), and he in turn recounted the gossip for Small's benefit. In the afternoon of January 2, 1800, the major called upon the Attorney-General, demanding that he admit or deny the fact that he had been spreading false reports. A contemporary letter describes what happened:

Mr. White answered that it being very possible that Mr. Smith might have said more or less than he told him he had better obtain from himself the exact Tale he had Communicated to the Chief Justice & and he should then very candidly tell him what parts of the Relation were true or false – Mr. Small not satisfied with this

First Parliament Buildings, Toronto – Upper Canada's second fatal duel occurred within the sound of a gunshot from the provincial legislature. (National Archives of Canada C-8780)

insisted on Mr. Whites going out with him immediately, which our friend having unfortunately agreed to, they met the next Morning....[4]

They met in a grove behind the legislative buildings of the day, near the present Front and Berkeley streets of Toronto, on the morning of January 3, 1800. Serving as seconds were Sheriff Alexander Macdonnell for Small (an incredible breach of duty by a man who should have been trying to preserve the peace) and Baron Frederick de Hoen for White. The Attorney-General had made his will the previous evening – a touching document, written in anticipation of dying. It began with a request "to be rolled up a sheet and not buried fantastically ... at the back of my own house," and concluded, "I forgive every one – I should like to have lived for the sake of my family – but I hope I am no otherwise afraid to die, than a rational being, ignorant of everything but his own insignificance and the power of the Almighty."

John Small killed John White in an 1800 duel over Mrs. Small's honour. Although Small continued to rise in society, the tragedy shredded the reputations of others, including Mrs. Small, who was ostracized by Toronto's aristocracy. (Toronto Reference Library, J. Ross Robertson Collection T15106)

White's pessimism was justified. In the first exchange of fire he received a bullet in the right side that passed between two lower ribs, shattered his spine and lodged near the left kidney. He was instantly paralysed from the waist down. He was carried to the home of his friend and executor, Peter Russell, where he lingered in agony for thirty-six hours and died.

The seconds fled for a time but promised to appear for trial. It was not necessary. Only Major Small was arrested. On January 20 he was tried for murder before Mr. Justice Henry Allcock and a jury in a hearing that lasted eight hours. Few details of this event are available. The judge may have briefed the jurors less on the law than on gentlemanly conduct, honour and the apparent "fairness" with which the duel had been conducted; Allcock most certainly remarked that the prosecutor had failed to produce evidence proving Small's guilt, adding that the jury should presume nothing. With a charge like this, from a man who claimed to have been a friend of the deceased (and who later wrote that he had advised White the night before the duel *not* to meet Small), the jury could do little other than to return a dutiful verdict of "not guilty."[5] The jury foreman was William Jarvis, already met, whose son would fight a duel years later. The presence of a man like Jarvis on the panel was questionable, as he was not only familiar with the slanderous stories about Mrs. Small, but had repeated them in correspondence two days before the trial! He had quarrelled with both White and Small in 1795; even in January 1800 there had been bad relations between him and White over money matters.

John White was buried, as he had asked, in the grounds of his home, but his remains were disturbed in 1871 by workmen searching for sand to be used in construction. His bones were reburied in the cemetery of St. James' Cathedral. The duel itself had created a stir throughout the province. The Niagara *Constitution*, on January 11, 1800, mourned the death of the Attorney-General and bitterly denounced duelling as "a custom falsely deemed honourable." Back in York, Major Small resumed his official duties. On two subsequent occasions he failed to win elective offices and society folk went out of their way to avoid him. He was finally appointed Clerk of the Crown and Pleas (a judicial position) and died in 1832.

Others associated with the incident had their reputations shredded. D.W. Smith, whose tale-bearing had led to the duel, found his advance in public life blocked. He had expected appointment to the Legislative Council; this was postponed indefinitely. As for Mrs. Small, she was long ostracized by York's upper crust. Eight years after the duel Mrs. William Dummer Powell, a leading socialite, was informed that a public gathering with even the Governor present would nevertheless include Mrs. Small. Mrs. Powell subsequently wrote:

I made no comment on her information [the informant was Mrs. William Jarvis], but as soon as she had gone ask'd my Daughters if they chose to go – Mary just finishing the trimming of a Gown for the Evening, laid it aside & with her Sister answered in the negative, – no more was said and we staid at home, convinced that those who had the same intelligence would do the same, – Mrs. McGill had long been determined not to be there, & I was much surpriz'd to find she had been there, and had induced by her example, other ladies to remain, who finding this infamous Woman had obtruded herself were inclined to retire.[6]

A duel almost occurred in March 1801. Joseph Willcocks (1773-1814), an expatriate Irishman living in York, was accused by William Weekes of being a government informer, a charge that Willcocks considered particularly odious in view of his own grudges against authority. He called Weekes a liar, Weekes demanded satisfaction the next day (the 20th), and Willcocks agreed, "but not so soon." On the morning of the 20th Baron de Hoen, acting as Weekes' second, called on the Irishman to determine a time and place. It was agreed that the duel would be held at 6:00 a.m. on the 21st near the Don River. James Ruggles consented to serve as Willcocks' second, though he advised that the hour be changed to 5:00 a.m., and spent the night with his friend. They probably did not sleep much; as of 4:00 a.m. they were setting out for the spot when the sheriff met them. They were arrested. Willcocks subsequently had to appear before Magistrate William Jarvis, post bonds and promise to keep the peace for six months.

Baron de Hoen, having participated as a second in two duelling incidents, plunged into obscurity and died about 1816. James Ruggles was drowned in 1804. Joseph Willcocks became a prominent opposition leader, initially fought on the British side in the War of 1812, went over to the Americans, and was killed at Fort Erie in 1814. William Weekes was to provoke and fight another duel.[7]

Weekes, like Willcocks, had been born in Ireland, and he had migrated to the United States before arriving in Upper Canada in 1799, where he practised law. He was elected to the legislature and had become an opponent of the government, all of which makes his dispute with Willcocks an ironic affair. In March 1800 he was active in having William Dickson made a "bencher" (Governor of the Law Society of Upper Canada). Dickson became a government supporter, though in other respects he and Weekes appeared to be friends.

On October 6, 1806, Weekes and Dickson were arguing a civil case in Newark (Niagara-on-the-Lake) before Mr. Justice Robert Thorpe, a curious figure who, though a member of the judiciary, was a known

William Dickson was expected to decline William Weekes' 1806 challenge; instead he killed his opponent. (Toronto Reference Library, J. Ross Robertson Collection T15286)

foe of the local government and entertained political ambitions. On this day, Weekes directed a scathing attack on the authorities, although his remarks had little connection with the case in hand. Indeed, his comments were not only irrelevant but in bad taste; he described former governor Peter Hunter, dead fourteen months, as a "Gothic barbarian whom the providence of God has removed from this world for his tyranny and iniquity." Thorpe did not object to this digression, so Dickson rose in his turn to defend the administration; he criticized Weekes personally in language as strong as Weekes had used in his address.

The inactivity of Thorpe was the most puzzling aspect of the incident; apparently he had encouraged Weekes to use the courtroom as a forum to oppose the government. The judge and his lawyer/ally met soon afterwards in a tavern where they concocted a strange scheme. Weekes, a bachelor, would challenge Dickson (married with a young family) to a duel. In the circumstances, Dickson might be expected to decline, thus embarrassing his Tory faction. Dickson, however, accepted the challenge, much to the dismay of Weekes, who made out a will in anticipation of the outcome. There was some manoeuvring by friends to prevent the duel, with suggestions that mutual apologies and explanations might be offered in open court. The principals did not agree. Selection of seconds was also difficult. Weekes' first choice, a Major Hart, was unacceptable to others and was ultimately replaced by one John McKee. Dickson's second was Doctor Robert Kerr.

These preliminaries took time, but on the morning of October 10 the party crossed the Niagara River to American territory. Near Fort Niagara they were placed twenty yards apart. At the signal they fired simultaneously. Weekes missed and was struck in the right side by Dickson's bullet. The wound was mortal, and Weekes died that evening. No judicial action followed; the duel had been fought on American soil and thus was deemed not to have happened at all!

William Dickson became a member of the Legislative Council of Upper Canada and promoted settlement around Galt; he died peacefully in 1846. Mr. Justice Thorpe sharply curtailed his political activities following the death of Weekes, was suspended from the Bench in 1807, and returned to England. Later he was appointed Chief Justice of Sierra Leone. He died in 1836.[8]

John Macdonnell (1785-1812) was the principal figure in Upper Canada's next duelling incident. Born in Scotland, he had emigrated to Glengarry in 1792. His family was prominent in the social, political and religious life of the colony. Embarking on a legal career, he studied law under William Dickson – and was probably articled to him at the time of the duel with Weekes – and in 1808 was called to the bar in his own right.

The young man had many admirable characteristics, but he had a quick temper. In the fall of 1808 the provincial Attorney-General, William Firth, made a disparaging remark about Macdonnell's practice in York. On September 16, Firth was confronted by Duncan Cameron, requesting a retraction on Macdonnell's behalf. When this was refused, Cameron went one step further, issuing a duelling challenge on behalf of his champion. Firth was fully aware of his legal responsibilities and dismissed Macdonnell's belligerent demand as being contrary to law. Given Macdonnell's prickly temperament, it was

John Macdonell may have been vain and egotistical, but he behaved honourably in his encounter with William Baldwin and died a hero's death at the Battle of Queenston Heights. (Toronto Reference Library, J. Ross Robertson Collection T17053)

to be expected that he would confront others. In the spring of 1812 he did.

Dr. William Baldwin (1775-1844), having emigrated from Ireland, had failed in both medicine and teaching, but had been admitted to the Upper Canadian bar in 1803 at a time when there was a shortage of lawyers in the colony (if one can believe that such a drought ever existed). In court he was often at odds with Macdonnell, who in 1811 had been appointed Attorney-General for Upper Canada. Baldwin regarded the young man with some sarcastic disdain; to Firth, now retired to England, he wrote of Macdonnell, "His honours rain not upon him – they come in tempests."

On April 1, 1812, their antagonism boiled over. In a hearing before Chief Justice Thomas Scott, Macdonnell used language which Baldwin considered "wantonly and ungentlemanly." He protested to the Bench, and the judge reprimanded Macdonnell. Still the Attorney-General did not curb his tongue. Baldwin had had enough. Through a friend, Lieutenant Thomas Taylor, he sent Macdonnell a letter requesting an explanation and apology for his remarks in court.[9]

Taylor reluctantly accepted the task. He had tried to persuade Baldwin to overlook the matter; indeed, he would apparently have to provide his own pistols if the doctor did "go to the turf." Macdonnell, on receiving Baldwin's note, expressed surprise that matters had run

William Baldwin (doctor, lawyer, politician) fought a duel on Toronto Island in 1812. (Toronto Reference Library, J. Ross Robertson Collection T31037)

so far. He declared that the offending words might have been explained away and a misunderstanding cleared up, but as Baldwin had now taken the offensive, the Attorney-General would neither apologize nor alter his remarks. By modern standards, this reply can only be described as being childish and pig-headed.

Macdonnell appointed as his second Duncan Cameron – the same man employed to challenge Firth. Baldwin was prepared to duel the following morning, but Macdonnell pleaded his public duties during the court hearings. A meeting was delayed until April 3, when the Spring Assizes would be finished.

On the night of April 2, Baldwin wrote a letter to his wife. He begged her forgiveness and understanding, signing off "Farewell – perhaps forever." He also drew up his will, leaving everything to Mrs. Baldwin while simultaneously damning Macdonnell, "borne down by an insolence which the opinion of the world forbids me to submit to …" and pardoning him – "I believe I forgive my antagonist." At dawn of the 3rd, a bleak, overcast morning, he met Taylor and walked across the ice to Toronto Island, pausing at Gibraltar Point to have members of the garrison witness the will. They then went on to meet Macdonnell and Cameron, who had arrived by sleigh at the rendezvous.

The principals were placed back to back, several paces apart. On command they were to turn and face each other. On the word "Fire," they would present arms and shoot. The signals were given. As Baldwin brought his pistol up, he realized that Macdonnell was standing firmly with his arm still at his side. Baldwin hesitated, loath to pull the trigger. Cameron shouted a question – why did Baldwin not shoot? Then Cameron called again, "He waits your fire." Baldwin took this to mean that in refusing to shoot, Macdonnell was admitting his callous behaviour. The doctor deliberately fired wide.

The two men advanced, shook hands and went their different ways, but they were never really reconciled. Baldwin became a prominent Reformer and was the father of Robert Baldwin, the Upper Canadian Reformer, statesman and judge. Macdonnell went on to a hero's death, sustaining a fatal wound at the Battle of Queenston Heights (October 13, 1812) while leading a bravely foolish charge. His friend Duncan Cameron was there to lead him, bleeding, back down the slope. Cameron came through a hail of bullets unscathed and lived until 1838; on the way he became a member of the Legislative Council, Provincial Secretary and a warden of St. James' Cathedral.[10]

If ever two families should *not* have fallen out, it was the Jarvis and Ridout clans of York. They had come from the United States with the Loyalist migrations; their sons had fought in the same regiments in the War of 1812; they had risen to be pillars of the colonial establishment. Yet the feud that grew up between them resulted in one of the most melodramatic stories in the history of Upper Canada. Moreover, it had political and social overtones; the Ridouts were to become moderate Reformers, the Jarvises high Tories, and each house would see the other as bent upon inflicting humiliation.

Early in 1815 Samuel Peters Jarvis (son of the foreman of John Small's jury) took his sister and one of the Ridout ladies to Quebec City for enrolment in a boarding school. Lieutenant Thomas Ridout, employed in the garrison, offered to keep watch on the girls' interests, paying some of Miss Jarvis's bills and drawing upon young Sam for repayment. A year later, Mary Ridout (mother of Thomas) visited Quebec. On her return she spread gossip that her son was not being repaid by Sam Jarvis. The Jarvis family protested to the Ridouts, asking that the story be denied. That was taken as an insult. On this occasion the spokesman for the Ridouts was George Ridout, who wrote young Sam Jarvis, stating that he was ready to defend the family's honour – another curious instance of attacking the complainant rather than the substance of the complaint. A duel was arranged, but circumstances forced a delay. Dr. John Strachan (later Anglican Bishop of Toronto) stepped in to mediate. In November 1816 George Ridout and Samuel Peters Jarvis signed a document; Ridout agreed to write a letter contradicting the gossip about unpaid debts, and Sam Jarvis withdrew an earlier letter that had complained about the stories. Peace reigned briefly, but the two families were now bitterly hostile. Time might have healed the breach, but little of that passed before another incident provided fuel for the fire.

William Jarvis was in confused, debt-ridden straits, with numerous creditors seeking payments. Samuel Peters Jarvis, seeking political office, may have been touchy about his father's financial difficulties. One creditor hired George Ridout as his lawyer, and George in turn employed his eighteen-year-old brother, John Ridout, to run errands. That meant dealing with Sam Jarvis, who had witnessed some of William's transactions and was trying to sort out the older man's tangled accounts. Given the bad blood between the families, the Jarvises would regard Ridout's activities on behalf of creditors as harassment by clan enemies.

On July 5, 1817, John Ridout called upon Samuel Peters Jarvis. Precisely what happened in that office is unknown; we have only Jarvis's version, stating that Ridout was offensive and insulting. In any case, Sam Jarvis forcibly ejected young Ridout. Four days later they came to blows in the streets of York. The fight was broken up by

Samuel Peters Jarvis – When Jarvis killed John Ridout in a duel, it was the culmination of a bitter quarrel between two prominent Toronto families. (Toronto Reference Library T30358)

Captain James Fitzgibbon (hero of the recent war) and another man, variously described as Robert Kerr or Dr. Robert C. Horne, the King's Printer. There could be no doubt that this quarrel extended to all of York's upper crust.

The affair now came to a head. Words had led to fisticuffs; the next stage was pistols. Ridout issued the challenge, Jarvis accepted, and the arrangements were made. The seconds would be, for Jarvis, Henry John Boulton (son of the Attorney-General, later Solicitor-General of Upper Canada, and still later Chief Justice of Newfoundland) and, for Ridout, James Small (son of Major John Small whom we have met, and later Treasurer of the Law Society of Upper Canada). The time would be dawn of July 12, 1817; the place, Elmsley's Farm, now the site of Yonge and College streets, well outside the boundaries of York at that time.

They reached the chosen site an hour before daylight. It was raining, and they found shelter in a barn. As dawn broke, the rain ceased and the principals took their places. From a common point they paced eight yards in opposite directions. The count, given by Small, was to be "One, two, three, fire." On the count of "two," Ridout raised his arm, fired, missed and began to walk away.

Ridout's premature shot was a terrible breach of the duelling codes. Was he nervous? Had he deliberately cheated with the intention of killing his opponent? Or had he intentionally fired wide, hoping Jarvis would do the same? Whatever the case, he was brought back by the seconds and a conference followed. He asked for another pistol, was given one loaded, and then had it taken away. Small and Boulton agreed that Sam Jarvis was entitled to his shot. Ridout stood in his place; the count resumed. On the word "Fire!" Jarvis brought up his arm and pulled the trigger. The report shattered the still morning air. Ridout collapsed, shot through the jugular and the windpipe.

According to medical testimony accepted at the subsequent coroner's inquest, John Ridout died instantly. This may seem improbable, but the description of his wounds suggests that he was incapable of speech, likely went into shock and quickly bled to death. Yet it was later stated by those present that he briefly stayed on his feet, remained conscious long enough to shake hands with all and forgave Jarvis! No matter what actually happened, the account that Jarvis and both seconds produced, then and in 1828, was a story painting them as honourable men, adhering strictly to a gentlemanly code and given final absolution by the dying victim. It was a good picture to present to any jury.

Boulton and Small left York for a time. Samuel Peters Jarvis was arrested immediately and imprisoned. Unlike many duellists, he had to wait a long time for his trial, which did not take place until October. During that interval he was allowed out once, to visit his dying father, but he was back behind bars when William Jarvis died and was buried.

Local opinion had been critical of Sam Jarvis. One story ran to the effect that, after his early shot, John Ridout had cried out, "Oh! Sam, I hope I have not hurt you," and that Jarvis had replied, "If you had, I would still have given you this one" before firing the fatal bullet. As the Jarvis/Small/Boulton version spread, the climate became more favourable. At the trial, Jarvis pleaded "not guilty." Although the presiding judge, Chief Justice William Dummer Powell, was a close friend of the accused's family, his charge to the jury included a stern lecture emphasizing the true nature of the law. Nevertheless, the jury was out only a few minutes and returned with a verdict of acquittal.

The Jarvis–Ridout duel of 1817 had many interesting aftereffects, great and small. John Ridout, who had gone to war at the age of fourteen, was buried in the churchyard of St. James' Church. A carved inscription was placed beside the grave; it is now preserved in the porch of Toronto's Anglican Cathedral and reads in part:

> In Memory of John Ridout… His filial affection, engaging manners, and nobleness of mind gave early promise of future excellence. This promise he gallantly fulfilled by his brave, active, and enterprising conduct which gained the praise of his superiors while serving as midshipman in the Provincial Navy during the late War. At the return of peace he commenced with ardour the study of law, and with the fairest prospects, but a Blight came, and he was consigned to an early grave on July 12th 1817, aged 18.

Mary Ridout, mother of the deceased, never forgave any of those present at the duel. She often stood by the door of St. James' Cathe-

St. James' Cathedral – The inscription to John Ridout, which can be seen today inside the porch of Toronto's Anglican cathedral, ascribed his death to "a Blight," a sophisticated insult directed at Samuel Peters Jarvis. (National Archives of Canada C-2790)

dral, waiting for Henry John Boulton to emerge, whereupon she would curse him publicly for his part in John Ridout's death.

The year after the duel, Samuel Peters Jarvis married Mary Powell, daughter of the judge who had tried him. She had previously been engaged to John Macdonnell, the near-duellist of 1812. Jarvis ultimately became Superintendent of Indian Affairs, and he died in 1857.

In 1828 Francis Collins, editor of the *Canadian Freeman*, wrote an article critical of Boulton (then the Solicitor-General), particularly for his connection with the duel of 1817. Collins was indicted for criminal libel, but in the process he managed to convince a grand jury that both Boulton and Small should be tried as accessories to murder. The two men, present in the court and wearing their gowns, were immediately arrested, tried over two days and acquitted; the jury was out only ten minutes. At the time of this *cause célèbre*, eleven years after the duel, several accounts of the earlier event were published, some repeating the versions of 1817, others with additional details. The Jarvis–Ridout duel is well documented in part because it was twice dragged through the courts.[11]

The Wilson–Lyon duel of 1833, otherwise known as the Perth duel, is probably the best known Canadian duel – and one that has been much misunderstood. A popular song by Stompin' Tom Connors has described it as "The Last Fatal Duel in this Country"; tourist literature, placemats and souvenirs distributed in Perth make the same claim. In 1982 the town even staged a "re-enactment" of the duel – a tasteless gesture, celebrating what was at best a stupid display of snobbish pride, if not a criminal act.

Perth had been founded in 1817 as a home for displaced Scottish weavers and a settlement for soldiers whose regiments had been disbanded after the Napoleonic Wars. Within a decade of its establishment, civilian colonists outnumbered military ones. Nevertheless, the former officers continued to dominate social and political affairs.

Their values, including exaggerated class snobbery and ultra-sensitive pride, were stamped upon the isolated community.[12]

Public rhetoric in Perth tended to be abusive and colourful, and personal disputes were bitter and uncompromising. The local aristocracy was prone to duelling. Although documentation is incomplete, it appears that most early encounters were harmless, akin to rough play-acting accompanied by crude public name-calling. In 1827 a lawyer named Daniel McMartin challenged someone to a duel; it is not known precisely who was his opponent or whether the challenge was accepted. In June 1830 lawyers Thomas M. Radenhurst and James Boulton, accompanied by seconds, rowed to an island near Brockville on the St. Lawrence River and there exchanged fire before reaching an "amicable arrangement." In January 1833 a more serious affray occurred; one Alexander McMillan (seconded by Radenhurst) fought Doctor Alexander Thom (seconded by Francis Henry Cumming, editor of the local newspaper). Doctor Thom had invited several of the town's upper crust to a party; McMillan had been asked to attend but his wife had been excluded from the invitation. This slight had led to a quarrel and hence the duel. The doctor received a minor leg wound, after which relations were patched. In April 1833 lawyers Daniel McMartin and James Boulton exchanged insults in printed notices; Boulton (who may have been McMartin's opponent in 1827) declined to be drawn into a duel on this occasion. McMartin called him "a liar, a coward, and a scoundrel," while Boulton described his enemy as a "low, insignificant scoundrel" unworthy of genteel combat.[13]

Perth, then, was a society with more than its fair share of prickly egos and pretentious parvenus. Community leaders talked incessantly of "honour" and "social position"; duels past and proposed were discussed. The highly-charged atmosphere must have affected the mental processes of John Wilson and Robert Lyon, though Wilson claimed to abhor duelling.

Robert Lyon had been born in Scotland in 1813 and had come to

Perth in 1829. His brother, a former army officer, was a prominent businessman, landowner and public figure whose own marriage linked him to Thomas Radenhurst and thus to the Ridouts of Toronto. By 1833 the younger Lyon was acknowledged as being handsome, charming and popular. He was also reputed to be a good shot with a pistol, the result of frequent practice.

John Wilson, born in Scotland in 1809, had reached Perth with his family in 1819. His father , a literate man with some medical knowledge, was considered to be above the level of the common herd, but as a former weaver his social rank – and John's – was below that of the Lyon family in the local pecking order. John Wilson apparently went into law in part to advance up the social ladder. He would be particularly sensitive to any event that might threaten his climb.

Wilson had been showing romantic interest in one Elizabeth Hughes, an English-born lady who had arrived in 1832. Her parents were dead; she was considered an "unprotected female," living with Mr. and Mrs. Gideon Ackland. Miss Hughes was also the object of attention from Henry Lelièvre, described many years afterwards as being "a well dressed idle nobody." That may have been true, but with his own colourful background (scion of a French Royalist naval officer who had switched to the British during the Revolution) and connections (his aunt was Mrs. Alexander Thom), Lelièvre still created interest in Perth's parochial upper crust.

Lyon and Wilson, friends and law students articled to Perth barristers, were visiting Bytown (modern Ottawa) on business in early 1833. At some point, Lyon spoke to Wilson about Elizabeth Hughes, mentioning that she seemed interested in Lelièvre and describing her as a woman who allowed men to put their arms about her in a manner "which no woman of spirit would permit." (Of course, in 1833, anything beyond tenuous hand-holding was considered lewd.) Lyon later claimed that his remarks were intended as a joke (though one in bad taste). He evidently had wanted to tease Wilson and make him jealous of Lelièvre.

Lyon clearly did not realize that Wilson had already turned his eye upon another lady, Joanna Lees. However, Wilson seized upon Lyon's scandalous allegations as a means of breaking off with Elizabeth Hughes. He wrote Gideon Ackland, reported Lyon's comments, and cited them as a reason for discontinuing his courting. In doing so he claimed he was mentioning her behaviour only as "proof of the young lady's good nature," then added that "there was a point when good nature itself became criminal." As an added touch of hypocrisy, Wilson declared that he "forebore to comment on the principles or honour of a man who could make such a statement relating to an unprotected female."

The letter did not remain private; its general contents were soon known to many. On his return to Perth, Robert Lyon discovered he was being frozen out of polite society. He soon found out why. Apart from Wilson's tale-bearing, Lyon was incensed at his companion's lofty moralizing about principles and honour. On June 12, 1833, they met in the street. Lyon demanded they adjourn to a private spot behind a wall. There he administered a beating, knocked Wilson down and called him "a damned lying scoundrel." Wilson wanted to offer some explanation (he had been surprised that Ackland had shown the letter around), but Lyon would have none of it. Nor could Wilson conceal his fight with Lyon; at least one man had witnessed it, while facial bruises showed the extent of the pummelling. The low-born, aspiring social climber had suffered a public disgrace; the professed enemy of duelling set out to protect his honour with a duel.

Although at least one person advised Wilson to let the matter rest, the young man sent a fellow law student, Simon Fraser Robertson, to Lyon, ostensibly for an "explanation." There was little chance of negotiations or compromise, and by late morning of June 13 a rendezvous had been arranged. Robertson would act as Wilson's second and Henry Lelièvre would serve for Lyon. They were to meet in a field beside the Tay River, a mile from Perth and just over the boundary that divided the Bathurst and Johnstown districts. Dr. William Hamilton would attend. The time would be 6:00 p.m., a very late hour for such affairs. Word of the impending confrontation spread, and several people set out for the spot, including Alexander Powell, a deputy sheriff, who claimed he had intended to stop the fight. In fact, Powell joined others in watching from a distance, assuming that this would be another instance of play-acting.

It was raining, and several of the parties had brought umbrellas. Percussion pistols were produced; the older, less reliable flintlock pistols would not have functioned in this damp weather. Lyon and Wilson were placed several yards apart, loaded weapons in hand. The signal was given; they fired; they missed.[14] Honour might have been satisfied at this point, and the affair could have ended on a handshake. Wilson, at least, apparently expected that matters would so proceed. He had gone to the field intending to fire wide (but not in the air – an obvious admission of guilt) and had hoped Lyon would do the same. He was shocked to discover that a second exchange was expected.

Often accounts of duels are based on self-serving statements of parties intent on saving their skins and reputations. In this instance, however, Doctor Hamilton may be considered to have been more disinterested than most, and his description of events confirmed those of Wilson, Robertson and the distant spectators. Wilson and Lyon, of course, could not communicate directly, only through their seconds. It is evident that Lelièvre was intent upon forcing the duel to a further exchange. His motives were not clear. Did he misunderstand the intermediary role of a second? Or did he mistakenly regard Wilson as a rival for Elizabeth Hughes and hope that the encounter would end in his death or disgrace?

Doctor Hamilton spoke to the seconds, begging that there be a pause while a reconciliation was attempted. Lelièvre flatly declared that such a course was out of the question. Hamilton, over Lelièvre's objections, spoke directly to Lyon, asking if there was no way to end the "unfortunate business"; Lyon said it was impossible. The doctor addressed Wilson and Robertson; both were anxious to have some peaceful settlement, but they were stymied by the intransigence of Lyon and Lelièvre, who declined any discussions or mutual apologies. The pistols were reloaded. The men prepared for the second exchange.

Wilson saw Lelièvre pointing out a ploughed furrow to Lyon, who seemed ready to use it in sighting his pistol. Sick with horror, certain that Lyon was aiming directly for him, Wilson turned his head away and pulled the trigger. Lyon collapsed, shot through both lungs, and died within minutes. The spectators rushed forward; Henry Lelièvre fled and was never seen in Perth again. John Wilson and Simon Robertson surrendered to the law at once and were imprisoned in Perth. The town was in an uproar. The malodorous role of Lelièvre was recognized at once, but it was also expected that things would go hard for the successful duellist and his friend. A coroner's inquest returned a verdict of "wilful murder."

In the immediate aftermath of the duel Perth's hotheads vented more dangerous blather. Lyon's employer, Thomas Radenhurst, railed drunkenly against James Boulton, who was Wilson's patron. For a time it was feared that these two enemies would face off again. The tempest passed; the courts would deal with the successful duellist and his companion.

John Wilson challenged and killed Robert Lyon in 1833 but won acquittal at a murder trial. One person attributed the outcome to the presence of many Irish on the jury. (Toronto Reference Library, J. Ross Robertson Collection T16864)

The choice of duelling ground meant that the crime had been committed in Johnstown District, and so the trial was to be held in Brockville. The two accused were taken there on August 6. On the 9th a grand jury returned a "true bill" or indictment for murder, and they were tried that day. The court room was packed, the case attracting the special interest of "respectable females."

Mr. Justice James B. Macaulay admitted a considerable amount of hearsay evidence that described the events leading to the duel as well as the combat itself. Neither defendant, by the existing law, was considered a competent witness, but they were allowed to address the jury, which they did with much contrition and eloquence, stressing that they had not sought Lyon's death. In his remarks to the jury, Judge Macaulay emphasized the charge. Murder, he said, was the causing of death with "malice aforethought"; manslaughter was causing a death but without malice. He accurately described duels as illegal residues of barbarous times, though he also let slip the phrase that "juries had not been known to convict when all was fair." He advised the jury that evidence explaining Wilson's actions "should be more properly addressed to another place" (a vague expression, possibly meaning that he would consider the evidence when sentencing, but the jurors should ignore it in reaching a verdict). It was a balanced charge, a fair statement of the law, and could well have pointed to a conviction for manslaughter. Nevertheless, after retiring briefly, the jury unreservedly acquitted both men. Back in Perth, the Reverend William Bell wrote in his diary of his surprise at the verdict. He credited it to many factors – the youth and eloquence of the defendants, the provocation Wilson had reputedly received and the Irish composition of the jury!

The courts could impose no penalty on John Wilson, but some other punishments could be inflicted upon him. His Presbyterian congregation reprimanded him and barred him from communion for three months. Joanna Lees, his undoubted favourite lady, took family advice and spurned him. In 1835 he married his second choice, Elizabeth Hughes, in a match that was more likely founded in her financial problems and his guilt feelings than in love. Their union put a romantic tinge on the duel – but it should be remembered that Wilson had fought for his own reputation, not hers.

Wilson became a successful lawyer, a middle-ranking moderate-Tory-turned-moderate-Reformer, and in 1863 was appointed to the bench. It is reliably reported that he was soon afterwards visibly shaken to find himself presiding over Assizes in Brockville. He had not been in the court house there since his own murder trial many years before. A legend that Wilson could never bring himself to pass a sentence of death on any offender is contradicted by the facts; in 1867 he condemned seven Fenians to hang, although the government later bowed to foreign pressure and commuted the sentences. A tale that on the anniversary of the duel he would lock himself in his room to brood is melodramatic but unsupported by any evidence. Undoubtedly, however, throughout his career he regretted the affair as the principal folly of his youth. John Wilson died in 1869, and Elizabeth survived until 1904.

Robert Lyon had been buried in Perth. His grave was long neglected but has in recent years been clearly marked for tourists to view. The inscription on his tombstone reads:

Friendship Offering
Dedicated
To the Memory of
ROBERT LYON
(Student-at-Law)
He fell
in mortal combat
13<sup>th</sup> of June 1833
in the 20<sup>th</sup> year of his age
Requiescat in Pace

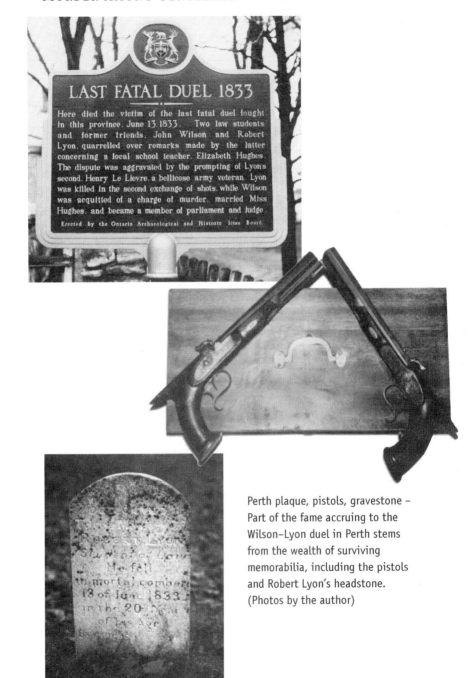

**LAST FATAL DUEL 1833**

Here died the victim of the last fatal duel fought in this province, June 13, 1833. Two law students and former friends, John Wilson and Robert Lyon, quarrelled over remarks made by the latter concerning a local school teacher, Elizabeth Hughes. The dispute was aggravated by the prompting of Lyon's second, Henry Le Lievre, a bellicose army veteran. Lyon was killed in the second exchange of shots, while Wilson was acquitted of a charge of murder, married Miss Hughes, and became a member of parliament and judge.

Erected by the Ontario Archaeological and Historic Sites Board.

Perth plaque, pistols, gravestone – Part of the fame accruing to the Wilson–Lyon duel in Perth stems from the wealth of surviving memorabilia, including the pistols and Robert Lyon's headstone. (Photos by the author)

The Wilson–Lyon duel is virtually the only such Canadian event to have been accorded some official recognition. The Ontario Archaeological and Historic Sites Board has erected a plaque in Perth which briefly recounts the story of the fight. As mentioned earlier, the community vehemently claims to be the site of the last fatal duel *in Canada*, but the provincial government's notice simply and accurately describes the affair as the last fatal duel in *Upper Canada*.[15]

T he Wilson–Lyon encounter was not the last in Upper Canada. It was followed by other challenges and exchanges, though none with a tragic outcome. There is a report of a duel at St. Regis, near Cornwall, in 1834. Donald Aeneas McDonnell (1794-1879), member of the Legislative Assembly for Stormont, had written a letter to a newspaper in which he criticized the accounting methods of Alexander McLean, then treasurer of the district. McLean sent a challenge, McDonnell accepted, and the pair exchanged shots without either being wounded.[16]

A curious incident occurred in Toronto in February 1835. About noon of the 25th a young law student named George Cooper was found in a side street, badly wounded and "weltering in his own blood." He was taken to a mansion and treated. The youth told a story of having fought a duel three hours earlier and, on being wounded, having been moved by his companions to a place where he would be found by passers-by. Cooper died the next day. A coroner's inquest was convened. Its members concluded that no duel had occurred. Cooper, they said, had shot himself in a bungled suicide attempt and had then invented the story of the fight in a pathetic attempt to salvage some honour and dignity. As another student-at-law said, he had a distorted view of duelling and its "respectability."[17]

A dispute rooted in banking and politics led to a duel in Toronto on March 19, 1835. George Truscott (1785-1851), an English capitalist, had founded the Agricultural Bank and then the Farmers' Bank, both headquartered in the provincial capital. Other bankers dis-

Although his pistol misfired, Allan Napier McNab wanted to continue his 1835 duel with George Truscott. (Toronto Reference Library, J. Ross Robertson Collection T15341)

trusted Truscott, whom they considered to be a sharp, possibly unethical character. The fact that the Agricultural Bank loaned money to Toronto while the hated Radical, William Lyon Mackenzie, was mayor also set Truscott apart from mainstream entrepreneurs.

His protagonist was Allan Napier McNab (1798-1862), whose many posts included being solicitor for the Commercial Bank, a Kingston-based institution. Truscott appears to have made some remarks in private that disparaged McNab, and these became public when Mackenzie repeated them in the Legislative Assembly. McNab was the probable challenger. At their meeting, Truscott had as his second an A. Turner; McNab was supported by one Radenhurst – almost certainly Thomas Radenhurst, who shared his politics. McNab's pistol misfired and Truscott discharged his into the air. McNab was anxious for another exchange, but the seconds persuaded him to end the matter there. Subsequently, McNab figured prominently in business and political affairs. He is best remembered for building Hamilton's Dundurn Castle and his remark, "Railroads are my politics," but he was also instrumental in advancing a protégé, John A. Macdonald. Truscott eventually confirmed the worst suspicions of his critics, fleeing to the United States to avoid imprisonment for embezzlement.[18]

Two newspaper items tell us of an affair between doctors in Brantford in 1836. The reports make fascinating reading, for they say as much about newspaper practices as about the event itself. The first is from the *Dundas Weekly Post*, March 8, 1836:

About the 20th of last month, Dr. Dowding, one of our medical practitioners, was called to attend a lady of this town in her confinement. He did so, and before the matter could be brought to a successful issue, thought it advisable to call in Dr. —, another gentleman of the same profession, to consult on the exigency of the case. Some difference of opinion arose, it appeared, as to the treatment of the patient, and from that a demand for satisfaction was made on the part of the former to the latter. After some epistolatory correspondence between them, the challenge was accepted by Dr. —, and the parties accordingly met on the morning of the 27th ult. After the exchange of two shots without effect, the seconds interfered.

The *Brantford Courier* of February 27, 1836, also reported the event:

A meeting having taken place this morning between Dr. Dowding and Dr. —, after an exchange of two shots each between the parties, the seconds interfered, and, although a reconciliation was not effected between them, it was agreed that Dr. Dowding would retract the words "liar, scoundrel and coward," applied to Dr. —, and the latter should in like manner retract the words "liar, villain, scoundrel and fool," as applied to Dr. Dowding; and that all reflections upon the character of either party as a gentleman, now published or in the press, should be considered as retracted.
Signed – Lloyd Richardson (in behalf of Dr. Dowding)
E. Saunders (in behalf of Dr. —)

The papers had only partly identified one participant, and had declined to name the other in any way. Why this was so is unknown.

For the record, the two were Drs. John Dowding (an English-born gentleman who practised first at Ancaster and then Dundas) and Alfred Digby (Irish-born, a reeve in Brantford, noted for introducing a motion in council that a councillor who arrived drunk should be ignored). We are left to wonder what happened to the patient.[19]

The Detroit *Daily Advertiser* of November 21, 1836, carried the report of another duel which began with a quarrel on Canadian soil and ended on American territory:

> An Affair of Honour – We learn that on Saturday last (November 19th), pistol shots were exchanged on the classic ground of Hog Island [now Belle Island, a Detroit park] between two "gentlemen" of Amherstburgh, U.C., one a lawyer, Richardson, and the other a gentlemen loafer, named Rankin. The causes of this honourable interview, grew out of a bar room quarrel in which said Rankin was injured, either in person or character to an extent which nothing could repair short of a duel. Challenge was sent and accepted, and according to agreement the parties met at 12 paces, with pistols and seconds. Upon firing, Richardson received a ball in the side, which passed through, caused a serious moving of the bowel. Upon his falling, the seconds were so much alarmed as to leave the ground with precipitation, and were soon out of view. Rankin receiving no serious injury, fled in a canoe, thinking perhaps that
>
> > "He who fights and runs away,
> > may live to fight another day"
>
> Richardson was taken by some men who were near the island in a canoe, and conveyed to Sandwich, where he is under the charge of a surgeon.

Newspapers in Upper and Lower Canada repeated the story, adding few details. *Le Minerve* of Montreal (December 29, 1836) stated that the victim had been the brother of the member of the legislature for Niagara, and grimly described him as having been abandoned "lying in his own blood." The *Constitution*, a Toronto paper, of December 14, 1836, reprinting an item from the *Detroit Spectator*, added that the quarrel had begun in bar room fisticuffs, and that Richardson had died on the 20th.

"Rankin" was no less that Arthur Rankin, a rising figure in political and military circles around Sandwich. In February 1839 he was in the papers again, this time denying that he had challenged Colonel John Prince. At that time the American papers referred to "Rankin, of Hog Island memory," indicating that the affair had gained notoriety along the border.

But who was "Richardson" and what had become of him? It would seem that the contemporary accounts were erroneous, for a modern writer, David Beasley, has identified the victim as Henry Richardson, a Sandwich-area lawyer, militia officer, future magistrate, and half-brother of Major John Richardson. According to Beasley, the duel was over a woman, and Richardson survived with a wound in the thigh. This, as much as the selection of American soil, would explain the lack of legal prosecution. However, Beasley dates the duel as November 23, 1836, which is clearly erroneous given the fact that it had been reported in a newspaper dated the 21st.[20]

John Prince (1796-1870) was one of the most colourful and controversial personalities in Canadian public life. As a magistrate and militia officer in the Windsor area in 1837-38 he was active in repelling attacks across the border by exiled Canadian rebels and their American supporters. These attacks were locally regarded as banditry; a comparison to 20th-century trans-border political terrorism is appropriate. On December 4, 1838, having taken many prisoners during one such raid (the Battle of Windsor), Prince ordered five captives to be shot. Although harassed citizens generally approved of this draconian act – the more so since American authorities were weak in preventing "Patriot" raids – others on both sides of the border condemned Prince.

In January 1839 the Detroit *Daily Advertiser* printed two letters, purportedly written by Canadians, which luridly described the executions and also criticized Prince's conduct as a magistrate. The letters were unsigned, but Prince set out to discover their authors and take action. He enlisted the services of Lieutenant Henry Rudyerd, 15th Regiment of Foot. Prince's diary records the subsequent dramatic events:

February 6, 1839 … At half past 4 I started for Malden on horseback with a view of seeing my friend Rudyerd and prevailing on him to stand my friend as against Col. [William] Eliott, Chas. Eliot, & the other Conspirators.

February 8, 1839 … At home all day long and very busily engaged in writing etc. Mr. Rudyerd called on me and wrote to Chas. Baby & other enemies of mine for Satisfaction. Answers tomorrow… At home all day and did not stir out. Unhappy at the base Conduct & ingratitude of C. Baby and others toward me.

February 9, 1839 … Engaged at Sandwich & at the Ferry all day. Horsewhipped Mr. Charles Baby because he refused to meet my challenge Except upon Hog Island, American soil, and I afterwards

John Prince took his politics and his personal honour very seriously. He duelled with at least one enemy, horsewhipped another, and sued a hostile newspaper for libel. (National Archives of Canada C4838)

posted him at Windsor, Sandwich and Malden as a Coward, a Liar, & a Poltroon – At home all the evening. Lt. [Allen] Cameron called [2nd Provincial Militia].[21]

February 11, 1839. A very snowy morning. Rose at 5 & accompanied by Capt. Rudyerd to the place of meeting. We arrived there half an hour before the Enemy. Very cold. Mr. W. [William] R. Wood [an architect, teacher, and District Treasurer] was attended by Lt. Cameron & I by Rudyerd. Distance 12 paces. At the first fire my Pistol missed fire. On the 2nd shot I hit Mr. Wood in the Jaw & the ball lodged there. He missed me both shots. Home by 8 to breakfast. I sent him home in my sleigh, & Rudyerd and I walked all the way.

John Prince never lived down the notoriety he achieved through his summary execution of prisoners. In 1849 the *Free Press*, published in London, Canada West, by William Sutherland, described Prince as "foul-mouthed, tyrannical and brutal." In May 1851 he brought charges of criminal libel against the paper. *The Queen vs. William Sutherland* was a landmark case in the history of Canadian libel law, for on this occasion the defence pleaded truth as justification, a tactic only recently allowed by legislation. The newspaper was acquitted, thanks in large measure to the work of John Wilson, one of the lawyers for the *Free Press*. His contribution to the cause of freedom of the press was significant, but it would remain overshadowed by his association with the Perth duel of 1833.[22]

Ironically for one so belligerent, John Prince in his capacity as a magistrate had to prevent a duel. On the night of January 21, 1856, he learned by anonymous letter that two men were planning "to meet in hostile array" at dawn. He ordered them both arrested. They were his own son, Albert Prince, and his political rival, Arthur Rankin, formerly a supporter during the controversies of 1839.[23]

In tracing the story of John Prince and his associates, we have left behind (chronologically) a duel at the other end of Upper Canada. On August 3, 1838, the *British Whig* carried the following item:

DUEL – An affair of Honour took place at Bytown on Saturday morning last [July 28], between Andrew Powell, Esq. – Barrister, of Bytown, and John Egan, Esq. – Merchant, of Aylmer, in which an exchange of shots and an explanation were the sole consequences. The duel arose from the circumstance of Mr. Powell's considering an intimate friend of Mr. Egan's to be no gentleman, which the latter resented. There is now no question as to the gentleman's gentility. Capt. Read, and G. Buchanan, Esq. were the seconds.[24]

The most notable figure in this incident was John Egan (1811-57), the Irish-born entrepreneur who was rising to prominence as one of the Ottawa Valley's most influential and creative timber barons. There is something appealing about his "going to the turf" on behalf of a friend, but we do not know the identity of the person whose honour Egan was defending.

One further duel occurred on November 28, 1840. Dr. Robert D. Hamilton of Queenston fell out with lawyer James Boulton, for business reasons that contemporary papers declined to describe. They crossed the Niagara River to American soil – another attempt to evade authorities by resorting to foreign territory. Two bloodless exchanges of fire healed wounded honour and the affair ended.[25]

Apart from those recorded duels, some further attempts were made in the eastern area. On December 19, 1839, two cases were heard in court in Perth involving a militia officer and two belligerent brothers. The newspapers reported them as follows:

The Queen at the suit of Lieutenant Bolton Read of March, versus John George Street, Esq. for being the bearer of a Duel challenge to the informant. The Jury, after three hours deliberation, gave a Verdict against the defendant. The Court deferred judgement, holding the defendant in recognizance for hereafter appearance when called on.

The Queen at the suit of Lieut. Bolton Read, versus Benjamin

Street, Esq. on three counts – first for writing a challenge; second for sending a challenge to the said Read; and third for posting him as a poltroon and coward. Mr. McMartin, for the defendant, had full scope for his usual zeal and ability. Mr. Radenhurst, for the informant, gave a clear exposition of the law in this untenable case, defendant – Acquittal.[26]

This incident, not fully explained in contemporary records, is all the more puzzling for the fact that the jury verdicts were apparently so contradictory. Subsequently, letters appearing in local papers indicated that John George Street had been challenged some three years earlier by a local schoolmaster, Dugald McNab. On that occasion Street had declined to duel – possibly because McNab was a cousin and hopelessly nearsighted.

Yet another duel may have been averted in romantic circumstances. Late in 1840 Lieutenant-Colonel Ogle R. Gowan (1803-76), a prominent Brockville lawyer, politician, and militia officer, challenged Lieutenant-Colonel Richard Duncan Fraser (1784-1857). The latter, a particularly quarrelsome figure, declared that Gowan was beneath the station of a gentleman and not a worthy opponent. However, he was willing to duel with Gowan's second, Lieutenant-Colonel Alexander Grant. A meeting was arranged, but on the intended morning Mrs. Fraser slipped out of her house and alerted the authorities. Brockville magistrates summoned Fraser and Grant and had them swear to keep the peace.[27]

Such at least was the contemporary newspaper account. Gowan's biographer tells a simpler tale. Fraser, disliking Gowan's political stands of the day, entered his office. In the presence of Gowan's son he accused him of being a coward and a fool. Gowan demanded satisfaction at twenty paces. The intended seconds, however, intervened to mediate a reconciliation before a meeting could be held.[28]

# Chapter 5

⋄

# Duelling
# in Atlantic Canada

The French colony of Acadia, after changing hands several times through wars and treaties, was ceded to England in 1713, although Île Royale and Île St. Jean (Cape Breton Island and Prince Edward Island) remained under French control. Acadia became Nova Scotia, and initially the seat of government remained at Port Royal (renamed Annapolis Royal for Queen Anne). However, a new capital was founded in 1749 at Halifax. Cape Breton Island, captured in 1745, returned to French rule in 1748. Ten years later the British seized it again, administered it for some years as a separate colony and finally annexed it to Nova Scotia.

French garrisons at Port Royal had been succeeded by British troops at Annapolis Royal, Halifax and other points along the coast. It seems logical that duels may have taken place in these years among the officers, but if so, they have gone unrecorded. The first known such affair occurred in Halifax on August 20, 1787. Two years earlier, Captain George Dalrymple, 42nd Highlanders, had made some scurrilous remarks about Lieutenant Charles Roberts, 57th Regiment, describing him as "unfit for the Grenadiers" and as having sold some books that did not belong to him. Roberts was in Europe at the time, and even after his return to Halifax he could not confront his enemy, who was stationed on Cape Breton Island. When at last they met, there was one exchange of shots. Dalrymple was wounded in one arm and the affair terminated.[1]

Simeon Perkins, a prominent citizen of Liverpool, Nova Scotia, kept a diary which has been a goldmine for historians. During a visit to Halifax he sparsely recorded a more serious encounter:

Wednesday, March 17 [1790] ... One Capt. [John] Lloyd of the troops is dead from a wound received in a duel with one Mr. Williams, a subaltern.

Thursday, March 18 ... The body of Capt. Lloyd buried. The Coroner's inquest brought in their verdict – wilful murder.

Friday, April 9th ... Mr Williams, the officer who killed Capt. Lloyd was tried and acquitted.[2]

Another duel, even more spectacular in its outcome, may have taken place some years later. On October 30, 1936, the Canadian Press carried the following story to newspapers across the nation:

North Aspect of Halifax, 1781. Canadian cities of the period were actually towns ringed by open country where duellists could find needed privacy. (New Brunswick Museum, Webster Canadiana Collection, W668)

Today when you trump your partner's ace the incident is usually dismissed with a frown or a mumbled oath, but there was a time in Nova Scotia when gentlemen took their cards seriously, and thereby hangs the tale of the last duel fought with swords.

Musty records take us back to a July evening in 1796, when the Duke of Kent, commander of the British forces in North America, entertained a large number of guests at the summer residence, Prince's Lodge, in honour of a visiting Baron. There were approximately 300 officers and civilian guests present. Card tables were set everywhere, wines were served freely, and a general atmosphere of civility pervaded.

About midnight most of the guests departed, leaving a number of the more engrossed card players to their own devices.

Among the latter was a group consisting of Col. Ogilvie, the Earl Ailsa, Capt. Howard of the Navy, and the Prince's A.D.C., Montague. They were seated in an alcove between the first and second lawns. All were wealthy and, though the stakes were high, seemed quite unconcerned and gay.

As the game progressed, however, the play grew intense, nerves were on edge and suspicion rampant. Suddenly an argument started between Ogilvie and Howard, turning quickly into a quarrel. A challenge was given and accepted; the point was to be settled by combat.

The quartet proceeded to an outpost guard room where rapiers were borrowed from Major Richard, and from thence went to the second lawn where the duel was to be held, Montague and Lord Ailsa acting as seconds.

The duel was fierce and bloody, both Ogilvie and Howard being expert swordsmen, and for some time neither had the advantage though both were receiving severe wounds. Suddenly Howard saw an opening in his opponent's guard, lunged, and Ogilvie fell dead to the ground in a wealter of blood.

Captain Howard's victory, however, was gained only at a great price; mortally wounded in the duel, he died soon after he had killed his adversary.

The duel created a great stir at the time, and the Duke of Kent refused to allow Col. Ogilvie to be buried with military honours.[3]

Unfortunately for the historian, the CP despatch carried no byline, and the "musty records" were not identified. The Halifax papers of July-August 1796 made no mention of the affair, but that was not surprising, since early colonial papers largely ignored local affairs (which were common knowledge from social gossip). More disturbing is that no Colonel or Lieutenant Colonel Ogilvie drops from the British Army List between 1795 and 1798. The spectacle of mutual mayhem makes for melodramatic reading, but was the CP report correct? Did the duel even happen? If so, how closely did events match the reconstruction of 140-odd years later?

Richard John Uniacke (1753-1830), the Solicitor-General, came near to duelling in the fall of 1791. He had dismissed a black servant who was immediately hired by the Attorney-General, Sampson Salter Blowers (1743-1842). This somehow provoked Uniacke, who expressed rude opinions of Blowers and was challenged for them. Cooler heads prevailed. The two men were compelled to post bonds and promise to keep the peace, and Uniacke may even have apologized. In 1797 Blowers became Chief Justice of Nova Scotia and Uniacke succeeded to the post of Attorney-General. The pair remained antagonists, and in the spring of 1798 they may again have come close to duelling owing to Uniacke administering a beating to one of Blowers' friends, with the city magistrates once more restraining two such august legal figures from taking the law into their own hands.[4]

Cape Breton Island was a colony distinct from Nova Scotia from 1784 until 1820. Although it lacked an elected legislature, it possessed its share of ill-tempered officials. One such was William McKinnon, a native of Scotland, veteran of the American Revolution, and in 1797 the Clerk of the Executive Council. Political differences also made him an enemy of Chief Justice Archibald Charles Dodd. When Mrs. McKinnon spread gossip about Dodd, the latter retaliated with uncomplimentary remarks about her ("a most infamous liar") and her husband (a "Damn'd Scotch Highland Brute"). In a meeting of the Executive Council on May 18, 1797, McKinnon sent Dodd a challenge to duel. His messenger, David Mathews, was both Attorney-General and acting Governor; having delivered the challenge, he promptly dismissed McKinnon from office. The duel might still have gone forward, but saner third parties intervened to prevent it.[5]

A court case argued in Halifax on July 19, 1819, led to a fatal duel involving Richard John Uniacke, Jr., son and namesake of the Attorney-General. In the heat of argument, Uniacke virtually accused a merchant, William Bowie, of being involved in smuggling and reacting to the production of a document "as a guilty man would have done." Incensed, Bowie wrote to Uniacke, describing these statements as "an untruth." He went on to demand that the lawyer retract the offending remarks. Bowie concluded:

> ... if this is refused, I shall be compelled to think you are losing sight of the high sense of honour you so much valued yourself on, and to say at once you are not a man of truth [a polite way of calling someone a barefaced liar].

Once again, pig-headed pride prevented a man from apologizing simply because an apology had been requested. Uniacke replied to Bowie on the 20th, stating that the merchant's letter closed the door to a retraction. The note, in Uniacke's words, "precludes the possibility of my placing myself on a par with you in explaining assertions made solely under the influence of your imagination." He went on to declare himself ready to duel, even though this would admit to their being social equals.

Richard John Uniacke Jr. refused to apologise for insulting language because the offended party asked for an apology. The foolish behaviour of duellists was often matched by their stubborn self-righteousness. (Nova Scotia Museum)

Seconds were chosen – Stephen W. DeBlois for Bowie, Edward MacSweeney for Uniacke. MacSweeney was reported to be indebted to Bowie, which may have been true, and to have been involved in several earlier duels in the West Indies, which he vehemently denied. The seconds met three times in attempts to prevent the duel from taking place, but their efforts were in vain. At 5:00 a.m., July 21, the quartet met two miles north of Halifax at the North Government Farm.

Arriving at the site, DeBlois called MacSweeney aside. The latter hoped that a reconciliation was still possible, but the conference was only to examine the pistols brought by Bowie. They were considered defective, so Uniacke's pistols were used by both parties. Twelve paces in opposite directions were measured out. Uniacke and Bowie were told to fire quickly, without aiming, on the signal.

On the first exchange, Bowie missed his opponent. MacSweeney described the moment from Uniacke's standpoint; ... the ball from Mr. Uniacke's pistol entered the ground a short distance from him, upon which he quitted his place and asked the cause of his pistol thus going off. I told him he had lost his fire and must return to his ground which he did.

Neither party showed any inclination to negotiate apologies or explanations, and neither of the seconds appears to have taken it upon himself to initiate such talks. In matter-of-fact fashion the pistols were reloaded and the principals readied themselves for another round. We may presume that the seconds had looked carefully to the weapons, perhaps adding more powder, so that there would be no repetition of Uniacke's misfire. Two shots rang out. Uniacke stood his ground; Bowie groaned and gradually collapsed. He had been hit in the right side, just above the hip. The bullet had passed through his intestines and had almost exited on the left. He was carried to the nearby farmhouse where a death watch began.

Uniacke, the victor, went frantic, rushing about, moaning and sobbing, calling for a horse. MacSweeney, having satisfied himself that Bowie was settled in the farm house, leaped into his gig, whipped his horse and made off to fetch a doctor. Eventually there were two surgeons on hand, plus an assortment of soldiers and civilians who made excellent witnesses at the trial to come. Acting either from foresight or formality, MacSweeney approached the dying victim and asked, "My dear Mr. Bowie, have you any charge against Mr. Uniacke or myself?"

The reply was, "No, my dear sir, I have not; all was fair and honourable."

Another witness would testify that Bowie declared, "I forgive Mr. Uniacke, and I hope he will pray for me." Absolution by the victim was a tasteful touch in these Georgian melodramas.

One of the doctors present extracted the bullet, although the case was clearly hopeless. Bowie lingered in great pain and died at 5:50 p.m., twelve hours after being shot. He was buried the next day amid a lavish show of grief on the part of the city's gentry.

One week later, July 28, Richard John Uniacke, Jr., and Edward MacSweeney were in court, charged with murder. Stephen Deblois was accused of a misdemeanour. The normal sitting of the High Court had been extended for one day to allow speedy trial, and presumably not detain true gentlemen in prison any longer than was necessary. The Solicitor-General, S.B. Robie, had declined to prosecute the case on the grounds of his friendship with Bowie. Samuel George William Archibald took the case for the Crown.

The trial was typical of those involving duellists: maudlin, indulgent to the accused and generous in the admitting of evidence. It began with a theatrical gesture. Richard John Uniacke Sr., snowy-haired and still the Attorney-General of Nova Scotia, entered with his son on his arm, proceeded to the bench and in a short, emotional speech formally surrendered him to the court.

Archibald presented the case for the prosecution, giving a fair description of the events leading to Bowie's death. He explained the law to the jury. In this he began well – "the deliberate killing of another in a duel constitutes murder" – but then he proceeded to undermine his own case. He stated that juries had never convicted when they were convinced that the duel had been conducted in a fair and honourable manner. The jury, he said, should convict if they found in the defendants "a rancorous and malicious disposition, which had hurried the parties beyond the bounds of reason and the law." On the other hand, declared Archibald, if they considered that no malice had been involved they should acquit the parties. The choice was either a verdict of "guilty of murder" or an unconditional acquittal. There was not a word about convicting on the lesser charge of manslaughter. Archibald's handling of the case made him almost indistinguishable from defence counsel. Crown witnesses eagerly reported Uniacke's most tentative hopes for a reconciliation before the encounter and Bowie's magnanimous words as he lay dying. Character evidence on behalf of MacSweeney was admitted in spite of much of it being hearsay.

An added touch of melodrama came when Uniacke faced the jury. After breaking down several times, he finally blurted out a defence statement. He swore that he had never intended to injure Bowie. Nevertheless, he stood firm in holding that his honour and that of his distinguished ancestors had been in danger – "My character, my honour, my all, were at stake on the one side, and degradation, disgrace and infamy assailed me on the other" – thus presumably justifying the murderous game played.

Mr. Justice Brenton Halliburton instructed the jury. Following the lead of Crown counsel, he first advised that the law regarded killing in a duel as plain murder, then went on to cite the precedents of other juries that had declined to convict if the duel had been "fair and honourable" – which, he added, all the witnesses had confirmed to be the case here. The jury retired for half an hour and returned with the customary verdict – "not guilty." The gentlemen of Halifax would be spared the spectacle of having the common herd witness the hanging of a colonial aristocrat, or the disgrace of having one of their own endure a prison sentence.

Not everyone was satisfied with the outcome. On August 10, 1819, the Fredericton *Royal Gazette* lamented that a charge of manslaughter had not been pursued. The editorial went on to say:

> The jury *acquitted* the Prisoners, and of course considered their conduct as *justifiable*, because it was *fair* and *honourable*. No case like this has ever, we believe, happened in this Province.

The Saint John *Star* of August 17, 1819, published an article entitled "Ought Duels to be Tolerated?" The piece was long and windy, but it did condemn duelling in harsh terms, describing the practice as illegal, foolish, immoral, unchristian, injurious to the peace, and undermining accepted legal procedures. Other newspapers carried the article. Nevertheless, gentlemen and juries continued to ignore these views. Throughout British North America there would be more such encounters, at least three of them fatal. In two cases there would be prosecutions and acquittals; in a third, a coroner's jury would refuse to identify the killer.

Richard John Uniacke, Jr., released from custody, went on to a moderately successful career in politics. In 1830 he was appointed to the bench; he died in 1834.[6]

A duel occurred on the Chebucto Road – then outside Halifax, now well within that city – on March 2, 1820. Lieutenant Joseph Armstrong, 15th Regiment of Foot, and Captain William Hull, 62nd Regiment, fired simultaneously. Armstrong was hit in the thigh and fell. The cause of their quarrel was not given in the papers.[7]

About this time (1820-21) another incident took place. The exact date is unknown, but there is little doubt that it was fought. Two lawyers, James William Johnston and Charles Rufus Fairbanks (the latter a character witness on behalf of Uniacke at the 1819 trial), had argued during a Halifax court case. Fairbanks used objectionable language for which he refused to apologize. A meeting was arranged in a field (now the corner of Spring Garden Road and Park Street). The Johnston–Fairbanks duel is attended by a curious story. According to tradition, Fairbanks fired first and missed. Johnston remarked, "I will stop you dancing," and fired at his opponent's heel. It is an unlikely tale, considering the notorious inaccuracy of the pistols of the day.

The two principals became major figures in public life. Johnston was twice Premier of Nova Scotia before his appointment to the bench in 1863. He died in 1873. William Hill, who had acted as Johnston's second, was also destined to become a judge. Johnston and Fairbanks became good friends after the duel.[8]

As in Lower Canada, the increasing tensions between Tories and Reformers brought many challenges to duel for political reasons. This may have been the cause of a bloodless affair fought in Halifax in 1838 between Edmund Murray Dodd (later a judge) and a lawyer named Nutting.[9] However, the object of most challenges was Nova

Scotia's leading editor, Reformer and gadfly, Joseph Howe. There can be no doubt about Howe's view of duelling. In a letter to his sister, written in 1840 shortly after his only duel, he declared:

> For my own part, I hate and detest duelling.... A person who engages in it lightly must be a fool – he who is fond of it must be a villain. It is a remnant of a barbarous age, which civilization is slowly but steadily wearing away, but still it is not worn out.

What drove Howe to risk his life in a ritual for which he had only contempt? He had begun as a publisher following a conservative line, but from 1834 onwards he had become increasingly critical of the ruling authorities. In 1835 he had been tried for criminal libel and had been acquitted. The following year he had won election to the Legislative Assembly. With that and his newspaper as his pulpits, Howe had criticized many public officials while advocating an overhaul of the colonial constitution. From 1837 onwards he was subjected to a series of challenges from angry politicians and members of their families. On at least one occasion, in refusing to apologize for a speech, Howe consulted with Dodd, the experienced duellist – whether for legal advice or duelling tips is uncertain. By one means or another, Howe managed to avoid "going to the turf."[10]

Early in 1840, however, the Reform leader made a speech that attacked many local personages including Chief Justice Sir Brenton Halliburton (the judge who had presided over R.J. Uniacke's trial). The text of his remarks is not available, but if they resembled that of a later address, Howe's comments were reasonable and moderate. Nevertheless, they roused the ire of the judge's son, John C. Halliburton, himself a lawyer, who sent a challenge to Howe.

On this occasion Howe accepted. In letters addressed to his wife, to the people of Nova Scotia and to his sister, he explained why he had finally done so. In part it was due to Halliburton's social position – "he was in the situation of a gentleman and had a right to make the

Joseph Howe, "The Tribune of Nova Scotia," was often challenged but fought only one duel; he demonstrated both courage and compassion on that occasion. (National Archives of Canada C-19997)

demand." It is rather difficult to see how the Reformer distinguished between one gentleman and another, but clearly he felt that Halliburton had special claim to attention – perhaps because he was ostensibly defending his father's reputation rather than his own.

Howe's other reason for accepting is much more easily understood. He was convinced that at least once he must make a show of physical courage, to protect his own reputation (and with it the political causes he had espoused), demonstrating that Reformers held as much contempt for Tory pistols as for Tory principles. He hoped, too, that if he survived with honour he might henceforth decline further challenges without risking disgrace.

They met at dawn of March 14, 1840, in Point Pleasant Park. Halliburton's second has not been identified, but Howe was attended by Herbert Huntington, a fellow Reformer. The latter had done his best to prevent the encounter through negotiations and had failed. Pistols were handed both men, the distance was paced off and a dropped handkerchief was the signal to shoot. Halliburton's bullet barely missed Howe. The latter had come with no intention of firing at his opponent. He looked at Halliburton, raised his pistol and fired into the air, saying, "I will not deprive an aged father of his only son."[11] The seconds advanced, and the affair was over.

Howe attained his purpose; only once more was he ever challenged to duel. Within days of his fight with Halliburton he received yet another deadly invitation, this one from Sir Rupert George, the Provincial Secretary. Howe described the outcome to his sister:

> My answer was, that never having had any personal quarrel with Sir Rupert, I should not fire at him if I went out, and that having no great fancy for being shot at by every public officer whose intellect I might happen to contrast with his emoluments, I begged leave to decline. This I could not have done had he come first [i.e. before Halliburton], but now, the honour was not equal to the risk – nothing was to be gained either for myself or my cause – they got laughed at and nobody blamed me.[12]

In reviewing the melancholy record of folly, bigotry, hypocrisy and plain bad manners that brought about so many duels, the example of Joseph Howe stands out as an exceptional case. In the opinion of this writer, he is the only man in Canada who earnestly went out to duel for a worthy or sensible cause.

The St. John River valley saw a great influx of United Empire Loyalists in 1782-83. To accommodate their demands for more efficient local government, the colony of New Brunswick was carved out of territory that had hitherto been part of Nova Scotia. The Loyalist aristocracy was as prone to duelling as were upper classes elsewhere in British North America. Unfortunately, the nature of early accounts does not permit us to identify some incidents precisely, particularly as to dates. Some folklore has also cluttered the records. For example, a fistfight between David Fanning and an unknown blacksmith, occurring on the ice of the St. John River about 1790, has been blown up in one narrative to a duel with axes. The veracity of this story is questionable.

The *Royal Gazette and New Brunswick Advertiser*, published in

View of Saint John, 1814. Like Halifax, Toronto and other pioneer cities, the small community seethed with class distinctions, with an upper class that flouted the law by tolerating duels. (New Brunswick Museum)

Saint John, carried a brief item in its issue of February 16, 1790, re-cording the first fatal duel in the province. It was very incomplete, stating only that a Dr. Cornelius Cobblestone had died the previous day of wounds sustained in a duel "fought between two and three o'clock in the afternoon of Friday last," February 9. His opponent, identified only as a "Mr. B__," had fled the next day to Annapolis, Nova Scotia.

A note found in Cobblestone's pocket partly explained the origins of the duel without shedding any light on the combat itself. The quarrel had apparently been a three-party affair – "B," Cobblestone and Christopher Sower, the King's printer. "B" emerges as a "foreign gentleman" (probably Danish, possibly German) and a surgeon whom Sower had injudiciously described as "a barber."

Dr. Cobblestone had written a letter, published in Sower's newspa-per, which stirred the wrath of "B" and led him to seek a duel with the publisher, who declined on the grounds that his work required him to attend Supreme Court sessions in Fredericton. "B" then wrote a windy, bombastic letter to Cobblestone, seeking "a reparation" – hence the fatal encounter.[13]

Another duel was fought on February 24 or 25, 1797.[14] On the one hand was Colonel John Coffin (1756-1838), a man of great courage and action. During the American Revolution his bravery had won him a battlefield commission, and his ruthlessness had led to a price being put on his head. In New Brunswick he was a fiery ultracon-servative. His opponent in the duel, Captain James Glenie (1750-1817), was an iconoclastic critic of the administration with an abra-sive personality. In the House of Assembly Glenie made some remarks to which Coffin objected. The colonel demanded an apology or satisfaction, and when the former was not forthcoming, they met in a wood near Fredericton for an afternoon engagement, accompanied by seconds identified only as "Capt. McL—" and "Mr. S." The former may have been Archibald McLean (1753-1830), a distinguished Loyal-ist, but one can only guess as to who was the latter person.

The Saint John *Royal Gazette* refused to print a detailed account of the affair, apparently fearing censure by either side, but it did go out of its way to assure its readers that "the contending parties on this oc-casion behaved in every point with the strictest honour, and distin-

Fredericton in 1818. Drink, cards, women, legal arguments and politics were the most common ingredients that led to duels. Fredericton, as a colonial capital, had its share of such incidents. (New Brunswick Museum, Mary Kearny Odell Bequest, 1938, 30188)

guished themselves as Gentlemen and men of valour." The Halifax
*Royal Gazette*, drawing courage from distance, published the following story:

> After the different overtures made by friends of both parties had
> proved ineffectual, the gentlemen met in the woods opposite F—n
> on Friday evening, the 24th of February, about five o'clock. The
> ground being marked out by the Seconds (Capt. McL— and Mr.
> S—) at 12 yards distance, they took their stands back to back. On
> receiving orders from the Seconds, they faced to the right and fired
> together. Col. C's shot went through Mr. G's thigh (a flesh wound).
> Mr. S— communicated the circumstances to the Colonel, and
> asked if he was satisfied. Col. C— replied that he wished Mr. G—
> to make an apology for the words which had given offence. Mr.
> G— told him he was not much hurt, would keep his ground and
> exchange another shot, if he was not satisfied. Both the Seconds
> then observed that it was too late to demand an apology, upon
> which Col. C—, in a manly manner, declared himself satisfied. Mr.
> G— afterwards told him, he did not mention it by way of an apol-
> ogy, but now that the gentleman had declared himself satisfied, he
> could say, upon his honour, he had no intention of conveying a
> personal insult in the language he made use of to Col. C— in the
> H. of A—. Col. C— proposed they should meet half way, shake
> hands, and bury in oblivion all former animosities, which was ac-
> cordingly done, and here the matter ended, and I am happy to
> think without any fatal consequence to either party.

On reading this, Glenie's friend Sir John Wentworth (Governor of
Nova Scotia) wrote him with advice to the effect that he should steer
clear of politics in favour of philosophy or science. Tradition had it
that a neighbour remarked to Mrs. Glenie, "It was a pity they fought."
She reputedly answered that if her husband had not duelled with
Coffin she would have done so herself![15]

Colonel Coffin was a pugnacious character who may have been involved in as many as five duelling incidents (from challenges to actual encounters) in his lifetime. On August 17, 1803, a bloodless confrontation took place between him and a Captain Foy near Fort Howe, Saint John, during which several rounds were exchanged. A newspaper of the day editorialized:

> The number of duels that are now fought proves the depravity of the times, and the little sense men have of another world. "If every one," says Addison, "that fought a duel were to stand in the pillory, it would quickly lessen the number of those men of imaginary honour, and put an end to so absurd a practice."[16]

New Brunswick's legal profession seemed particularly prone to duelling. It has been suggested that this grew out of two factors – an unusually large number of lawyers coupled with such stiff court fees that people were discouraged from litigation. Competition for clients was fierce, and arguments over fees only aggravated the situation.[17]

A court case in January 1800 produced a remarkable spate of duels and challenges. The issue was the ownership of a slave claimed by Stair Agnew, who had five distinguished lawyers appearing on his behalf. The slave had two lawyers pleading her case, in which she ultimately succeeded. In the course of the trial, Agnew took exception to remarks made by Samuel Denny Street (1752-1830), one of the counsel appearing for the woman, and challenged him to a duel. Details of the encounter are vague. Apparently neither party was injured, and although charges were laid against Agnew, Street and their seconds, they were never brought to trial, the excuse being that the indictment had been badly drafted. Agnew, greatly upset at the manner in which the slave case was handled, also sent a challenge to Judge Isaac Allan, one of the four judges presiding. The judge declined this invitation, which some considered a more courageous act than if he had met Agnew[18]

Meanwhile, in the course of a different jury trial, Samuel Denny Street (who had fought Agnew) and John Murray Bliss (who had been Agnew's second) flared up at one another. Street's second on the earlier occasion had been a Mr. Anderson, whom he now sent with a challenge to Bliss in the late afternoon of January 16, demanding satisfaction the following morning. Bliss replied through his second, Stair Agnew, that he had other commitments on the 17th and proposed that they duel in an hour. The answer (promptly returned through the seconds) was that half-an-hour was acceptable, although eventually it was agreed that supper should precede any meeting.

The brief delay was used by the seconds, Agnew and Anderson, to attempt negotiations. Agnew suggested that Street alter the wording of his challenge and thus give Bliss a graceful exit. Anderson refused to carry that idea to his friend, so certain was he that Street would hold to his original message, Agnew conveyed the same appeal directly to Street and was turned down. It was now late in the evening when the principals and seconds met at the Court House, ready to have at each other in what appears to have been the only duel in Canada held indoors.[19]

The pistols were loaded by Agnew, who, in spite of his own recent displays of belligerence, was determined to play peacemaker. He suggested that the principals submit to the wills of the seconds, and that the affair should end with one exchange of fire, even if no injuries were incurred. Street angrily rebuffed this idea, and even asserted that the distance, nine paces, was too great. In this he was overruled by both seconds.

The exchange of fire that followed did no harm to either opponent. Street and Bliss declared themselves ready to continue, and Street spoke of having either an apology or the blood of his adversary. Anderson and Agnew were adamant in refusing to let matters continue and attempted to shoo their champions from the room while some compromise was drafted. Anderson assured Street that an apology would be forthcoming, then went directly to Bliss (with Agnew's consent – formalities had to be observed). At length, Bliss was persuaded to make a carefully worded statement to the effect that he had not intended to offend or personally insult Street, nor to charge Street with having lied to the jury that day. One is left to wonder exactly what Bliss *had* said and what he had *meant* to convey. In any case, harmony was restored and the men apparently parted as friends.[20]

Another tempest arose in Saint John in 1818. Once more, Colonel John Coffin was involved. His schooner *Martin* had been seized by the Controller of Customs, Robert Parker, for carrying contraband goods. The Parker family was very close to another local dynasty, the Chipman clan. It appears that these two families fell out with Coffin, who received a challenge from one of Robert Parker's offspring. The elderly colonel wrote instead to the senior Parker with a classic challenge of his own:

Sir, – I have the honour to communicate the following note received from your son, Neil, last Sunday morning. I am not in the habit of entertaining young gentlemen at this inconvenient place, but, sir, harbouring no vindictive resentment against you, and our ages being more equal, if you will attend me upon a party of pleasure to Moose Island, I shall be very happy to entertain you. I regret very much that I cannot offer you a passage in the schooner *Martin* as she is at present out of commission.

There is no record of the date of this incident, but the invitation was probably declined. In the same year Coffin was hailed into court for having sent a duelling challenge to Ward Chipman Jr. The old firebrand found few so belligerent as he.[21]

The most notorious duel in the history of New Brunswick was that of October 2, 1821, at Maryland Hill, four miles from Fredericton. It was connected to earlier incidents through family ties; the successful duellist, George Frederick Street, was the son of the

George Frederick Street (1787-1855) killed G.W. Wetmore in a duel. Street's subsequent trial was orchestrated to ensure his acquittal, enabling him to continue his career in politics and the law. He was appointed a judge in 1845. (New Brunswick Museum)

high-spirited lawyer who had been so prominent in the incidents of January 1800.

On September 29, 1821, George Ludlow Wetmore, son of the Attorney-General, was acting as lawyer in a civil case. Counsel for the other party was G.F. Street. Hot legal arguments in court led to bitter words outside. Some said that Street struck Wetmore; others reported that he only raised his hands in a threatening gesture. Whatever happened, Wetmore thought it over that night, then sent a challenge to Street through his appointed second, John Winslow (later Sheriff of Carleton County). Street replied through Lieutenant Richard Davis, 74th Regiment of Foot, then in garrison in Fredericton.

According to Street, who later wrote a detailed though self-serving account of the incident, Wetmore asked that they meet two weeks later. Street claimed that he considered duelling repugnant, advised Wetmore of that view, but also added that if a duel could not be avoided then it should be fought immediately. Winslow, unable to dissuade his friend from seeking satisfaction, found himself in protracted negotiations over time, place and weapons. Oddly enough although he was the challenger, Wetmore was allowed to provide the pistols, reported to have been used in the Glenie–Coffin dispute of 1797.

In Wetmore's eyes, Street's words had started the quarrel, and Street must retract them before any reconciliation could be arranged. Street refused to make any major concession, and he stood by earlier remarks that Wetmore had acted in a manner unworthy of a gentleman. The negotiations dragged on to their inevitable conclusion. On the morning of October 2 the principals and seconds met at the appointed place. Street's narrative describes what followed:

> The ground was measured by the seconds, when Wetmore immediately went and took his stand where his second stood. I then took mine where Davis stood. Nothing was said. The seconds retired for a few minutes and then came to us. Lots had been drawn between them for the choice of pistols, which on the first fire fell to Davis, who chose what (if there was any difference) was considered the best pistol, that is, the one that had not the stiffness in the

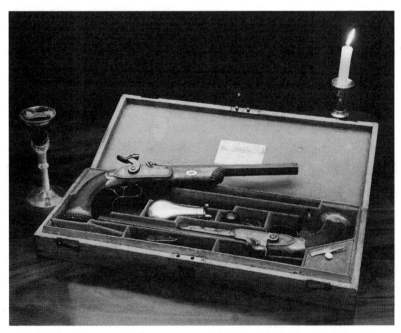

The best pistols came complete with powder flask, loading tools and extra flints. (New Brunswick Museum, Mary Kearney Odell Bequest, 1938, 29942)

cocking. Davis then informed us both that we must keep our pistols down until the signal for firing was given, when we must raise the arm and fire as quickly as possible, without aim or cessation. We received our pistols on the cessation. We received our pistols on the full cock. I put my arm down close to my side, and when the signal was given, half raised it and fired on the ground. I did this from a desire to prevent accident on my part, having from the beginning no wish or intention to take his blood, having gone there solely with the view of defending my character from imputation, and not from any feeling of revenge or malice against him, and with the most desire that it should not end in an accident to either of us.

Street may have fired low deliberately, but Wetmore's shot had been more seriously aimed, though it missed. Davis and Winslow attempted to end the matter there, but neither side was ready to yield or apologize. The affair continued. Again, Street's account describes the tragedy in detail:

The pistols were reloaded by the seconds, though not in our view. Winslow then said that as I had the choice of pistols in the first fire he thought that his friend had the right of choice in the second fire. Davis replied that the choice having been made by lot in the first fire it ought to be so in the second, but as he knew that I would rather that the advantage, if there was any, should be against me rather than for me, he would give him the choice; upon which Winslow chose (for Wetmore) the pistol I had fired with as the one supposed to be the best, if anything, and which had been reloaded by Davis; and I received the pistol Wetmore had used in the first fire, which had been reloaded by Winslow. When the seconds came to the ground Winslow went up to Wetmore and had a minute's private conversation with him, in which, as he has since informed me, he communicated to him what had passed between him and Davis on the subject of stopping proceedings; but as he (Wetmore) still persisted in saying he would have another shot, and then he would stop and leave it to professional men, or something to that effect.

In the second fire I did not think I ought, in justice to myself and my family, to purposely throw it away, having thrown it away in the first; and he persisting in proceeding and, apparently to me, with a determination to hit me if he could, especially as he in the second instance kept his arm half raised before the signal was given, which would naturally enable him to bring his pistol to the level quicker than I could. I kept my arm down close to my side, as in the first fire, until the word was given, when I raised my arm at hazard and fired as quickly as possible. Wetmore did the same. Winslow says his (Wetmore's) pistol went off first. I think they went off as near as possible together; and Davis is of my opinion. I had no view in my second fire whatever, nor had I the least expectation of hitting him. My intention was only to show him that I did not intend to throw away my fire purposely a second time and that if he proceeded he must risk his own life as well as mine. I hoped my fire had missed him – but fatal chance ordered otherwise. The ball struck his pistol arm, glanced, and entered his temple. He fell and never spoke again. We ran to him. I was like one distracted. I raised him in my arms; and we all tried to make him speak, but without effect.

Winslow ran to a nearby farmhouse owned by one Segee, while Street despatched a servant boy to fetch a surgeon. Davis and Street remained with the body until they heard someone – Segee – approaching, whereupon they retired to the woods, mounted their horses and made off, being joined on the road by Winslow. Street claimed later that he had narrowly escaped death; Wetmore's first or second ball, found in a tree stump, had passed dangerously close. Since neither he nor the two seconds, by their own accounts, remained to go over the ground at the time, it is hard to believe this, which reeks too much of rationalization.

The three men fled to Robinstown, Maine. Behind them was raised a traditional hue and cry. Notices printed in the newspapers and posted in public places linked them to Wetmore's death and offered £10 each for their arrest. Samuel Denny Street (father of George Frederick), assisted by friends, angrily tore down many of these broadsheets, for which they would be reprimanded later by the courts. On the other hand, associates of the Wetmores clamoured for justice and retribution.

So long as the trio remained in the United States they were safe from the law and free to negotiate for terms by which they might return to New Brunswick. At length Street and Davis recrossed the border and surrendered to the authorities. Winslow prudently remained in Maine for the time being, a tactical decision that would affect the trial of the other two.

On February 21, 1822, George Frederick Street and Lieutenant Richard Davis stood trial for the murder of George Ludlow Wetmore. Judges in the case were Ward Chipman and John Saunders. Mr. Justice John Murray Bliss declined to sit on the case because he was connected by marriage to Wetmore's family. Curiously, the prisoners were defended by Ward Chipman, Jr. (son of one judge) and Henry Bliss (whose father had declined to participate in the trial).

No full account of the trial itself has survived, but Mr. Justice Saunders' charge to the jury has come down to us. It is an incredible speech, for it shows contorted, convoluted logic as the judge virtually ordered the panel to bring in an acquittal. In fact, his instructions may have been part of an elaborate script drawn up even before Street and Davis left Maine, as Fredericton's elite once again strove to protect some of its members from the rule of law.

Saunders began by ordering the jury to be guided only by such evidence as had been presented in court, ignoring all "stories told out of doors." That was sound law, though it weighed in favour of the accused, since what passed as "common gossip" was virtually common knowledge – that Street had killed Wetmore in a duel and that Davis had been one of the attending seconds. The handbills and newspaper advertisements raising the "hue and cry" with rewards had said as much and more, pointing out that the accused men had absconded – yet Saunders did not refer to that aspect of their behaviour.

The death of Wetmore by gunfire could not be denied, but the aristocratic judge reasoned that no evidence actually placed the murder weapon in Street's hand. All the high words exchanged earlier between the two principals, he said, did not prove that they regarded each other with malice. Segee, the farmer who had been summoned to the dying, unconscious victim, had seen only Winslow (the man who had fetched him and who had wisely remained in Maine). Moreover, Segee could not positively identify either of the accused, who had fled at his approach. There was some confusion about the clothing worn. Segee stated that he had seen a man wearing a blue or blue-black coat; Street's brothers (being gentlemen, considered reliable witnesses!) said that their sibling had never owned such a coat. The judge gave great weight to character evidence adduced on behalf of the defendants, described all else as "presumptive," and sent the jury off to deliberate. They dutifully returned with a verdict of "not guilty."[22]

Street's attempt to duel again arose from a legal case between Edward W. Miller and a Fredericton merchant, Henry George Clopper. Miller had employed Street as his lawyer. In May 1832, Clopper wrote to Miller, complaining that Street was using shady tactics and that the lawyer was promoting discord between the two contestants in order to keep the case (and his fees) going. Street had a letter delivered by hand to the merchant, denying misconduct, demanding a retraction, and adding that if one was not forthcoming he (Street) would "be driven ... to the unpleasant necessity of taking such steps as I may think necessary to protect my honour and character."

Clopper scribbled a reply on the spot, but the messenger refused to deliver it, claiming that he intended only to act as a conciliator, not to bear notes that would aggravate the situation. Clopper then had the message delivered to Street by ordinary mail. Although he moderated some of his language, admitting that Street may not personally have been taking legal shortcuts, he said that the lawyer's employees (for whom Street was responsible) certainly were. As to Street's motives, Clopper stated bluntly that he was free to draw his own conclusions.

Street had not issued a formal challenge, and he seems to have expected Clopper to do so. When the merchant refused to rise to the bait, Street let the matter drop. The whole affair would have remained private had not an unrelated issue, the authorship of an anonymous letter in the press, started them slanging at one another in print some twenty-two months later. In the course of this tedious debate, which filled column after column over several weeks, Street went after Clopper again. On February 22, 1834, in the body of one such attack, Street wrote of his enemy:

> He has experienced, that when a man intentionally gives me personal offence, I am not the person who will seek redress through the medium of the public prints; I am the keeper of my own honour, and know how to protect it.

Clopper was outraged, in another letter to the press he reminded the world of the 1821 tragedy and chastised Street for even hinting at a duel either in 1832 or 1834. In blunt language he described their earlier dispute, quoted the correspondence of 1832 and declared:

> I did not expect such an outrage upon the feelings of this community as that the Honourable George Frederick Street should have sought another duel, and another victim, among its members.

That did not end the bickering, but it did put Street on the defensive. He wrote again, claiming (without conviction) that he had sought no combat with Clopper and that he regarded the events of 1821-22 with sorrow. Nevertheless, he had only insults for Clopper, whom he described as "despicable." Against an adversary who scorned duelling, Street could attack only with words.[23]

The Street–Wetmore duel did not end duelling in New Brunswick, though its fatal outcome may have helped curtail it by giving further proof that "little boys should not play with guns." There were at least two challenges in 1831. Saint John was the site of one such melodrama. Henry Chubb, editor of the *New Brunswick Courier*, wrote something that offended John Hooper, publisher of the *British Colonist*. No copies exist of the *Courier* issue which carried the article, so exactly what Chubb said is not known. What is clear is that Hooper despatched a note to Chubb, railing about having been defamed and calling for satisfaction. This letter was printed in the *Courier* of April 2, 1831. It would seem that Chubb declined to meet his enemy.

On May 28, 1831, the Saint John papers carried a report from St. Andrews, a picturesque community on the Bay of Fundy. Colonel Thomas Wyer, a member of the Legislative Assembly, had criticized one Captain Spearman for acts unworthy of a public official. Again, the precise nature of the charges is unknown, but Spearman sent a challenge to Wyer through a half-pay officer named Jones. Wyer not only refused to duel – he turned to the Attorney-General of New Brunswick and had the pair prosecuted for attempting to disturb the peace.

In his memoirs, *Seventy Years in New Brunswick Life*, Lieutenant-Colonel William T. Baird provides the following story of an event in Fredericton:

> The departure of the stage, driven by Larry Stivers or "Green," every morning in the winter at eight o'clock, from Fredericton for Saint John, was a common event; but a stage driven rapidly down

Queen Street one morning in 1836 at an earlier hour, attracted my attention. It contained five persons; two principals, two seconds and a surgeon. Words uttered in hot debate on the preceding day by Thomas Gilbert (the honourable member for Queens), insulting Dr. Wilson (the honourable member for Westmorland) were to be atoned for in blood. A retired spot three miles below the city was the place selected for a duel with pistols. After two exchanges of shots, the seconds considered the honour of the parties vindicated, and they returned scatheless.[24]

One further duel apparently occurred in Fredericton in October 1848. William Hunter Odell quarrelled in a tavern with a Lieutenant Jones, 36th Regiment of Foot. Odell accused Jones of involvement with his daughter, and the officer replied that nobody would be interested in Miss Odell. That brought a challenge from the fiery-tempered lawyer. In the subsequent exchange of fire, both parties missed. Odell was reported as being ready to fire again, but Jones was unwilling to proceed.

William Hunter Odell had been appointed a judge of the Court of Common Pleas in 1847. If the account is true, he would have been the only judge in Canada ever to duel while on the bench. The duel had a curious outcome. William Franklin Odell, father of the duellist, had died in 1844; his family had subsequently had a memorial plaque made for installation in Christ Church Cathedral. Bishop John Medley, hearing of the duel, ordered that the Anglican sacraments be denied both parties until they had publicly apologized. Lieutenant Jones did so, but William Hunter Odell did not. That proud family boycotted the Cathedral; the plaque was placed in storage and never installed.[25]

There are few reports of duels in Newfoundland, a situation that probably reflects the state of records (there was no local newspaper until 1807) rather than a shortage of encounters. Garrison troops and maddening isolation were frequently the ingredients of 18th-century quarrels, but none of a duelling nature has been found. A letter published in the St. John's *Mercantile Journal* suggests that an actor, Mr. Marcus, and one "A.Z." fought a pistol duel at fifty paces on the night of February 23, 1819, the issue being the actor's theatrical skills.[26]

The Rudkin–Philpot duel of 1826 was a *cause célèbre* in the history of St. John's. It involved officers of the Royal Newfoundland Veterans Companies – contingents of experienced soldiers who had replaced British regulars in many post-Napoleonic garrisons. On the night of March 29 there was a party in the quarters of Captain M.H. Willock. In the early hours of the 30th, as some guests departed, Captain Mark Rudkin sat down to a game of cards with Ensign John Philpot. Philpot had already exchanged hot words with another guest who had suggested they should all leave.

An argument arose over the division of the "pot" (roughly $12 in value), Rudkin claiming the whole and Philpot demanding half. Captain Willock, the host, was called to adjudicate and ruled in favour of Rudkin. The irate Philpot scooped up the money and pocketed it. That led to more bitter comments. Willock, by now outraged at the behaviour of his guests, ordered Philpot out, but it was Rudkin who left first. Philpot followed; in the hallway he threw a jug of water on Rudkin, then kicked him before another officer broke up the scuffle. The party dissolved as the guests scattered to their quarters, queasy from having witnessed an embarrassing incident.

By morning the officers in St. John's were aware of what had passed. Philpot was urged to apologize to Rudkin, who was not only the injured party but the ranking one. He refused, and Rudkin then demanded satisfaction. The seconds were to be Captain George Morice (for Philpot) and Dr. James Strachan (for Rudkin). After some haggling over details, it was agreed that the duel should take place at Robinson's Hill (now inside the city) in the mid-afternoon of March 30.

The distance between the two was measured out – fifteen paces (about forty feet). Philpot, who normally wore a velvet jacket, had removed this garment; above the waist he wore only a light undershirt. Apparently he feared that he would be hit and wanted to eliminate fabrics that might irritate or infect the wound; later this would be cited as proof of his harbouring murderous intentions.

Rudkin and Philpot kept their pistols at their side until the call of "Ready! Fire!" (given by Strachan). Both men fired without effect. The seconds reclaimed the weapons, conferred about a possible reconciliation, found Philpot adamant in his refusal to apologize, and reloaded the pistols. This time Morice called, "Ready! Fire!" whereupon Rudkin shot Philpot through the heart. The latter groaned, collapsed and died without uttering a further sound. Once it was clear that the wound was fatal, Rudkin dashed to Fort Townshend, where he reported the incident to his commander.

The law moved with its customary swiftness. By April 17 Rudkin and the two seconds were before the Supreme Court of Newfound-

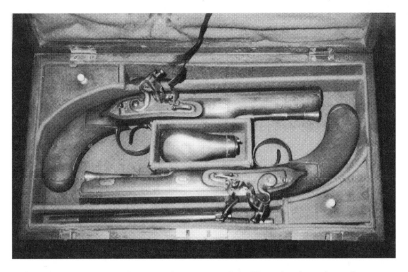

The Rudkin–Philpot duelling pistols. Cases and duelling pistols such as these showed high craftsmanship, although the weapons themselves were inaccurate and frequently unreliable. (Newfoundland Museum)

land and a jury of twelve men. The charge was murder. Public opinion, initially sympathetic to the victim, swung round to the accused as the trial went forward. The events leading to the quarrel and the course of the duel itself were described by witnesses and by the defendants. Rudkin made a long speech to the jury. It is interesting to read this address, for in one way or another he used every form of defence that had helped or would help other successful duellists in escaping the hangman.

He began by expressing regret: "I have unhappily, though unintentionally, deprived a fellow being of existence." He seized upon the judge's comments defining murder – "symptoms of a wicked, depraved, and malignant spirit; a heart regardless of social duty, and deliberately bent upon mischief." With the charge framed in that manner, Rudkin went on to describe himself (with the help of character witnesses) as anything but the depraved monster who would commit murder. As proof of this (and to blacken poor Philpot a bit more) he grandiloquently mentioned that he had been insulted by the deceased on other occasions, and had been able to forgive him in dignity:

By some means, Gentlemen, it has acquired publicity, that the insults offered me by the deceased, on the night previous to the fatal meeting, were not the first that I had received from him; it is, indeed, but too true. However, I should not have alluded to the subject, but that I am most anxious to efface from your minds any impression, which such a report might have created, that I was actuated ... by any vindictive feelings for former occurrences. For his previous conduct he had apologized; and, I most solemnly declare ... that I had, with all that candour and sincerity which are the characteristics of my countrymen, with all my heart and soul forgiven him, and that I entertained the same friendly disposition towards him, which I had felt from our first acquaintance.

From there the captain went on to describe the insult, a kick, as the most dreadful calamity that could befall any officer:

> ... he followed me out of the door and kicked me -yes, gentlemen, I blush to acknowledge that I suffered the vile indignity; aye, and in the presence of a gentleman.... Of all the personal insults one man can give another a kick is, gentlemen, the most galling and degrading ... in a kick contempt is coupled with violence; it sinks you in your estimation, as it were, below humanity; it is an act which a man of correct and humane feeling would scarce commit towards a dog he regarded; it leaves a stain upon the character of the injured party, especially, in military life, which verbal apologies never can efface.

So much for the horrendous nature of the kick. Rudkin immediately pressed on to demonstrate the inevitability of his subsequent action in requesting a duel:

> ... had I not redeemed my character, by pursuing the course I did (however much the event of it is to be deplored) I should have been scouted by my brother officers, and held in contempt by my men. Vain would it have been for me to quit my present Regiment; the disgrace would have stuck to me through the Army, would have driven me from it, and have followed me even into the retirement of private life.... Had I submitted to this degrading indignity without resenting it, as an officer and a gentleman, I should, notwithstanding, for ever have been branded as a poltroon and a coward.

There was, of course, the awkward fact that Rudkin had challenged and Philpot was dead – indeed, had expired without decently forgiving those present. As was the case with other fatal duels, something must be said to the effect that the survivor had gone out with innocent intentions while the victim had been the one with murder in his heart. Rudkin put that forward too:

We went, gentlemen, to the fatal field – but with widely different feelings, and for widely different purposes – I, gentlemen, to repair my injured honour, and he, to seek my life. Had that, gentlemen, not been his fixed determination, he might, without even the shadow of an imputation on his courage, or indeed even without submitting to an apology, have averted his untimely fate. He might have fired in the air, and then the matter might have ended – he was by a mutual friend advised to do so, and in full confidence that he would have followed that advice, I did as it will be proved in evidence fire the first shot in a most careless manner, purposely to avoid injuring him – but when I found, that instead of doing so, he did deliberately fire at me – that he afterwards resisted all the earnest entreaties and endeavours of our seconds, who were alike the friends of both, to effect an accommodation – when I saw him change his position, and fix his eye upon me as if to make sure of his intended victim – I was compelled in defence of my own life to fire the second time. But gentlemen you will be satisfied from the evidence that I fired in the most fair and honorable manner. My pistol was not raised till the word was given, and we fired instantaneously – The distance was unusually great – The pistols I had never seen before – they were not adapted for duelling, but were of the commonest description – such as must convince even the most inexperienced in such matters, that the fatal result was the effect of chance, and not of superior skill or deliberate aim.

Rudkin pulled out more emotional stops by describing his military service – twenty-two years in the army, a veteran of the Napoleonic and American wars, several times wounded and taken prisoner at least once. He then raised the precedent of the Uniacke-Bowie duel seven years earlier. His use of this case shows how viciously the cycle of forced acquittals simply encouraged further duels and hypocrisy. Rudkin virtually stated that Uniacke had had less at stake, had received less provocation than himself, and had been let off, so why not him?

In that case the parties were not military men, neither was the provocation of such a nature, but that it might have been decided by a legal tribunal, without any imputation upon the courage of either party. Mr. Uniacke, however, was a man possessing high spirit and honourable feelings, and preferred appealing to the laws of honour, instead of those of his country. He called Mr. Bowie out – they fought – and at the second fire the latter fell. Mr. Uniacke and his second, Mr. McSwiney, were, as I before stated, indicted for wilful murder – but as it appeared from the whole of the evidence, that the unfortunate transaction had been fairly and honourably conducted, the Jury, (after an impressive charge from the Judge, in which he recapitulated the evidence, laid down the law on the subject, and pointed out the general conduct of Jurors on such occasions) returned a verdict of not guilty.

Rudkin cited a few English cases involving acquittals of military duellists, appealed to the jury for fair treatment and rested his case. The seconds, Captain Morice and Dr. Strachan, then made shorter statements, the tenor of which was that Philpot had been an aggressive hothead who had behaved badly in the first place, had refused to apologize either before the meeting or after the first fire, and who had been amply warned by his friends that he would be responsible for any outcome of the event. Captain Morice testified that on being advised that Rudkin sought an apology, Philpot had stormed, "Does he think me a damned poltroon? I will convince him to the contrary of that. Parade the bulldogs (pistols) at once, and let us have it over." Still later, following the first exchange of fire, Morice had urged Philpot to make amends, and threatened to leave the field after the second exchange.

The presiding judge was apparently more conscientious of his duties than many other judicial figures.[27] The *Mercantile Journal* of April 20, 1826, stated that in summing up the evidence and the law he noted "a wide distinction between the Law of England and that which duellists falsely call honourable contest." Captain Morice, he felt, might well be acquitted, but in the case of Rudkin and Strachan he made it clear that the jury must convict on either murder or manslaughter, depending on how they interpreted the motives and contrition of these two defendants.

The jurors retired. They were out for an hour, and when they returned it was to report that they could not agree on a general verdict, and could they bring in a special verdict? They were told this was possible only if it did not conflict with legal principles. Coming down squarely on the fence, the foreman announced that they considered the defendants innocent of "malicious intentions." The judges were not satisfied. This did not address the charge itself, and the jurors must clearly state whether they were convicting of manslaughter or acquitting altogether. The panel retired again, and after twenty minutes they re-emerged to announce an unqualified verdict – not guilty. The prisoners were immediately released, to be welcomed by a crowd that had come to see them as heroes persecuted by a ruthless judge.

For some years local legend had it that the ghost of Ensign Philpot haunted the area where the duel had taken place. Time and urban sprawl obliterated the site, and both the legend and the ghost faded away. It is difficult to associate gas stations with restless spirits. The pistols themselves have survived and are now held by the Provincial Museum of Newfoundland.[28]

Prince Edward Island, "The Garden of the Gulf," had one recorded duel, although accounts of it are contradictory. The affair took place on June 25, 1851, at the "Government Farm" near Charlottetown. The principals were George Coles (1810-75), a businessman and Reform-minded politician (seconded by Thomas Heaton, who held several official posts) and Edward Palmer (1809-89), the leading Tory politician of the day and virtual Leader of the Opposition (seconded by Andrew Mitchell of Halifax). The cause of the quarrel is not known; a contemporary account mentioned only that Palmer fired and Coles did not.

On March 23, 1872, a letter was published in the Charlottetown *Examiner*, signed by Jacob Carvell, alleging that Palmer had challenged, that he had fired prematurely, and that only Coles' leniency spared Palmer his life. Palmer sought proof to rebut these claims and got it from his former second, Mitchell. In a letter to Palmer, dated March 28, 1872, he declared:

> I now have simply to state in proper justice to you, that Mr. Carvell has misrepresented you in connection with that affair. And firstly you were the *Challenged* and not the *Challenger*, as Mr. Carvell has asserted, and secondly his averment that "you fired before the word was given" is groundless in fact. The duty to order the fire devolved upon me, and I distinctly remember that you discharged your pistol when and not before the word fire was uttered by me, and I justly add, that your demeanour in this affair was that of a gentleman of honour and courage.[29]

*Chapter 6*

&

# Patriote Days
# in Lower Canada

From 1830 onwards, duelling in Lower Canada assumed epidemic proportions. Political differences boiled into personal disputes as Reformers, Radicals and Tories quarrelled ever more bitterly while the colony drifted towards rebellion. Political debates and editorial comments alike stirred fierce passions. Not only were challenges more frequently delivered and accepted, but certain figures emerged as repeated duellists, or acted as seconds on more than one occasion. Some men were principals in certain encounters, seconds in others. Fortunately these incidents smacked more of theatrics than serious combats, and through the period of "political" duelling no one was killed and injuries were rare.

Though it was a relatively bloodless period in the history of Canadian duels, it was also a time when these incidents swept around the leading figures of the day, including the central political player, Louis-Joseph Papineau. Twice he was challenged to combat, but each time he declined to duel. He explained his refusals in *La Minerve*, newspaper of the radical *Patriote* party, in its issue of December 8, 1834.

The roots of his disputes went back to May 21, 1832. A long election campaign had erupted into a riot, and the Montreal magistrates had called on the military to restore order. The troops had opened

Louis-Joseph Papineau declined several duelling challenges. His extensive correspondence provided information on many duels involving his contemporaries. (Toronto Reference Library)

fire, killing three people. Thereafter the officials who had requested soldiers became the special objects of *Patriote* ire. One of them, Dr. William Robertson, finally lashed back at Papineau for an article that had appeared in *La Minerve*, accusing him of abusing his powers as a justice of the peace. Papineau argued that he had attacked his challenger for his public acts rather than his private character, and that such behaviour did not justify seeking personal satisfaction. Another challenger, William Walker, he dismissed as a hooligan who had tried to whip up mob action against Papineau himself.[1]

Journalism, politics and duels seemed to go together in the early 1830s, but these encounters were not always well covered. In 1836 Thomas Mitchell Smith, editor of the Montreal *Morning Courier* was described by the rival *Herald* as having fought three duels in as many years. None, however, was reported at the time, and in only one case have any details come down to us. At some unknown date – but before the summer of 1835 – Smith had duelled with Samuel Revans, then with the Montreal *Daily Advertiser*. On that occasion Smith shot and missed; Revans waited until his opponent had fired, then discharged his pistol in the air.[2]

On April 26, 1834 the newspaper *L'Ami du peuple* published an anonymous letter accusing Reformer Edouard Rodier of having paid people to attend a meeting at Saint-Philippe and applaud him. That sort of rhetoric was fairly common in those heated times, but Rodier was more bellicose than most politicians. The following day he wrote to the paper's owner, Pierre-Édouard Leclère, asking for the name of the correspondent or for personal satisfaction from Leclère himself.

The publisher replied on the 28th, refusing to divulge the name, accepting responsibility for the paper's contents and expressing his willingness to meet in battle. The seconds, through whom these communications passed, would be John Bélestre-McDonnell for Rodier and Alfred Rambau (editor of *L'Ami du peuple*) for Leclère. They met at 4:00 p.m. that day at the foot of Mount Royal. There was an argument over the distance to separate the principals – twelve or eighteen paces – and a compromise was reached in fifteen paces.

On the agreed signal the two men turned and faced each other. Rodier struck his chest dramatically and shouted, "Straight to the heart, my friend," fired his own weapon and missed. Leclère deliberately fired wide.

The seconds tried to negotiate a settlement, but Rodier was adamant – Leclère must reveal, retract or continue. Rambau had not expected the encounter to go this far, and certainly had not anticipated a second exchange. He threatened to withdraw, leaving McDonnell to supervise the proceedings. The hapless Franco-Scot noted that one of the pistols was defective and Rambau went to fetch another pair. In the interval, Rodier spoke directly to Leclère, observing that he was a bad shot. The latter declared he had no intention of firing directly at his opponent, which forced Rodier to admit his unwillingness to shoot either. He did not wish to be an assassin, but he rebuked Leclère for withholding an apology as well as his fire.

Rambau, the reluctant second, came near to re-igniting the duel by asking Rodier if he was calling Leclère a coward. Impulsively, Rodier said, "Yes, so long as he does not wish to fire on me." Only minutes before Rambau had been threatening to leave; he now urged his employer to shoot, but the publisher remained firm in his refusal. McDonnell was urging Leclère to retract or apologize if he would not fight. At last it was agreed that Leclère would sign a statement declaring that he personally considered Rodier innocent of the accusations made by the anonymous correspondent. That was considered acceptable, and the various parties went their ways.[3]

December 1834 was a busy month in the story of Lower Canadian duels. On the 13th John Bélestre-McDonnell (Rodier's second)[4], exchanged fire twice with James J. Day. The two lawyers had quarrelled in court and adjourned behind Mount Royal; neither was hurt.

That same month an article appeared in *L'Ami du peuple* which insulted Louis-Victor Sicotte (1812-89), then an ardent nationalist and a founder of the St. Jean-Baptiste Society. He sent a friend to the editor, Alfred Rambau, demanding an explanation or satisfaction. Rambau asked if Sicotte's complaint was against the newspaper or the author of the article. When told that the grievance was with the author, Rambau stood firm. He could not reveal the name. However, he said, the writer of the piece would be available at 10:00 a.m. the next day to duel with swords.

In 1834 Louis-Victor Sicotte was unsuccessful in his bid to duel with the anonymous author of an article published in a newspaper. (Archives of Ontario, S670)

This unexpected reply stirred consternation among Sicotte's friends, although he was willing to fight on these terms. He was advised that pistols were now customary, and he knew nothing of swords. Besides, how could he be expected to duel with a hitherto-anonymous opponent? Another approach to Rambau, aimed at getting the name or changing the weapon, failed completely. Some suspected that there was no "anonymous author" – that Rambau had written the offensive piece himself and was hiding behind a fictitious front. At length, Sicotte challenged Rambau directly, but the editor refused on the grounds that Sicotte had declined satisfaction offered by the writer, and he (Rambau) owed Sicotte nothing.[5]

Another instance of a duel avoided occurred in December 1834. Thomas Storrow Brown, merchant and Reformer, had been insulted during an election campaign by another merchant, George Auldjo. According to Brown, he had let the matter go, assuming that Auldjo had been drunk, and Brown also explained that he did not wish to introduce further turbulence into a tense contest. Having waited six weeks, Brown sent a challenge to Auldjo, but the latter declined to accept it on the grounds that Brown had waited too long. The would-be duellist retaliated by announcing his challenge and the refusal in the Montreal papers, adding that Auldjo was a liar and a scoundrel. The latter did not respond to these insults and died peacefully in 1846. Thomas Storrow Brown became a noisy, officious *Patriote* general in the 1837 Rebellion who virtually abandoned his men at the Battle of St. Charles. He fled to the United States, returned under an amnesty in 1844 and died in Montreal in 1888.[6]

Alfred Rambau, who had avoided Louis-Victor Sicotte in December 1834, had to dodge another duel in July 1835. *L'Ami du peuple* had described a rock-throwing incident near the Montreal Seminary, ascribing the riot to revolutionary elements. No names were cited. Nevertheless, one gentleman, J. Siméon Neysmith, sent a letter to Rambau, claiming libel and demanding retraction or satisfaction. This time the editor was more forthright in his refusal, which he printed on July 22. He began by saying that Neysmith had not been named in the article, that he had waited three days before challenging, and that his chosen second, Napoléon Aubin, was already party to a plot on Rambau's life. In publicly avoiding a duel, Rambau hinted that Neysmith might still have been a party to the original violence, and that Aubin had been insulting and dishonest in his meetings with the editor. The claim that Aubin had been part of a murder conspiracy was unfounded. In spite of Rambau's abusive account, there were no counterattacks, physical or literary.

While various minor figures were issuing or avoiding challenges, the Governor of British North America was himself beset by a would-be duellist. James Stuart, veteran of a duel in 1819,[7] had been suspended in 1831 from the office of Attorney-General by Lord Aylmer, following a petition from the Legislative Assembly that the ill-tempered Stuart be dismissed. After unsuccessful appeals to London for reinstatement, the aggrieved Stuart turned upon Aylmer, first berating him for lack of support and at last, in November 1834, demanding a gentleman's satisfaction. The Governor haughtily declined, pointing out that as the king's representative he could not stoop to such action. Stuart wrote again, stating that he would be happy to fight Aylmer once that man had vacated the governorship.

Lord Aylmer – Matthew Whitworth-Aylmer (5th Baron Aylmer), Governor-in-Chief of British North America from 1831 to 1835, was challenged by a former Attorney-General to duel in 1834. (National Archives of Canada, C-4809)

It happened that within a month word of Aylmer's recall arrived at Quebec, and Stuart sought another meeting. He claimed a fresh cause to challenge: his name had been omitted from a list of executive councillors. This had been merely a printer's error, but most people felt that the former governor would have to accept the challenge, no matter how flimsy the pretext. To the surprise of many, Aylmer once more declined to meet his enemy, stating that the cause was trivial and that he was forbidden to duel by higher orders – whether spiritual or temporal he did not explain. On that note, he departed for England. Stuart's career was not adversely affected by this incident, and he went on to become Chief Justice of Lower Canada – yet another example of a duellist or aspiring duellist finding his illegal challenges no barrier to legal advancement.[8]

A more serious, yet curiously laughable, affair occurred on November 26, 1835. The new Governor of Lower Canada, Lord Gosford, had thrown a glittering party in Quebec. It had begun on the evening of the 25th and went on well into the morning with heavy dining and repeated rounds of dancing. One suspects that alcohol and fatigue contributed to sparking a duel between two guests – Marc-Pascal de Sales Laterrière (1799-1872, doctor, member of the Legislative Council) and Elzéar Bédard (1799-1849, lawyer, member of the Legislative Assembly). The incident was described by Louis-Joseph Papineau in a letter to his wife dated November 30, 1835, but it was not reported by local newspapers.

The quarrel was rooted in a legal dispute that had flared up the previous summer. Bédard, arguing on behalf of a debtor, referred to Pierre-Jean de Sales Laterrière (1790-1834), the deceased brother of Marc-Pascal, as having demanded usurious collateral and interest in lending money to Bédard's client. Eventually the case went against the Laterrière family, not because of the usury issue but on a legal technicality. The matter rankled with Marc-Pascal, who resented the accusation made against his dead brother and who also questioned the outcome of the court settlement. He continued to grumble about

Bédard to anyone who would listen. In the crush of people attending Lord Gosford's party, Laterrière stepped on Bédard's foot. Papineau's letter recounts what followed:

> Bédard said to him, "Sir, was that accidental?" The other replied with a laugh, "What! Does that offend you? It is less than words can do!" The next day Bédard asked for an explanation; Laterrière said that his views were well known.
>
> A meeting was inevitable. Bédard had cheerfully dined until 2:00 a.m. and had danced until 4:00 a.m. Several hours later he went forth to fight. Laterrière fired three times without effect. Bédard fired twice; on the third exchange his pistol misfired. The seconds, who had waited too long to play their parts, persuaded Laterrière to explain himself. Our champions have given authentic proof that they are maladroit. Laterrière has gone home to console his young wife. It is not the first time he has shown a violent streak. Bédard has also gone to the country with his wife to reassure, console, and distract.[9]

The remarkable thing here is that the seconds would have allowed the affair to go to three rounds of fire. Moreover, the fact that neither man was hurt in those three exchanges suggests that the parties were either drunk, hung-over or simply going through the motions to satisfy appearances. We must also assume extraordinary bullheadedness that prevented them from seeking reconciliation until one weapon had failed.

Charles-Clément Sabrevois de Bleury (1798-1862), lawyer, member of the Legislative Council and prominent enemy of the Reform movement, must have set some form of record, for he is credited with having fought seven duels – with John MacDonald (a lawyer), an unidentified army officer, Ludger Duvernay, James C. Grant (a Montreal lawyer, who was wounded in the affair, June 1822). William

Henry Scott (member of the Legislative Assembly for Deux Montagnes), Charles-Ovide Perrault and Joseph Goddard (a Montreal merchant). Little is known of the affair with Grant, while the duels with Scott, MacDonald, Goddard and the officer are undocumented.

Sabrevois de Bleury, with his conservative views, was a natural enemy of Charles-Ovide Perrault, a dedicated radical *Patriote*. On January 8, 1836, in a Legislative Assembly debate, Bleury insulted Perrault. That evening, on the icy streets near the legislature, Perrault confronted his antagonist and gave him a beating; they were separated by two other MLAs. Word of this incident spread rapidly. All members of the legislature were aware of what had happened and anxiously waited for developments.

Very early the next morning, when still in bed, Perrault received a message from Bleury, asking that they meet at 7:45 a.m. Perrault tried to delay an answer, but when pressed by the messenger (Quebec lawyer Aaron Ezekiel Hart) he replied that he would give a definite response in two hours. He consulted other MLAs who boarded in the same house, then went to the legislature itself to discuss the matter further. He was clearly reluctant to duel, particularly with one so experienced as his challenger. His friends were divided as to whether he should accept or decline the challenge. Perrault finally decided to meet Bleury, fearing that if he refused he would become "a pole that every little dog could piss on." His associate, Doctor Edmund Bailey O'Callaghan, consented to attend as physician but not as a second; that function was assumed by MLA William Henry Scott. The encounter was to take place at 3:00 p.m. in a wood six miles to the west on the road from Quebec to Ancienne Lorette.

Perrault had lunch with his friends but found he had no appetite. About 2:45 p.m. O'Callaghan and Dr. Jean Blanchet left in a carriole. Perrault and Scott left in a coach and another carriage joined them with Bleury and Hart, while a fourth vehicle brought up the rear with two more of Bleury's friends, a Mr. Maxham and a Dr. Bardy. There was to be no shortage of medical talent available!

Côme-Séraphin Cherrier, MLA for Montreal and an opponent of duelling, had heard of the proposed encounter and tried to stop it. He rushed to a court clerk and obtained arrest warrants to be served on both principals. These were given to a bailiff who completely botched his assignment. Meeting Bleury in the street, this official accepted assurances that the gentleman was going to see a justice of the peace. The bailiff stopped at a tavern before going on to Perrault's quarters, only to find that the MLA was gone. The legislature was officially advised of the impending duel and a search was begun – but the officers charged with that task headed east, towards Beauport, rather than west.

Meanwhile, undisturbed by the authorities, the duellists had reached the chosen site. The seconds placed Bleury and Perrault thirty-six feet apart and loaded the pistols. Dr. Blanchet asked if some arrangement might yet be made, and Perrault referred the matter to his second, Scott. Hart (Bleury's second) asked if a settlement was possible; Scott inquired about what Bleury wanted, and Hart replied, "An apology." Scott's response was negative. Bleury, he said, had been the aggressor.

Perrault stood aside, watching, while the seconds parleyed with each other, with Bleury's friends, and with Bleury himself. At last a solution was worked out. The opponents were to advance towards each other, grasp hands and say, "I am sorry to have insulted you" (Bleury) and "I am sorry to have struck you" (Perrault). These words were to be spoken simultaneously, and they were to reply in unison, "I accept your apology." The two men were coached in the agreed words, then strode to their meeting. Bleury held back his lines, allowing Perrault to apologize and he to accept, but the seconds refused to recognize this attempt to renege. They started again, this time speaking in chorus. The pistols were discharged in the air and all returned to their respective carriages, proceeding to a tavern for a drink before going back to Quebec about 5:30 p.m. They were welcomed by the Legislative Assembly, where members had waited fearfully for news of the outcome.

Charles-Ovide Perrault, whose letter to his brother-in-law provides the most detailed account of this incident, joined the rebel *Patriotes* the following year. He was wounded at the Battle of St. Denis (November 23, 1837) and died the next morning.[10]

Sabrevois de Bleury had yet another duel. This arose from an article in *Minerve* in March 1836, attacking him for alleged electoral misconduct in the Richelieu riding. He wrote to the owner, Ludger Duvernay (a Reform leader and another founder of the St. Jean Baptiste Society), demanding an apology. When this was not forthcoming, a duel behind Mount Royal was arranged for 5:00 p.m. on April 12. Bleury had as his second John McDonald, whom he had reportedly fought *against* in an earlier duel. Duvernay's second was Edouard Rodier, the principal of an encounter two years earlier.

The two opponents were placed twelve paces apart. This time there was no early reconciliation. On the first exchange of fire Duvernay's vest was brushed by a bullet that carried away his handkerchief. This was serious business! Three further exchanges took place without effect. On the fifth fire Duvernay was hit, the bullet passing through the fleshy part of his right thigh and scratching the left one. Blood had been spilled and the field was abandoned; neither party apologized or forgave the other. In describing the fight in his newspaper, Duvernay defiantly took another swing at his enemy: "The blood spilled by Mr. Bleury will not erase what has been written; fire and brimstone won't make black into white."[11]

It was not long before Sabrevois de Bleury was involved in yet another quarrel, this one involving Amury Girod – soldier of fortune and *Patriote* supporter who, on April 7, 1836, assaulted de Bleury in a Montreal street, climaxing a series of newspaper attacks that had been in progress. He was rebuked for not having at least sent a challenge to de Bleury. In *La Minerve* of April 12 Girod heaped further abuse on his political adversary, accusing him of both corruption and cowardice, daring the old conservative to send him a challenge. This time, however, de Bleury pursued his antagonist with a defamation suit in the courts. Girod blustered for some weeks, then lamely and abjectly retracted everything he had ever written about de Bleury, and apologized in print for his assault.[12]

The political climate was heating up in 1837; differences between *Patriotes, bureaucrats* and governing officials were irreconcilable. In this highly charged atmosphere, duelling was discussed commonly, although the practice was losing respectability. When the editor of *Populaire*, Montreal-based Hyacinthe-Poirier Leblanc de Marconnay (1794-1868), used his paper to mount stinging attacks on leading *Patriotes*, and virtually invited Robert-Shore-Milnes Bouchette to send a challenge, the young radical contemptuously ignored the dare, regarding de Marconnay as no more than a windbag. He would not duel so lightly as he had done in 1827.

Given the tense politics of the day, it is surprising to find that the first gentlemanly shoot-out of 1837 involved two English lawyers who had fallen out over a bill. William Collis Meredith (1812-94) and James Scott met at 8:00 p.m. on August 9 near Mount Royal; their respective seconds were James M. Blackwood and Joseph-Ferréol Pelletier. At the first exchange of shots, Scott was badly wounded high in one thigh, the bullet lodging in the bone in such a way that it could not be removed by doctors. The duel ended on the spot. Although he lived until June 6, 1852, Scott was probably pained for the balance of his days by the bullet. There was a peculiar rough justice to the inci-

William Collis Meredith wounded his opponent, James Scott, in a duel over a disputed legal bill. (Toronto Reference Library, J. Ross Robertson Collection, T32084)

dent. As a law student, unaccustomed to such affairs, Scott had du-elled with Campbell Sweeney, Jr., and had wounded him in the leg. As to Meredith, he went on to be knighted and became Chief Justice of the Superior Court of Quebec.[13]

Politics, however, was at the heart of other duelling incidents in Lower Canada that autumn. At Saint-Benoît (now the site of Mirabel Airport), a government Indian agent and justice of the peace, Dominique Ducharme (1765-1853), found himself arguing bitterly with his rebellion-minded neighbours. When someone called him an official toady, Ducharme exploded. A distinguished veteran of the War of 1812 – almost certainly the true victor at the Battle of Beaver Dams – he demanded a duel with his antagonist. The challenge was not taken up; after all, Ducharme was seventy-two years old! Some weeks later, however, the veteran campaigner was sheltering fleeing rebels from the wrath of Loyalist forces.[14]

Politics, too, was the inspiration for a duel fought at Quebec in October 1837.[15] On one side was Robert-Shore-Milnes Bouchette, who only three months earlier had ignored another man's provoca-tions. Against him was Thomas Cushing Aylwin. Their respective sec-onds were M.A. Taschereau and S. Lelièvre. The precise course of the duel is uncertain, for it was subsequently reported by two newspapers so intent on blackening the reputation of one or another of the prin-cipals that it is hard to believe they were describing the same incident.

According to *Le Liberal* (supporting Bouchette), Aylwin fired in the air while Bouchette's bullet landed at the feet of his enemy. Aylwin was described as being visibly frightened, with muscles twitching, and refused to expose himself to a second exchange. Bouchette, the challenger, was anxious to continue the affair, and ac-cused Aylwin of cowardice on the spot. Even that insult did not bring the much-sought second round, and the parties left the field.

An opposing newspaper, *Populaire*, viewed the affair very differ-ently. Its editor suggested that either Bouchette or *Le Liberal* were lying about a second exchange being demanded and refused. If that had been so, the paper continued, then it would have been very base conduct, for Aylwin had already proven his courage by accepting Bouchette's shot and had shown his pacific nature by firing in the air.

As to the quarrel that had brought the men to duel, the papers were equally unable to agree. *Le Liberal* claimed that its own editor had first challenged Aylwin for uncomplimentary remarks, that Bouchette had merely delivered the invitation, but that Aylwin had basely refused to meet. Bouchette, finding his mission to be a failure, accused Aylwin of cowardice and thus provoked a duel on his own account. The paper went on to praise Bouchette extravagantly as a dignified gentleman, while describing Aylwin as a drunk, blackguard and poltroon. The paper concluded its account by saying that difficulties had been encountered in getting a surgeon for the duel, as none of that profession believed that Aylwin would risk a meeting. Ultimately, *Le Liberal* declared, Aylwin had consented to duel out of despair rather than courage.

*Populaire* was equally antagonistic towards Bouchette and supportive of Aylwin. By its account, an incident in court had been the genesis of the duel. Aylwin had tossed a note to someone, but it had landed in the hat of Charles Hunter, editor of *Le Liberal*. Aylwin remarked in jest that he was annoyed that anything should have even modest communication with Hunter's hat; the editor had taken offence and sent Bouchette to deliver a challenge. The lawyer had declined, stating that he considered Hunter too base an opponent, and Bouchette had then challenged on his own account.

The duel itself was a minor event, and the manner in which it was described says more about contemporary journalism than about duelling itself. Charles Hunter, who so viciously attacked Aylwin, was a co-worker with Bouchette on *Le Liberal*; he was also a fiery *Patriote* supporter whose intemperate writings led to several terms of imprisonment for perjury and sedition. The editor of *Populaire*, so anxious to blacken Bouchette's reputation, was H.-P. Leblanc de Marconnay, whom Bouchette had recently spurned as a buffoon unfit to duel in his own right.

As tensions mounted between *Patriote* radicals and the authorities, an incident in a Montreal street illustrated how much that city had become a flashpoint on the eve of the 1837 rebellion. On the night of October 29 Lieutenant Augustus Howard Ormsby, 1st Regiment of Foot (also known as the First Royals or the Royal Scots), was making his rounds. One of his sentries made a disturbing report. Two Radical gentlemen had tried to force the soldier from his post and to seize his musket. Ormsby advised the guard to use his bayonet if they persisted.

One of the sentry's tormentors stepped forward. It was Edouard Rodier, and he took exception to the orders just given. Rodier stated that he had been publicly insulted and that he held Ormsby responsible. Whether by this, Rodier meant that the soldier had somehow provoked him before the officer's arrival, or that Ormsby's instruction to use a bayonet was itself the insult, one is left to wonder. Nevertheless, Rodier had challenged the lieutenant and the young officer was uncertain about how he should respond.

On the morning of October 30, Rodier sent two friends, Thomas Storrow Brown and Ludger Duvernay, to the regimental mess, there to arrange the details of an encounter. The English officers considered the Radicals to be impertinent, but they finally agreed that Ormsby should meet Rodier. However, his second, Captain John Mayne, had instructions to allow only one exchange of fire before removing the younger man from the field.

The party met at the Côte St. Pierre racetrack. Fire was exchanged, both men missed, and Ormsby was hustled away. Rodier and his companions had not expected this. Once more they presented themselves at the mess, seeking an explanation from Mayne. They were told that no other officers would be taking up a similar challenge, and that General Sir John Colborne had been informed of the incident. Colborne later expressed his displeasure, but conceded that Ormsby had perhaps responded honourably. Word of the duel spread through the *Patriote* forces, and Rodier was made out to be at least a moral victor, having faced a proud English adversary as an equal. The symbolism of the event may have cheered the rebels at St. Denis, when they scored a striking victory over British regulars. It did them no good at St. Charles and St. Eustache. By the end of 1837 some *Patriote* leaders were dead – Amury Girod, having abandoned his men on the eve of battle, had shot himself – and the rest were in exile, quarrelling among themselves, plotting armed returns, and ultimately waiting for amnesties that would allow them to creep back to Canada. In their absence, duelling incidents were less frequent. All the same, Lower Canada was to witness one more such encounter – this one with a tragic outcome.[16]

The death of Major Henry John Warde, the last duelling fatality in Canada, was swift, dramatic and mysterious. The facts of the duel itself are clear enough, but the nature of the dispute which led to the deadly encounter with Robert Sweeney is clouded by myth and uncertainty.

Warde, a handsome and popular officer with the 1st Regiment of Foot, had distinguished himself under fire during the rebellions of 1837. Sweeney, a native of Ireland, had come to Canada about 1820, and he was respected as a successful Montreal lawyer, man of letters, militia officer, and expert on duelling. It will be recalled that in 1834 he had insisted on such strict observance of the customary rules concerning seconds as to prevent an encounter between two gentlemen.[17]

About 5:00 a.m. of May 22, 1838, near the Verdun race track, Warde and Sweeney faced each other some fifty feet apart. Warde was accompanied by Captain John Mayne – the man who had seconded Lieutenant Ormsby the previous October. Sweeney had as his second Lieutenant Dionysius Airey, Royal Artillery, while Doctor Alexander Knox of the First Royals stood by as medical attendant. On the command "Ready, Fire!" they raised their pistols. Only Sweeney fired. Warde leaped convulsively and collapsed.

The duel had been witnessed by a farmer, J.B. Lanouette, who came up just as Major Warde expired. The others brusquely ordered him off the field. Lanouette at first refused, but then he obeyed. As he passed Sweeney he remarked, "You have had a bad beginning to the day." The victor did not reply. Instead, he threw down his weapon and began to sob.

Having shooed Lanouette away, the party now sought help in carrying Warde's body to the Pavilion or headquarters of the race course. John McDonald, a passing farmhand, was asked to help move the corpse. McDonald curtly refused, adding that the major's killer should be punished. However, he finally consented to carry the body, aided by two other farmhands. Apparently, Warde's friends drew back at touching his bloody remains.

W.H. Lavelock, a cabinet maker and carpenter residing in the Pavilion, was wakened about 5:30 a.m. by a man seeking a room for Warde's body. It was brought in and laid out on a couch. Someone stripped the corpse and began washing it. As this was going on, the fatal bullet fell free. It had passed clear through the major's body, from right to left, before lodging in the victim's left arm. A man claiming to be Captain Mayne's servant later identified Mayne, Knox and Warde, adding that although he did not know the other parties, "the gentleman who shot Major Warde lived near the Haymarket, and that his name was Sweeney." All were grieving at Major Warde's death.

These facts were brought forward at a coroner's inquest held on the afternoon of the 22nd. Doctor A.H. David probed the body in the presence of the twenty-man jury, revealing how the bullet had torn apart Warde's chest. Yet only Lanouette, McDonald and Lavelock were called as witnesses. Those who had played the grisly game itself were not summoned, and Sweeney had apparently fled to Vermont with the seconds to wait upon events.

He had no need to worry. He was counted as a gentleman by polite society – the same society whose members now investigated the affair. Having heard but three witnesses, one of whom had named the killer, the jury brought in the most incredible, disgraceful verdict possible:

> We are of the opinion that the late Major Henry John Warde came to his death, in consequence of a gunshot wound inflicted by *some person unknown* in a duel this morning.

The newspapers of the day immediately gave the lie to this finding, openly reporting Sweeney as the other principal. However, the contemporary press was also momentarily mystified as to why the duel had taken place.

What had caused Warde and Sweeney, reported to have been good friends, to meet in such deadly fashion? The most widely accepted story is that Warde, as vain as he was handsome, had for some months been receiving gifts of flowers, accompanied by love letters, from an anonymous admirer. He imagined that his admirer was Charlotte Sweeney, the wife of Robert Sweeney.

A near-contemporary account, published in *The Times* of July 14, 1838, has it that Warde withdrew from the family for two months, during which time he received neither flowers nor notes. On May 21, however, a further bouquet was delivered with an unsigned letter, declaring that this was the last such gift he would receive. Having behaved prudently for two months, Warde now wrote to Charlotte Sweeney, who opened his letter in the presence of her husband. Robert Sweeney read it and demanded to know if she had sent flowers to the major. This she denied. The outraged husband now sought out Warde, insisting upon an explanation. The officer blandly stated that he was sorry if he had written to the wrong woman. That did not satisfy Sweeney, who requested and got the meeting of May 22.

This account was apparently published to offset earlier reports that Warde had previously sent some "highly offensive anonymous letters" to Mrs. Sweeney. Still another version has it that Warde had despatched flowers and a letter to a French-Canadian lady which had been delivered to the wrong address. A more romantic tale is that Warde, curious about who his anonymous admirer might be, had his servant follow the messenger who brought the last bouquet. The latter dropped by the Sweeney residence to visit a servant employed there, but Warde drew the wrong conclusion and wrote a passionate letter to Mrs. Sweeney. She in turn concluded that Warde had gone mad and showed it to her husband.[18]

None of these accounts rings absolutely true; most reflect efforts by friends to make Warde out as an appealing victim of circumstance. The "wrong address" story was put forward by Major General John Clitherow, commander of the Montreal garrison, but one would think that *something* in such a letter would have indicated that a lady other than Mrs. Sweeney was the intended recipient. The version published in *The Times* of July 14 leaves one asking, why would Warde suddenly write to Charlotte Sweeney if he had tried to avoid her company for two months? The tale of the messenger followed is put forward by A.W.P. Buchanan, who is unreliable as an authority and does not give his own sources for the account. The determination of the coroner's jury to get Sweeney off the hook might have meant several different things – an upper-class cover-up, popular support for a wronged family, or even an odd attempt to minimize dishonour for the protecting British army at a time of rebellion and border unrest.

Anther version of the duel's origins differs so much that one must ask whether it describes the same event, yet it has as much credibility as the stories put out by the friends of Warde and Sweeney. E.B. O'Callaghan, as a *Patriote* sympathizer, had no warm feelings for either party. Writing to his fellow exile, Louis-Joseph Papineau, he passed on the news as he heard it second hand:

I learn from a man from Montreal the following particulars as the cause of the affair. Miss Sweeny (R. Sweeny's sister) was at some ball or party with Mde R. Sweeny where Major Warde also attended. In the course of the evening the latter made some reflections on Miss S. as to her appearance, dress, carriage, etc. This was resented by Mde S. who appeared to have spoke rather high. Her husband came up; got into words with Major Warde, whereupon the latter struck him with his glove across the face.[19]

Affairs following the duel were tumultuous. Warde himself was buried on May 25 with full military honours. Later a tombstone would be raised identifying the victim as a lieutenant colonel, his promotion

DUEL FATAL..—Hier matin une rencontre fatale eut lieu entre le major WARD des Royaux et ROB. SWEENEY, Ecuier. Au premier feu le major Ward tomba mort d'une balle qui lui traversa le cœur. Ainsi a été terminée, la carrière d'un homme brave qui déjà avait à St.Charles, rendu des services importants à la patrie. On ne saurait trop réprouver la coutume barbare des duels. Le courage du major Ward ne pouvait nullement être mis en doute. Il était un des officiers de Sa Majesté, qui avait fait ses preuves sur le champ de bataille ; il est à regretter que les services d'un officier de talents et dont la bravoure était reconnue, ait été perdu dans une querelle privée. Mr. Sweeney est un des citoyens les plus respectables de cette ville, et il est malheureux pour lui que cette affaire ait eu lieu.

In the early 19th century, few newspaper articles carried headlines. Even this story, on page 2 of *L'Ami du peuple*, May 23, 1838, had only a modest banner.

having been promulgated in London on June 5, before news of his death reached there.

Newspapers denounced the hypocrisy shown by the coroner's jury, which so evidently did not wish to pronounce the truth. The Montreal *Herald* remarked bitterly, "The value of an oath in Canada is not much," even though the editor of that paper, Robert Weir, had sat on the coroner's panel! With greater honesty, Protestant and Catholic clergymen attacked duelling from their pulpits. Bishop Jean-Jacques Lartigue, horrified at recent "affairs of honour," ordered that one Lieutenant Leclère of the Montreal Volunteer Rifles be excluded from street-lining duties during a religious procession because he had recently been connected with a duel. Leclère's superior, Captain De Bleury, refused because he had also been concerned with a duel. In consequence, the whole of the Montreal Volunteer Rifles was banned from the occasion. The climate of public opinion was suddenly turned against the sickening practice.

All the same, with the air cleared by the blind verdict of the inquest, Robert Sweeney was able to return to Montreal, and he retained his militia commission which was another mark of upper class gentility. If he was guilt-ridden by the affair, he did not have long to bear his burden; a little over two years later, on December 15, 1840, he died at his home. The newspapers of the day respectfully mourned his passing, recalling his reputation as that of a scholar and gentleman. Charlotte Sweeney later married John Rose, another Montreal lawyer, who became the second minister of finance in post-Confederation Canada. He settled in England, where Charlotte died in 1883.

Spokesmen for Perth, Ontario, bent on maintaining that town's claim to being the site of the last fatal duel in Canada, have repeatedly described the Verdun affair as not being a duel at all. Their reasoning has been that only gentlemen could conduct duels, that in fleeing the law, however briefly, Robert Sweeney revealed himself to be no gentleman, and thus the Warde-Sweeney incident was merely a vulgar shootout between two scallywags.

The argument is ingenious but strained and pointless. The duelling codes themselves did not require that duellists surrender to the authorities. Indeed, in one of the most famous of duels the victor (Aaron Burr) fled from New Jersey after killing his opponent (Alexander Hamilton) in 1804. As has been seen in the case of New Brunswick's Street-Wetmore duel, the flight of the successful duellist did not prejudice his trial following his surrender six months later, nor did anyone ever question whether the events of October 2, 1821 had been anything other than a duel.

The fact was that the contemporary view of a "gentleman" had relatively little to do with one's behaviour. Had that been the measuring stick, then both the Perth duellists would have been considered utter cads, Lyon having slandered a lady and Wilson having libelled her. Instead, polite society judged a "gentleman" in terms of birth and upbringing. Even by those terms, the backwoods affair in Perth would have been *déclassé* compared to that at the Verdun racetrack, for both Sweeney and Warde were much higher on the social ladder than either Lyon or Wilson.

Certainly the upper crust of Montreal considered Sweeney a "gentleman" even after the duel and his brief, easy evasion of the consequences. His peers quickly got him off the hook through the blind coroner's inquest, and he was welcomed back at once. The obituaries of 1840 were glowing and sympathetic, befitting the prejudices of the day.

A British case about this time illustrates the curious, hypocritical and class-ridden nature of duelling. In August 1838 a Mr. Mirfin was killed in a duel on Wimbledon Common. The successful combatant, a Mr. Eliot, absconded and was never taken. The seconds were tried as accessories to murder. The presiding judge declared that the encounter had been managed "with a strict regard to the practice usually followed on such occasions." His only complaint was that there had been an unusually large number of spectators.

The British press was more critical of the Wimbledon Common

duel, but not because the victor had fled. The affair drew ridicule because some of the participants were not deemed sufficiently genteel; the deceased had been a linen draper, while one of the seconds had been the son of a bricklayer. How would the English papers have regarded an incident like that at Perth, where one of the principals had been the son of a weaver?

Verdun, Quebec, has never boasted of the Warde–Sweeney duel, and no plaque commemorates it. That is probably more tasteful, considering the true nature of duelling – colourful, immature, and unlawful. That fact was starting to take hold of public sensibilities, as demonstrated by the outcry in the wake of Major Warde's death. Duelling would now begin to fade from the scene.

*Chapter 7*

〜

# Duels in the West

The Prairie and Pacific regions of Canada were frontier areas at the close of the 18th and beginning of the 19th centuries. European settlements were scattered and invariably tied to the fur trade. There were few magistrates, no superior courts, no newspapers, no lawyers, no political parties, and no permanent military garrisons. Most of the ingredients for duels, as fought in the East, were absent west of the Great Lakes.

There were, however, disputes among fur traders, some of whom were as pugnacious as any urban dandy. One such was John McDonald of Garth (so called to distinguish him from many other McDonalds in the business), who sailed from Scotland, bound for Quebec, in April 1791. During the voyage young McDonald (he was only seventeen) picked a quarrel with his cabin mate, one Ensign Kennedy. On a dark night they went on deck to duel with pocket pistols. Neither was hurt, and fellow passengers, hearing of the incident, considered it amusing. Soon after his arrival in Lower Canada, McDonald was hired by the North-West Company and headed for the west. At the Grand Portage (now in Minnesota) he challenged Edward Harrison, a clerk, to a duel with pocket pistols. The latter had thrown a bun at the touchy Scot. Harrison took a piece of rope and threatened to whip the upstart. The incident ended there. In later years McDonald actually commanded Harrison in trading posts, and their earlier dispute seems not to have affected their working relationships.[1]

Other duels arose from fur trade rivalries as the Hudson Bay Company, North-West Company, Pacific Fur Company and the American Fur Company struggled over a diminishing supply of pelts. Competition intensified, threatening mutual bankruptcy, and violence flared between employees of the various firms. This ranged from simple harassment and fisticuffs through to raids and ambushes, with a few duels in between. The records of these, however, are so sparse (given the lack of newspapers and judicial documents) that we must rely on sparse personal accounts and company journals for information. In some cases it is uncertain whether the incidents were duels or brawls.

The rivalry was particularly intense around Lake Athabaska, where a ramshackle Hudson Bay Company post (Fort Wedderburn) stood only a mile and a half from the more substantial Fort Chipewyan, operated by the North-West Company. In October 1816 these posts were respectively commanded by John Clarke and Roderick McKenzie. It is McKenzie's post journal or fort diary entry of October 5 that gives the primary account of a duel – with swords – in this unlikely corner of the world.

A stranger, later identified as Hector McNeil, NWC, approached Mrs. John McVicar as she was drying clothes at the HBC fort and asked if she came from Glasgow.[2] She refused to answer what was somehow considered an indecent question. McNeil next challenged John Clarke to a duel, but Clarke declined to fight a social inferior. John McVicar accepted the challenge. Simon McGillivray (NWC) gave his sword to McNeil, who in turn handed his own weapon to McVicar, and the battle was on.

The two men went at each other for six minutes, an unusually long period for swordplay. The post journal account stated that McVicar received a minor wound in the forehead and was disarmed; McNeil was intent on finishing him off when Mrs. McVicar ran screaming and scratching between the combatants. Both men were hauled before A.N. McLeod (an NWC employee who doubled as justice of the peace) and ordered to keep the peace.

Fourteen months later McVicar swore a deposition in which he claimed that McNeil had been the wounded party, that he (McVicar) had abandoned his sword after it became lodged in a door frame, and that it was A.N. McLeod (rather than Mrs. McVicar) who prevented McNeil from killing his unarmed opponent. About the same time, McNeil swore another deposition, in which he claimed that McVicar had provoked the duel on the orders of John Clarke. In other respects his account confirmed that of the Fort Chipewyan post journal.

An American adventurer, Ross Cox, was on the Pacific coast as the fur wars heightened. He subsequently published a book on his experiences, *The Columbia River*, in which he recorded the following amusing incident:

Mr. Pillet fought a duel with Mr. Montour of the North-West, with pocket pistols, at six paces, both hits; one in the collar of the coat, and the other in the leg of the trowsers. Two of their men acted as seconds, and the tailor speedily healed their wounds.

The date was early 1817, and the place Fort Okanagan, a North-West Company trading post in the mountains. Nicholas Montour the younger, a Métis employee of the NWC, remained in Western Canada. François Benjamin Pillet, born at Lac-Deux-Montagnes, was employed by John Jacob Astor's Pacific Fur Company. Pillet stayed with the fur trade for many years and retired to New York, where he was living in 1853.[3]

Île-à-la-Crosse, in what is now northern Saskatchewan, was an important fur trade post and the focal point for much of the HBC/NWC rivalry. In May 1819 the truculent John Clarke had moved there on behalf of the Hudson Bay Company. He frequently taunted Angus Bethune, his NWC opposite number, demanding to meet him "as a gentleman" while threatening to horsewhip Bethune. The latter declined. In October 1819 one Paul Fraser (NWC) threatened to fight; he was told that only "blackguards" tried fisticuffs, but that his enemy, John McLeod, would willingly settle their dispute with pistols in some nearby bushes. McLeod and his second, one McKenzie,[4] went off to the spot, but Fraser's superiors detained him. After twenty minutes, McKenzie returned to the post to tell Fraser that they were waiting for him. He returned to McLeod and fifteen minutes more passed before the two men abandoned the place. The incident had ended in the humiliation of Fraser.

On November 26, 1820, Alexander McDonnell, a Nor'Wester, wrote a letter from Green Lake (northern Saskatchewan), describing tension in the area. It read, in part:

Clarke and party are seemingly anxious to shed blood. There have been three duels fought within a month's time, one by Halcro at Lac La Cloche with the famous John M'Leod (no blood), one at Ile à la Crosse between young Douglas and a Pat Cunningham (no blood) and the third can hardly be called a duel, it is rather an attempt at an assassination.

The third incident, the "assassination," is the only one that McDonnell describes. It occurred at Lac Cariboux and involved a Mr. Heron (probably James Heron) of the North West Company and a Mr. Leslie (HBC). Their argument was over the allegiance of an Indian.[5] Leslie produced a pair of pistols, but Heron was similarly armed. Leslie appeared to retreat. He suddenly turned and offered to shake hands. As Heron held out his hand, Leslie fired one of his pistols. Although the range was point-blank, he did not injure his opponent; he either missed or the bullet lodged in Heron's heavy clothing. Heron discharged one of his "pocket pups," and although it misfired, he reportedly wounded his enemy. How he managed this is difficult to say, but perhaps the powder flash singed Leslie.

Of the other two incidents, nothing is known beyond McDonnell's brief references. The participants were John McLeod (already met), Joshua Halcro (a little-known HBC trader), Patrick Cunningham (an affable HBC employee, more often considered a peacemaker), and James Douglas, a seventeen-year-old mulatto NWC clerk who was beginning a fascinating career that would eventually make him the most powerful figure on the Pacific coast and earn him the title, "Father of British Columbia."[6]

The merger of the Hudson's Bay Company and the North-West Company in 1821 ended a protracted feud. Men who had been bitter rivals now worked for a common employer. Duelling might have passed from that region but for a new element that disrupted the Pacific Cost – gold. In 1858, gold was discovered in the Fraser River, and a stampede of miners began. Most came from California, and their first stop was Victoria, on Vancouver Island, where they stocked up on supplies before heading for the mainland. In the first days of the gold rush, colonial authorities were overwhelmed by the numbers of men who had to be regulated. Most of the prospectors were orderly, decent fellows, but among them were violent elements, including a few who had been run out of San Francisco by vigilantes. This was the backdrop for the only fatal duel (if we may call it that) in the history of Western Canada.

The event grew out of a dispute aboard the steamer *Sierra Nevada,* which sailed from San Francisco to Victoria early in July 1858. During the passage, a woman named Bradford died and was buried at sea. Her beautiful daughter, aged eighteen or twenty, immediately became the object of pity among the male passengers. Two of these, George Sloane and John Liverpool, attempted to take her under their respective wings. From that moment onwards, they took a violent dislike to each other. Sloane's was a gentle approach; Liverpool virtually expropriated the girl. When the former passed a hat among the passengers, Liverpool seized the money and pitched it overboard, snarling that he would care for Miss Bradford himself. Sloane protested, Liverpool struck hard and the fist-fight ended only when the two men were pulled apart by fellow travellers.

The *Sierra Nevada* arrived at Esquimalt (near Port Victoria) on the morning of July 19. Her passengers disembarked and soon were dispersed in the tent city that had sprung up nearby. Liverpool and Miss Bradley quickly occupied a tent together, a development which infuriated Sloane. Friends counselled him to keep clear of the couple, and he reluctantly did so. Liverpool, however, was not content. He had captured the spoils, but for him the war continued.

That evening, Liverpool sought out Sloane amid the tents and demanded satisfaction. His stated cause was that Sloane had offered money to Liverpool's wife, the marriage supposedly having taken place immediately after landing, and that Sloane had been the aggressor in the shipboard brawl. It did not matter that the money had been intended as a charitable gift, or that it had been proffered a day before the "marriage." Sloane attempted to put off his enemy, but Liverpool now hurled curses and insults, denouncing Sloane as a liar and coward. Nothing less than immediate combat would satisfy him. Sloane, taking up the challenge, might still have been dragged away by a friend, but one of Liverpool's cronies pulled the would-be peacemaker away. A duel there would be – crude by standards elsewhere, and more deadly for that reason. There was no time for sober second thoughts, and only the briefest of formalities were observed.

A bystander offered Sloane his revolver and consented to act as a second. Liverpool was probably armed already. The "duellists" were placed ten paces apart. By some means – the roll of dice, the toss of a coin – the challenger had secured a position whereby the setting sun shone in his opponent's face. At a signal, both men fired. One missed; a bullet drilled through George Sloane's heart.

An inquest was held at once; it returned a verdict of "wilful murder." The law could do little more, however. John Liverpool evaded arrest and retreated swiftly to San Francisco, taking Miss Bradford with him. It was later reported that he had committed another murder and paid the penalty, while the lady ended up in prostitution.[7]

Assuming this account to be accurate, one is left to wonder whether this should be considered a duel. If one accepts it as such, then the Sloane–Liverpool shootout succeeds the Warde–Sweeney affair as "the last fatal duel in Canada." On the other hand, the Victoria tragedy smacks of a frontier gunfight rather than an urbane settling of accounts. In the final analysis they may not be so different, the one being a vulgar, brutal incident, the other a polite, brutal incident. The essence of duelling was the element of violence; formal duels simply added ceremony and hypocrisy.

*Chapter 8*

# Canadian Duels
# Abroad

Many of the duels fought in Canada, especially during the post-conquest period, were conducted by mere transients who happened to be passing through (as with British army officers) or who used Canadian territory in the hope of evading American law (as happened at Windsor in 1820, see chapter 4, note 8.) By the same token, some Canadians were involved in duels on foreign soil. The Weekes–Dickson duel of 1806 and the Rankin–Richardson affair of 1836 have already been mentioned. In both cases the parties simply crossed water to American territory and the victors were not prosecuted for their misdeeds. However, other Canadians had gone further afield when they became embroiled in affairs of honour.

Charles Petit de Levilliers was born at Boucherville in June 1698, the son of an officer in the forces of New France. He followed his father into the military and eventually was stationed in Louisiana. He survived at least one wound in an Indian campaign, but was less fortunate in a later incident. He duelled with another officer, Barthélemy, chevalier de Macarty, received a serious injury, and died some days later on April 1, 1736. The victor returned to France, where he was in disgrace for several years.

About twenty years later another Canadian-born soldier fell in a duel. Baptiste Tisserant de Montcharvaux, who had been born at

Quebec, was serving in the Illinois country, possibly at a post commanded by his own father, when he was killed in a duel with one Vergès. It was a particularly hard blow for the father, whose wife and three other sons had drowned years earlier.

Among *les canadiens* of Montcalm's defeated army was a dashing young officer, Laurent-François Lenoir, sieur de Rouvray, who remained in the service of France after the capitulation of New France. His subsequent career saw him rise to the rank of marshal; he would die in Philadelphia in 1798. At some point before the French Revolution, while holding the rank of colonel, he sought a duel with another officer who had offended him. His opponent wanted to use pistols, but de Rouvray maintained that officers and gentlemen duelled only with sabres. A council of officers weighed this dispute and came out for swords. In the battle that ensued, both men were wounded.

The family d'Irumberry de Salaberry was one of the *canadien* families most dedicated to the new English regime. The most famous of its members was Charles-Michel de Salaberry (1778-1829), who commanded at the Battle of Châteauguay (October 26, 1813), one of the most striking victories of the War of 1812. Three of his brothers had previously died while on duty with British regiments overseas, and Charles-Michel had served in the West Indies and the Low Countries.

Sometime around 1799, while stationed in Martinique with the 60th Regiment of Foot, Charles-Michel de Salaberry reportedly fought a bitter sabre duel. The story is recounted by Philippe Aubert de Gaspé, and though the tale is undocumented, certain facts – notably that his friend Hippolyte Desrivières of the same unit died about this time – lend credibility to the account.[1]

The 60th Regiment was reportedly led by a ragtag collection English, Swiss and German officers; also in the unit were two French-Canadians, Lieutenants Desrivières and de Salaberry. One day, as the latter was dining in the mess, a particularly quarrelsome Prussian entered, glared at de Salaberry, and announced that he had just killed

Charles de Salaberry's duel in the West Indies has been described in great detail, in spite of meagre evidence that it even happened. (National Archives of Canada, C-9226)

Desrivières. "Very well, sir," said de Salaberry, most calmly, "we shall dine and then you may have the pleasure of despatching another French-Canadian to the hereafter."

At the battle's outset, the young *canadien* was slashed about the forehead, scarring him for life. His friends wanted to intervene, but de Salaberry would have none of it. He was granted a few moments to bind his wound with a handkerchief, then the savage combat resumed. The outcome is not clear; de Gaspé merely says that "the German captain thereafter never slew a French-Canadian nor anyone else." Another writer claimed he sliced his opponent in two.[2]

Another "foreign" duel took place in the remote expanse of the Indian Ocean. Louis or Louison Baby, the youngest son of Jacques Duperron Baby, had been born at Detroit in 1781 but had been raised at Sandwich (modern Windsor). The Baby family were prominent in Canadian commercial and political affairs and, like the de Salaberrys, very sympathetic to British interests. Young Louis Baby joined the British army and travelled far with the 5th Regiment and later the 69th Regiment, surviving at least one shipwreck off the Isle of Wight. At length he attained the rank of captain and was stationed, with his brother Antoine Baby, on Île Bourbon (now known as Réunion), where he was killed in a duel about 1812 or 1813.

A family history gives few details of the event.[3] Louis was reported to have been a notorious duellist, unpopular with his fellow officers. Antoine Baby, in a letter to another brother dated February 2, 1816, wrote: "After poor Louis' death I sent a whole account of it to Bellingham in England, which I hope was forwarded to the family. It is too distressing to repeat." It is unfortunate that Antoine did not expand on his younger brother's death, for apparently the account sent to England has not survived. We can only wonder why or how Louis Baby came to his violent end.

Yet another duel abroad with close Canadian associations occurred on November 19, 1835. The cast of characters was as follows:

John Arthur Roebuck (1802-79, a member of Britain's House of Commons, resident for a time in Canada (1807-24) and a spokesman for Canadian Reformers, especially Louis-Joseph Papineau. Roebuck was outspoken to the point of being abusive.

John Black, editor of England's *Morning Chronicle.*

Samuel Revans (1808-88), former founder and editor of the Montreal *Daily Advertiser* and another supporter of Reform causes, but in 1835 a lawyer in England, having left Canada because of "indiscreet articles."

Simon McGillivray (1783-1840), a former partner of the North-West Company, now settled in England and part owner of the *Morning Chronicle.*

Roebuck, as MP for Bath, often published his views in pamphlets. In one of these he wrote of Mr. Black in very unflattering terms, describing his conduct as "base" and "utterly disgraceful." He particularly rebuked Black for dishonourable dealings affecting a Mr. Goldsmid, claiming that the editor had printed correspondence with Goldsmid in the *Morning Chronicle.*

John Black assigned Simon McGillivray to be his messenger and second. On November 13 he wrote an angry note to Roebuck, challenging him to duel if he were the author of the offending brochure. McGillivray had some trouble locating Roebuck, but finally delivered the note on the 17th. Roebuck admitted having written the item, retracted nothing and advised McGillivray that he would provide a second on the 19th. On that day Samuel Revans appeared on behalf of Roebuck. By now the politician was willing to admit one mistake – Black had *not* published the Goldsmid correspondence in his paper. A contemporary report went on to describe Roebuck's curious hedging: "Mr. Revans also felt authorized in saying that Mr. Roebuck had never intended to impute cowardice to Mr. Black; that he really believed him to a philosopher, and, as such, would of course not fight."

Black was not satisfied; he insisted that words like "base" and "disgraceful" required retractions. Roebuck would not concede this, and the two principals came forward to conduct their business with pistols. At the first exchange, Roebuck received Black's inaccurate shot, fired in the air, and repeated his earlier concessions as expressed by Revans. Yet he finished by repeating that he considered Black's conduct with Goldsmid to have been unworthy, and maintained his right to make public statements about public men. McGillivray stated that the duel must continue, given Roebuck's intransigence and Black's continued outrage. There was a second exchange of shots; it is not known if Roebuck again fired in the air, but in any case the two men were unhurt.

It was now the turn of the seconds to quarrel, Revans stating that a third round was needed, McGillivray saying that as part-owner of the *Morning Chronicle* he did not wish to expose his editor to further dangers. Revans replied that, as a mere second, McGillivray had no say in the principal dispute. It appeared for a time that the seconds might also duel, but Roebuck turned diplomat to prevent that. However, McGillivray arbitrarily declared that the whole affair was at an end. Nobody apologized or forgave; the outcome was unsatisfactory to all.[4]

Major John Richardson (1794-1852), born in Queenston, Upper Canada, had a colourful career that included combat in the War of 1812, service in the British army, a period as a mercenary soldier, journalism, politics, police chief along the Welland Canal, and prodigious writing of histories, historical novels and personal accounts. He was notorious for his quick temper, rash judgement and pig-headed pugnaciousness which even a sympathetic biographer could not fully justify. Richardson vies with John Prince and Charles-Clément Sabrevois de Bleury for being the most belligerent Canadian duellist, for he was associated with at least nine duelling incidents involving eleven men that included an assortment of military officers, public officials, a jealous husband and his personal attorney.[5]

Richardson left Canada in 1815 and spent many years living as a half-pay officer in London while attempting to launch his reputation as a writer. Soon after his arrival in Britain he had exchanged shots in Hyde Park with an officer who had criticized an actress of whom the Canadian was fond. Neither man had been hit. Later he had duelled in the Bois de Boulogne, near Paris, this time against a French nobleman, again for the honour of a lady. A bag with six clumsy horse pistols was produced, and each man reached in and drew a weapon. Richardson's aim was thrown off by a sticking trigger; he was shot in the Achilles tendon and was unable to stand for a second exchange.[6]

In 1835 the Liberal-Conservative politics of Spain had erupted into the Carlist Wars during which the British Auxiliary Legion was recruited by the Liberal side with the active support of the British government. It was an ill-prepared force; the officers were mad for promotion and honours while the soldiers were common mercenaries. Discipline was lax and the leadership erratic. More than one officer supplemented his pay by writing despatches for English newspapers in which the correspondents belittled their seniors and glorified themselves.

By June of 1836 Richardson and the British Legion were at San Sebastian, on the Bay of Biscay. In a quarrelsome, back-stabbing fraternity of officers he had more than his share of enemies. A clique was regularly harassing the Canadian in petty and major ways. It was whispered loudly that Richardson had defamed deceased officers in correspondence and had been cowardly under fire. Both claims were false but rebutting them was difficult. He demanded an inquiry into his conduct and at length a Legion tribunal vindicated him. Soon after that he was promoted to major.

Yet the campaign of surreptitious slander continued. Two officers wrote abusive reports of his regiment that reflected on him. Richardson called one a coward and duelled with him. Several shots were exchanged without injury to either man, and the Canadian finally stated that his opponent had proved by his coming to the affair that he was no coward. Within hours the other critic challenged Richardson, but that was avoided by third-party intervention.

The bad blood between Richardson and his brother officers reached its peak in "the affair of the Spanish Club." On November 4, 1836, at an officers' club he had joined, Richardson had an altercation with a waiter. He never stated what had started this dispute, but his enemies claimed he had refused to pay for a deck of cards. Other members sided with the waiter and insisted that Richardson leave the premises.

The next day Richardson tried to resign from the club, but a meet-

Belligerent and eccentric, John Richardson issued more duelling challenges than any other person in Canadian history. In his memoirs he tried to justify each incident. (National Archives of Canada, C-31606)

ing of officers had tried him *in absentia* and had voted to expel him. There was violent talk of horsewhipping and more duels, none of which translated into action. The expulsion/resignation incident would still make a damning story if published in *The Times.*

Richardson asked permission of his superiors to embark for France, and he left on November 16. Before leaving he sent letters to four officers who had been instrumental in his expulsion to meet him at Bayonne, just over the border, there to duel one after the other. None turned up, and after three days he went on to Bordeaux and thence to London, leaving word of his movements should any of his enemies choose to accept his challenges. His struggle to redeem his honour went on for two years – a tempest in a teapot, petty to all but him.

Word of his expulsion from the club had been published in a military journal, the *United Service Gazette,* as early as December 3. Richardson defended himself ably in the same paper, but when he went over to the offensive, writing scandalous letters about his enemies, the *Gazette* refused to print them. The editors saw no point in being instruments to personal quarrels among disputatious officers.

By late January 1837 a Captain Kirby, one of the four challenged by Richardson, had arrived in London. The Canadian sent his enemy a note, reminding him of the San Sebastian affair and renewing his invitation to duel. Kirby agreed to meet, but then was persuaded to write a conciliatory note. In it he stated that he had not realized the gravity of expelling Richardson and pleaded that he had merely followed the lead of another member, General Charles Chichester. This note, published in the *Gazette,* was acceptable to Richardson, who turned his wrath to his remaining foes.

Early in 1838, Richardson ended a twenty-three-year exile and went back to Canada, now the centre of much British attention following the rebellions of the previous year. On May 30 he learned that General Chichester was now in Montreal, one of many officers in the expanded garrison. Acting through a lawyer, Murdock Morison, Richardson raised the San Sebastian affair once more. Chichester declined to apologize for his part in the club incident (he had seconded the motion of expulsion), but referred the matter to his superiors. Once again, third-party diplomacy came into play. Chichester signed a statement to the effect that he had not understood the resolution of expulsion, that he bore no ill will towards Richardson, and that the Canadian had been innocent of the accusations laid against him. This document – which suggested that Chichester was a muddle-headed fool – was printed later that year in Richardson's memoirs. Thus ended one of the most protracted attempts to duel in the history of that foolish custom.[7]

William Epps Cormack (1798-1868) was a native of St. John's, Newfoundland. In the early 1820s he was prominent among those who were trying to contact and save the last of the Beothuk Indians. In the course of this work he crossed the island on foot in 1822, the first man to do so. Subsequently he moved to Australia, then to New Zealand, before settling in British Columbia.

His farming days in Auckland, New Zealand, included an odd duelling note. On March 17, 1842, he quarrelled with Captain A.D. Best. Cormack recruited Dr. S.M. Martin to deliver a verbal challenge, and Best appointed Dr. Edward Shortland to act on his behalf. At 6:00 a.m. of the 18th, Best, Martin and Shortland met. An hour passed during which the seconds argued as to whether Best's or Cormack's pistols should be used. It was all academic, for Cormack himself did not appear. Martin finally withdrew, but returned later with an offer to reopen the affair. Captain Best declined, stating that he did not wish to play the fool for his opponent's pleasure.[8]

Such incidents as these demonstrated that Canadians were neither more nor less belligerent than other people, whether they were at home or on foreign soil. The wounding of de Salaberry and the death of Baby indicated how earnest were the duellists of their time; the bloodless nature of later encounters reflected how much "going to the turf" had degenerated into pompous ritual, marked by bluff and bluster rather than deadly purpose.

*Chapter 9*

༚

# Duelling
# in Decline

Throughout British North America, duelling challenges were regularly being issued during the 1840s. Nevertheless, the practice was rapidly falling into disrepute. When in 1838 Robert Sweeney killed Major Henry Warde at a Verdun race track, the public reaction was one of mixed grief and outrage. The coroner's jury which blandly stated that Warde had died at the hand of "a person unknown" was particularly subjected to contempt; some crimes might be forgiven, but not hypocrisy or stupidity. In England, societies were being formed to suppress duelling. They were not unlike modern societies that work towards ending fox hunts.

However, it was Queen Victoria who did more than anyone else to bring the practice to an end. In March 1844 she discussed the problem with her Prime Minister, Sir Robert Peel. Hitherto, the Mutiny Act had included a provision for officers being cashiered if they failed to uphold their honour by duelling. This was repealed, and the Articles of War amended to require the court-martial and dismissal of any officer who duelled, challenged, acted as a second or failed to prevent a duel. Almost immediately, duelling ceased within the British army, and civilian society followed suit.

In 1838 the most active duellists were the exiled rebels from Lower Canada. As they paced about Vermont and New York, planning

Ludger Duvernay was one of Lower Canada's most frequent duellists; George-E. Cartier sought his advice before one encounter. (National Archives of Canada, C-46210)

fantastic raids and contemplating ignominious defeats, they quarrelled with each other. Ludger Duvernay in particular considered challenging Dr. Cyril Hector Coté, a disputatious gentleman who brooked no disagreements. Edouard Rodier persuaded his friend not to go through with it, citing "the customs and manners of Vermont" and the possibility of ridicule as reasons not to duel. Nevertheless, Duvernay wrote to Coté, declaring his intention to fight should they ever return to Canada – a threat both men forgot when their exile at last ended. Duvernay also came near to duelling with an American supporter, Charles Bryant, in February 1838, but Bryant wrote a conciliatory letter which disarmed the *canadien*.[1]

Meanwhile, Toronto society seethed with its juicy scandals. In June 1839 Elizabeth Van Rensselaer Stuart, the wife of lawyer John Stuart of London, went to Toronto, ostensibly to visit her mother. There she was seduced by Lieutenant John Grogan, 32nd Regiment of Foot, with whom she eloped, leaving behind her husband of five years and their three children. Since Grogan and his unit had only recently been stationed in London, it is possible that the adulterous couple had formed their attachment earlier.

John Stuart went after Grogan. On June 27 they met on Toronto Island. One newspaper reported that "two shots were fired by the parties, without effect." By another account, Grogan virtually admitted that he had wronged the husband by accepting Stuart's fire and withholding his own. Stuart also took his enemy to court, where he was awarded £672 14s. 3d. Subsequently, a statute went through the Legislature of Upper Canada granting a rare divorce.[2]

Larratt Smith was twenty-one years old when, in July 1841, he ran afoul of Aemilius Irving. Both were young lawyers. Irving reportedly made rude remarks about Smith's mother; Smith wrote a challenge and waited for a meeting. Mutual acquaintances intervened, and when Smith and Irving met at Toronto's race track it was to shake hands, Irving having written a letter (presumably either an explanation or an apology) that satisfied Smith. The two men had been friends before the incident and resumed their camaraderie afterwards. One might ask if the challenge had been serious or a piece of bravado.[3]

Hamilton, Canada West, came near to having a duel in January 1843, thanks to the fiery temper of Doctor Gerald O'Reilly. It was prevented by the other party apologizing by way of an advertisement printed in the Hamilton *Argus*:

> … I, Richard Howell, having on the 21st January last published a statement reflecting on the professional character of Dr. Gerald O'Reilly of Hamilton, inasmuch as I accused him of extortion in charging me with a sum of four pounds 1 shilling 6 pence for one visit … now declare that the whole of that statement as made by me was totally without foundation … and now express my deep regret in having been the cause in any way of injuring Dr. O'Reilly.[4]

The Warde–Sweeney duel had not ended duelling in Lower Canada. Robert Weir (editor of the Montreal *Herald*) and William Kemble (editor of the *Quebec Mercury*) were reported to have exchanged shots in July 1838. It will be remembered that Weir had played a minor role in the events following the death of Major Warde;

the editor had served on the coroner's jury that had ignored Sweeney's part in the duel, even as the *Herald* denounced the jury's conclusions. Ten months after Weir and Kemble had blazed away at one another, in May 1839, a terrible fracas erupted in Montreal involving Major John Richardson.

We have already met Major Richardson and his various disputes in London, France and Spain.[5] Richardson had returned to Canada in 1838. An attempt to duel with an officer of the Montreal garrison for an incident months earlier in Spain had come to naught, but he had acquired a malodorous reputation among the military. About April 1839 he came into collision with his own lawyer, Murdock Morison. Richardson complained that in his absence Morison had barged into his home and, before Mrs. Richardson, had searched through his papers for evidence of Richardson having written ill of the military. The author declared Morison to be no gentleman; the lawyer sent a challenge which Richardson declined on the grounds that the messenger/second was also an inferior.

Riding into Montreal, Richardson found that he had been "posted," public notices having been put up accusing him of cowardice. Morison rode up to him and openly whipped him when Richardson tried to drag him from his horse. Shouting that he would fight Morison within an hour, Richardson turned to two officers to stand as seconds. Both refused and civilian friends also declined to participate. He offered to fight alone, but that was unacceptable to Morison. When at last a second was found, Richardson was such a nervous wreck that his second persuaded Morison's to postpone the encounter one day. Once he finally presented himself at the agreed-upon hour and place, Richardson was haughtily informed that he had lost his right to duel by virtue of undue delay. Once more he was "posted" and humiliated.[6]

His subsequent efforts to duel with others ranged from farce to melodrama. In June 1840, while paying an extended visit to friends in Detroit, one George Meredith, who was separated from his wife, imagined Richardson to be paying too close attention to the lady – who was also Richardson's cousin. There was bombastic talk of duels; the affair was no secret in Detroit. A meeting was arranged on Fighting Island (Canadian territory), but the intervention of a law officer prevented any shooting.

Richardson moved on to Brockville, and by September 1840 he was embroiled in yet another dispute, this time with Colonel William Williams, who commanded the garrison there. The colonel forbade his officers to associate with Richardson, suggesting that the newcomer was a notorious gambler and was neglecting his wife. That led to a furious barrage of notes between the two, intervention by a magistrate, a challenge to Williams by public placard, a suggestion by the colonel that they shoot it out at five paces, and a further "posting" of Richardson by which he was accused of cowardice. In this ludicrous affair both disputants published and distributed abusive pamphlets in support of their views.[7]

His next run-in took place three years later in Kingston, temporarily the capital of the United Canadas. By now he was publishing a newspaper, the *Canadian Loyalist*, which was as partisan as any other periodical of the day. His particular *bête noir* was Stuart Derbishire, the Queen's Printer and representative for Bytown. Richardson heaped assorted insults upon the man. His claim that Derbishire was secretly editing a Kingston newspaper was false. A charge that Derbishire had changed sides during the Spanish Carlist Wars appeared true. An accusation that Derbishire was working against the political interests of his constituents was partly true – the man was an ineffectual member of the Legislature.

An Orangemen's demonstration and riot provoked the first dispute. A youth was killed. Derbishire sympathized with those who had started the disturbance, and Richardson heaved fresh abuse on his enemy. On October 17, 1843, they faced each other, pistols in hand, attended by seconds. Richardson had provoked the affair, even though Derbishire had finally issued the challenge. Richardson had promised to stand his ground until his opponent was satisfied. The argumentative major apparently conceded that his was the weaker case, for he said that he was ready to aim low and that he bore no personal grudge against the gentleman. On the word "Fire," Derbishire missed; Richardson's shot landed at his feet. The seconds intervened. Richardson offered to shake hands, but Derbishire interpreted this as an apology, and Richardson withdrew the invitation, but the seconds declared the matter settled with honour to all.[8]

Richardson was involved in at least one further essay into the duelling sphere. On May 18, 1848, a letter appeared in the Montreal *Morning Courier*, written by him, suggesting that the human race was facing imminent destruction. Charles Dawson Shanley ridiculed the aging war horse in his Montreal *Transcript*, then declined to explain his motives. Richardson despatched a friend with a note, asking that Shanley appoint a second to arrange a meeting. Shanley went to the police. On May 21, Richardson was tried before a magistrate and ordered to keep the peace for six months.[9]

While Major Richardson was making his erratic way through Canada, others were also doing their best to perpetuate the archaic custom. In 1841 two gentlemen, Joseph Yule of Chambly and Timothée Franchère of Saint-Mathias, attempted to organize an encounter. They were frustrated when Franchère's second refused to have any dealing with Yule's man. The element of farce was becoming increasingly prominent in duelling affairs.

In the 1840s such incidents were centred upon Montreal. Upper and Lower Canada had been united in a shotgun union in 1840, and from 1844 to 1849 that city served as capital of this hybrid political unit. With so many politicians about, it was to be expected that Montreal would be the locale for numerous challenges.

Colonial aristocrats were finding ways to avoid duels; it was becoming easier to decline them honourably. In March 1844 Sydney Bellingham (Tory) declared that Lewis Thomas Drummond (Reformer) had uttered some derogatory statement which caused Bellingham to send a cartel.[10] Drummond, however, explained away his statements, and the challenger went no further than publishing their correspondence in the Montreal *Herald*. More forthright was Francis Hincks, the Reformer-publisher of the Montreal *Pilot*, who wrote an uncomplimentary article about Ogle Robert Gowan, the prominent Orangeman and politician. Gowan confronted the publisher, demanding that he designate a second to arrange a duel. Hincks denounced the practice as repugnant to his principles and refused to play what he described as a detestable game. His stand, taken publicly, denoted considerable moral courage. It was a good omen for Hincks' subsequent career – one of the most honourable in Canadian public life.[11]

The year 1844 appears to have been infected with duelling madness. Ludger Duvernay, back from *Patriote* exile, quarrelled with Joseph Guillaume Barthe, member of the Legislative Assembly and editor of *L'Aurore*, a Montreal newspaper. On July 25 the former rebel despatched his second, A. Desmarais, to arrange a meeting. Barthe, however, brusquely ejected the messenger. The next day he laid a complaint before the justices of the peace charging Duvernay with having sent a challenge and Desmarais with having communicated it. The two men were summoned into court and ordered to keep the peace for six months – especially with regard to J.G. Barthe. In subsequent newspaper wars, when even Barthe and Hincks were tossing insults at each other, there were those who compared their behaviour. Hincks, it was said, had been content with stating his principles and had left matters at that; Barthe had not made clear why he declined to duel, and then had run for cover under the law's protection.[12]

A duel avoided, by more laborious means, centred on George-Étienne Cartier, a rebel in 1837, a Father of Confederation in 1867, but simply a rising lawyer-politician in the 1840s. In June 1844, at a public meeting in Montreal, he quarrelled with Guillaume

Levesque, another former rebel and exile. The latter raised his hand as if to strike Cartier but did not actually hit him. The incident touched off a round of letters, transmitted through R.A. Hubert (acting for Cartier) and A.A. Dorion (acting for Levesque). Cartier stated that his opponent had committed an unforgivable offence and demanded satisfaction. Levesque replied that he too had been insulted – Cartier had called him "un petit impertinent" (a little upstart) – and he suggested that one offence cancelled the other. Nevertheless, he was ready to duel if his enemy insisted.

Cartier admitted to having spoken rudely, but claimed that he had suffered a greater insult – a threat to his person. The seconds now came into play as intermediaries. Dorion suggested that they sign a document admitting mutual injury. Cartier insisted upon one in which Levesque would admit to offering a greater offence and would abjectly apologize. Levesque would have nothing to do with it. An encounter with pistols, timed for 7:00 p.m., appeared inevitable.

At the last moment, Levesque signed an apology which Cartier accepted. The document, redrafted to save Levesque's honour, was probably the work of Dorion. It stated that Cartier had also given offence, but admitted that Levesque's sin had been somewhat greater. By such

In his youth, George-Étienne Cartier was a brave rebel and pugnacious duellist. Few Fathers of Confederation had such a colourful past.
(National Archives of Canada)

hairsplitting devices did statesmen refrain from "going to the turf." Cartier was one of the most pugnacious politicians of that era, notorious for demanding apologies, retractions, clarifications or satisfaction from his various political foes. He was particularly touchy about those who questioned his physical courage in the recent rebellion.

On November 23, 1837, Cartier had participated in the Battle of St. Denis, the only *Patriote* victory of those times, when rebels firing from stout stone buildings had repulsed British regulars supported by cannon. Cartier had been prominent in the defence, and had brought reinforcements across the Richelieu River while under fire. Later he had fled to the United States, returning through an amnesty in 1843. In the cut and thrust of 1840s politics, Cartier found himself at odds with many opponents, some of whom had been his comrades-in-arms in 1837. The newspaper *L'Avenir*, devoted to the unrepentant radicalism of Louis-Joseph Papineau, was particularly anxious to belittle Cartier, who had made his peace with authority and had entered the moderate Reform movement. On August 9, 1848, that paper carried a letter accusing Cartier of cowardice under fire, abandoning the field on the pretext of going for ammunition and returning only when the enemy had fled.

Cartier was furious. He stormed into the offices of *L'Avenir* demanding to know the author of this libel. Joseph Doutre, aged twenty-three, admitted responsibility for the article and accepted the politician's challenge. They were to meet on Mount Royal. Cartier prepared for the encounter by seeking instruction from Ludger Duvernay. On the appointed morning, Cartier and Doutre reached the spot with their seconds and took up their positions. Abruptly they were interrupted by Montreal police, summoned by Cartier's brother. The duellists were ordered home. The next day they appeared before a magistrate, charged with disturbing the peace. The charge was dropped and the two men were let off with a warning.

A week later *L'Avenir*'s editors circulated a rumour that the Cartiers had engineered the police intervention. Cartier set off again with a renewed challenge. On this occasion he and Doutre sought a more secret rendezvous, south of Montreal, on the Chambly road. They were placed twenty paces apart. On the first exchange of fire both missed. They were given fresh pistols and tried again. This time Cartier put a bullet through Doutre's hat-brim. The seconds then halted the affair, and the principals returned separately to Montreal. They long remained enemies, but in 1873 Joseph Doutre served as a pall bearer at Sir George-Étienne Cartier's funeral.[13]

Meanwhile new duelling characters emerged to join veterans in the field. Thomas Cushing Aylwin, whose 1837 encounter with R.S.M. Bouchette has been mentioned,[14] fought a more dangerous affair on March 25, 1845. He had traded angry words in the Legislative Assembly with Dominick Daly, the member for Megantic; Aylwin may have been drunk at the time. In a single exchange of shots, Aylwin missed, and Daly's bullet went through his opponent's flapping coat tail. The parties declared themselves satisfied and left the field. This was truly a legislative affair; the seconds (Etienne Taché and Stuart Derbishire) were members of the Assembly, as was the doctor in attendance, Thomas Bouthillier.

Another duel was staged near Kingston on February 19, 1848. This was a further example of the legal profession setting a bad example. The principals were a Captain (or Major) Henry Saddlier (also spelled Sadlier), described as being a local militia officer and prison inspector, and Christopher Armstrong, a magistrate from Bytown. The quarrel began at a land auction sale. The Kingston *Argus* described the affair with heavyhanded sarcasm under the headline "NOVEL, INGENIOUS AND EXPEDITIOUS MODE OF SETTLING A LAWSUIT."

On Friday last there was a sale of some property in this city belonging to a learned Judge of a Lumbering District who had come here to attend it. At the appointed time advertised the audience collected, amongst whom was a somewhat well-known Major of Militia of this city. Some observations were made at the sale, in disparagement of the title, by the Major, who was anxious to purchase the property in question, and made a *miserable* bid of £5 upon it. In consequence of this the sale did not go off, and the learned Judge feeling aggrieved, commenced an action against the Major for "Slander of Title." On receiving the Writ the Major placed it in the hands of a friend, also a member of the Canadian Bar. The two legal gentlemen considering pistols to be better than pleas, agreed that the best way of settling the case before them would be to place the Judge and the Major in an upright position at 15 paces distant, so that the Judge might try to shoot the Major and the Major attempt to bore a hole through the Judge. Accordingly ... the litigants, instead of "putting themselves upon the country," agreed to put themselves *into* the country, and proceeded to the edge of the marsh, about a mile and a half from this city ... and "did then and there wilfully and with malice aforethought seek to do each other grave bodily harm, against the peace of our Lady the Queen, Her Crown, and Dignity, and to the evil example of all others in the like case offending."

After one explosion of "villainous saltpetre" the Defendant told the Plaintiff he was a gentleman, whereupon the latter agreed to withdraw the suit ... thinking it would be rather dangerous work to explode any more "villainous saltpetre," went out of Court, accompanied by their Attorneys in the "cause," or to speak more intelligibly, left the bog to which they had trotted. Thus was a case, which the regular course of Law might have taken years to decide, settled between sunrise and sunset.

Another Kingston paper, the *Upper Canada Herald,* denounced the duel, expressing particular anger that lawyers should be involved in such breaches of the peace. This brought a stinging reply from the seconds, Charles Stuart and Archibald (Greenfield) MacDonell, described by another journal as "two very green limbs of the law." MacDonell denounced the *Herald's* account as being "false in every particular." Yet another Kingston editor was ambivalent; the *British Whig* admitted that "duels in themselves may be improper and un-called for" and stated, "We ourselves arc opposed in principle to du-elling." At the same time it noted that English lords and cabinet min-isters had duelled within the last three decades, and it also cited the recent Aylwin–Daly encounter as an honourable example of legislators duelling. The *British Whig* even chided the *Herald* for having criticised Major Saddlier but not having attacked its "friend," Aylwin, for similar conduct. The *British Whig's* editor concluded his contradictory re-marks by writing, "We do not see how he [Armstrong] could well avoid a meeting with … Saddlier, when called out by that gentleman."[15]

Between the Aylwin–Daly affair of 1845 and the two duels of 1848 (Armstrong–Saddlier, Cartier–Doutre) lie several rumoured and half-reported meetings with pistols. A pamphlet published at Quebec in 1871 suggested that about this time Bartholemew Conrad Augustus Gugy fought several duels; the author, Thomas Willan, was Gugy's brother-in-law. He gave no details, but stated that Gugy had strained the rules in encounters with Aaron Hart and a man named Grant, while behaving shamefully in the face of provocations by two other gentlemen named McCord and Ryland. Considering the parti-san nature of the pamphlet, coupled with Gugy's reputation for su-ing opponents rather than fighting them, plus the lack of corrobora-tive evidence, these accusations may be more sound than substance. A combat between lawyers L.T. Drummond and W.H. Fleet is hinted at, but supporting evidence is again lacking. A duel between Robert Abraham (editor of the Montreal *Gazette*) and William Bristow (re-placing Francis Hincks as editor of the Montreal *Pilot*) is more sub-stantially suggested, although no precise date can be assigned to it, and it may have been averted on the field by negotiation of the seconds.[16]

The citizens of Bytown (modern Ottawa) were accustomed to street disturbances. Two decades of brawling lumbermen and assorted disputants had given it a reputation as the roughest town in British North America. Yet they must have been surprised on August 19, 1848, to discover their community plastered with notices as yet another would-be duellist "posted" his uncooperative opponent. The handbills read:

TO THE PUBLIC

Having been grossly and wantonly insulted yesterday, in the streets of Bytown, by Edward V. Cortland, and having promptly demanded from that individual (through a friend) the usual satisfaction, which that cowardly miscreant, without assigning any reason, refused to grant,

I have no other recourse left to me, but to proclaim to the world and now I do so, that Edward van Cortland, Surgeon, of this place, is a mean and contemptible liar, slanderer, and ruffian; a miserable, drivelling, cowardly scoundrel, a pitiful poltroon, and utterly unworthy of the notice of any one having pretensions to the character of a gentleman.

R. Hervey, Jr.

Fighting words indeed! The local newspapers for the month are either missing or silent on the affair, and we may never know what insult, real or imagined, so aroused the ire of Robert Hervey (1820- ? ), a Scottish-born Tory lawyer who, for about ten years, was a man of some importance in Bytown, being its third mayor in 1849. His enemy, whose surname had been misspelled, was Doctor Edward van Cortlandt (1805-75), a mildly eccentric, argumentative, widely-read Bytown pioneer who made enemies easily but was respected for his intellect. Certainly one issue on which they differed was the hospital operated by the Grey Nuns. Van Cortlandt was quite at ease working there, while Hervey denounced it as a place where sick Protestants were exposed to Popish propaganda (shades of the origins of the O'Sullivan–Caldwell duel of 1819). In this instance, Doctor van

Cortlandt seems wisely to have avoided Hervey, whose judgement was never particularly sound in such emotional affairs as politics or religion. They did not have to bear each other long as in 1852 Hervey moved to Chicago.[17]

To the 1848 tally of duels and near-duels could be added an incident involving Charles-Joseph Coursol (a future judge) and Pierre Blanchet (editor of *L'Avenir*). Coursol, whose politics were marked by passionate, even violent attachment to Reform causes, was appointed coroner for Montreal on June 30, 1848. Blanchet wrote an editorial critical of Coursol's qualifications and past. The new coroner flew into a rage and despatched a friend to Blanchet to secure either an explanation or a rendezvous.

Blanchet's editorial may have been unfair and cruel, but the writer was not inclined to compromise. In the July 22 issue of his paper he attacked Coursol again, this time for seeking a duel, a practice which Blanchet described as "ferocious and barbarous." Not only did he refuse to go through the motions of appointing a second, but he described Coursol as setting a "scandalous example of violence and disorder" when his public duties were to "enforce the laws while preserving peace and social order." Having bludgeoned Coursol in print, the irate editor went on to ridicule and denounce the very concept of preserving honour by duel. The social underpinnings of the practice were collapsing rapidly.[18]

In February 1849 there unfolded one of the most remarkable legislative sessions in Canadian history. A particularly divisive subject, the Rebellion Losses Bill, was being debated. A dozen years of past history were hurled at each other by Reformers and Tories in mutual character assassinations. The Assembly was in an uproar. Spectators in the public galleries plunged into fist-fights, and female onlookers were escorted to a neutral area behind the Speaker's chair.

At the centre of the tumult was William Hume Blake, the Solicitor General, who privately disagreed with much of the bill which he now so vigorously supported in public. Blake's speeches of February 15

In 1849, William Hume Blake (left) and John A. Macdonald were prevented from duelling through the intervention of the Legislature's Speaker and Sergeant-at-Arms. Who says that politicians are dull? (Toronto Reference Library, J. Ross Robertson Collection, T16843; National Archives of Canada, C-6959)

and 16 (Friday and Saturday) turned into verbal assaults on leading Tory politicians. So vicious were his extemporaneous orations that Blake himself later regretted their tone. In the heat of debate, however, several Tories spoke of challenges, and the honourable member for Kingston, John A. Macdonald, actually delivered one by note in the chamber.

Abruptly the Speaker was informed that the two men had left the Assembly, apparently to arrange an encounter. The galleries were cleared and the Sergeant-at-Arms, ceremoniously gowned and carrying the mace, set off with orders from the House to fetch the honourable members before the chair. Macdonald was found almost at once. He submitted to the Speaker's authority, gave assurances that nothing had happened so far, and that he would behave in an orderly manner. Blake was not at home, and there were crude suggestions that he was hiding from Macdonald's second. On Monday, the 18th, the Solicitor-General himself returned to the Assembly and explained his Saturday absence. Having promised good behaviour, Blake and Macdonald resumed their public careers.[19]

Another incident involving the dignity of the Legislative Assembly occurred in 1854. John Gleason, a mere elector, felt he had been defamed by Louis Napoléon Casault, the member for Montmagny, during discussions of a legislative committee. A written challenge reached Casault, who showed it to his colleagues. A motion by A.N. Morin, seconded by John A. Macdonald, summoned Gleason to the Bar of the Assembly, there to apologize abjectly for having offended the dignity of that body.

Nevertheless, Casault felt that in his private capacity he owed Gleason some personal satisfaction. On December 18 he wrote to that gentleman, explaining that the challenge had been an offence to the Chamber, and thus the Assembly had been obliged to act. Once it adjourned, however, he would consider himself free to meet Gleason. Apparently there was no response. Casault went on to become Chief Justice of Quebec, his reputation unsullied by any personal involvement in deadly child's play.[20]

In Quebec City itself another lawyers' quarrel produced another shootout. This incident began on December 6, 1854, when two attorneys were discussing whether they could proceed with a case the following day. Thomas Pope indicated that he would be ready and signed a document to that effect. Nevertheless, on the 7th Pope stated that he was not prepared to complete the business that day. His adversary, George Irvine, remarked that in signing a paper the previous day Pope had either been meaning to follow their case through or had been trying to mislead those involved in the business at hand. "That is not true" retorted Pope.

Irvine, twenty-eight years old and rising in the legal profession, brooded over this exchange for the rest of the morning and concluded that Pope had called him a liar. He appointed John Pentland to be his second and sent a message to Pope, asking if he was prepared to apologize for his words. Pope, feeling that Irvine had been the first verbal aggressor, replied, "Decidedly not," whereupon Pentland declared Irvine's intention to seek traditional satisfaction and asked

Pope to "name a friend." The task fell to John Young. That evening saw a brisk exchange of notes between Young and Pentland while they arranged a meeting. The seconds also discussed whether the duel might be averted by means of one party or another apologizing. Their correspondence, later published, was an elaborate waltz of words which ultimately failed because both principals felt they had been unjustly insulted, and neither was willing to back down before the other.

Initially the duel was to take place at 7:30 a.m. on December 8, but this proved inconvenient to Irvine, so it was postponed to 11:00 a.m. Where it was to occur is not known, but almost certainly it would have been outside the city limits. At 9:30 a.m. John Young called on John Pentland, at which time the latter stated that he had been unable to secure pistols for his friend – a rather odd situation, considering that Irvine had challenged in the first place. Young replied that this need trouble no one, as he had spoken with Mr. Pope the previous evening, the problem had been anticipated, and Pope was happy to make his pistols available to both sides. A doctor was recruited – the final detail – and the parties converged upon the chosen spot. John Young later described the formalities and exchanges that followed:

At 11, we arrived on the ground together. The principals bowed to one another, and Mr. Pentland and I loaded the pistols. We then measured off fourteen paces as the distance. We then returned to the place where we had left the principals. I then proceeded to conduct Mr. Pope to his place, when Mr. Irvine said, "Gentlemen, may I be permitted to make a few observations?" The seconds acquiesced – Mr. Pope said, "Not the slightest objection." Mr. Irvine then said, "Before doing an act which may be fatal to one or both of us, I wish to say that I had no intention to injure Mr. Pope's feelings, no desire to hurt him in any way. I had no intention to throw any disreputable imputation on his character. Mr. Pope is under a misconception as to my words." Mr. Pope then replied, "That is the same as was stated in the correspondence. The words still remain and the public will give a meaning to them. If they are withdrawn, of course, I shall have no objection to withdraw mine, but unless that is done, and as we are here, we had better finish the business for which we came." I then conducted Mr. Pope to his place – Mr. Pentland did the same by Mr. Irvine. The parties were placed back to back, and at the words, "one, two, three," they fired simultaneously. Mr. Irvine fired in the air. Mr. Pentland said to me, "It appears but as one shot, they have both fired simultaneously." I then walked up to Mr. Pope and he said, "Tell Mr. Pentland that if Mr. Irvine wants another shot I am willing." I replied, "No, it is settled, there shall be no more," Mr. Pentland having told me that he would not have more than one. We then left the ground. As we approached the gateway leading to the high road, Mr. Pope asked me "if it was true that Mr. Irvine had fired in the air?" I said, "Yes"; "Then," said he, "I'll speak to him." Mr. Pope and I then walked towards Mr. Irvine and Mr. Pentland, and Mr. Pope said, "Now, Mr. Irvine, after what has just taken place, and as the matter is now over, I feel that I am in a position to say that I am very sorry that any words used by me should have led to a meeting of this kind between us." We then shook hands. Mr. Irvine said, "I hope you saw that I did not intend to do you any bodily injury." Mr. Pope replied, "I suppose that the usages of society require this sort of thing, but I think it is a most absurd way of settling a difficulty." We then walked to our carioles and returned home.

*A most absurd way of settling a difficulty* – this from a person challenged who seemed more determined to duel than the challenger! George Irvine, the reluctant challenger, went on to a career in Parliament and as a judge in Admiralty cases. The encounter itself, though not reported in the Quebec press, stirred enough gossip that Irvine and Pope published a pamphlet describing the incident; it included all the letters that had passed between their seconds.[21]

Duels were becoming so repugnant to society that publicity fell off. In the 1850s they were most frequently mentioned in the press by persons *denying* that they had been involved in such incidents. One man, André Auclaire, claimed in the Montreal *Herald* of June 16, 1859, to have exchanged shots on Mount Royal with an opponent who did not identify himself and of whom Auclaire did not demand a name. The dispute had grown out of a city council meeting and a chance encounter on the street. Nevertheless, the tale was questioned at the time and since as being too bizarre to be credible.

An encounter between Michel Vidal, editor of Quebec's French language *Journal*, and Télésphore Fournier, employed by *Le National* of the same city, undoubtedly took place, but the details are not known with certainty; the earliest accounts were not published until 1890 and 1899, decades after the event. The year has been variously given as 1850, 1851, 1856 and 1860; the 1856 date is most likely, since *Le National* existed only from 1855 to 1859. Nor is it clear which newspaper published an article that provoked the other's champion. Through their seconds, Fournier and Vidal agreed to meet in Sherbrooke. After a three-day carriage ride to that city they lodged in a hotel where detectives apprehended them, returned the party to Quebec and brought them before a magistrate. They gave assurances that they would not duel anywhere in Canada. That done, they travelled to Rousses' Point, New York, to try again.

Poor documentation of some duels raises many questions; Télésphore Fournier is known to have duelled – but precisely when? (Archives of Ontario, S177)

Accounts of the duel differ; one version has it fought at twelve paces, another at fifteen paces. A melodramatic narrative states that Vidal fired and narrowly missed, his bullet whistling by Fournier's ear. The other man had waited motionless to receive his opponent's shot; he glared coldly at Vidal, aimed deliberately for ten seconds, then fired contemptuously in the air. The two men were instantly reconciled. Fournier went on to become a minister of the Crown and later a justice of the Supreme Court of Canada. Vidal migrated to the United States, where he was elected to Congress and later served as a diplomat. Their chance meeting in Ottawa in February 1890 generated the first recounting of their story.[22]

The institution of duelling received a well-nigh fatal blow in May 1861. Once more, two prominent French-Canadians squared off at each other for no better cause than touchy sensibilities. This time the results were less than farcical. Louis-Siméon Morin (1832-79) was Solicitor-General for Canada East, a rising young man doomed ultimately to disappoint the hopes of those who sponsored him. Louis-Antoine Dessaulles (1819-95), a prominent *rouge*, was editor of *Le Pays* and a member of the Legislative Council. He was incensed by articles critical of him and of the council which appeared in the newspaper *Minerve*. Believing Morin to be the author of these attacks, he wrote an angry letter to the Solicitor-General. Morin replied by denying authorship of the offending pieces. Dessaulles wrote again, stating that he did not believe Morin – that if Morin did not compose the articles, he at least inspired them. In an escalation of rhetoric, Morin replied in an abusive letter calling Dessaulles a duplicitous, cowardly liar. That was the last straw; Dessaulles despatched a challenge directly to Morin, without even resorting to a second acting as courier.

Morin appointed Thomas Kennedy Ramsay (1826-86), a future judge, to act on his behalf. Alexander Edward Kierskowski (1816-70), another member of the Legislative Council, performed as second for

Louis-Siméon Morin's 1861 "duel" with Louis-Antoine Dessaulles was more farce than fury. Their seconds were either incompetent or determined to sabotage the event. (Livernois, Archives nationales du Québec)

Dessaulles. They entered into complex negotiations, much of which they confirmed in writing. Morin, aware of his political position, insisted that the duel should take place on American soil. It was therefore agreed that they should go to Island Pond, Vermont. Kierskowski was to find a surgeon, and Ramsay would secure the weapons. Apparently this was a difficult matter; in a note written at 2:45 p.m. of May 11 he reported, "I have been unable to get the implements required."

By 5:00 p.m. of the 11th he had bought a brace of pistols, but they had not been thoroughly cleaned or inspected. The group caught a ferry to Lévis, took a train to Sherbrooke, then another train to Vermont. By about 5:00 a.m. of May 12 they were on the chosen ground. Ramsay, the veteran of an earlier duel (date unknown) with Louis Labrèche-Viger, had not been able to buy any bullets in Quebec, a fact that astonished Dessaulles and Kierskowski. Evidently he did

Volume 12 of the *Dictionary of Canadian Biography* has a long entry on Louis-Antoine Dessaulles which does not even mention his attempt to duel with L.-S. Morin. (Livernois, Archives nationales du Québec)

have a bullet mould and some lead, and with these the parties fashioned crude balls on the site. Once the weapons had been loaded, the principals were planted some fifteen paces (about forty feet) apart.

At this point someone noted that one pistol was defective. *Le Pays* virtually accused Ramsay of deliberately handing Dessaulles a faulty weapon, yet *Minerve* reported Ramsay as having warned of the situation. In any case, the duel could not continue. Even now the seconds communicated with each other in writing. Ramsay handed a stilted note to Kierskowski, mentioning the "unfortunate incident which necessitated the adjournment of our proceedings." On behalf of Morin he offered to meet again, anywhere over the border, "after having procured proper weapons to the satisfaction of both." Failing that, he suggested that the dispute be submitted to some umpire at home. The disappointed group retraced their steps to Quebec.

*Le Pays* and *Minerve* subsequently published voluminous correspondence, charges and countercharges related to the incident. Kierskowski and Dessaulles were furious with Ramsay and Morin. It seemed incredible to them that there should have been difficulties in buying either good pistols or proper ammunition in a city like Quebec, which was, after all, the capital of Central Canada at the time. They railed against what they viewed as stupidity or worse on the part of the Solicitor General and his second. Dessaulles was now angry at Morin for seeking to duel outside Canada, citing other public figures as having been willing to duel on home soil without regard for their offices.[23] The Morin–Dessaulles fiasco brought a roar of laughter from polite society. It might be said that duelling henceforth succumbed to ridicule, but there were a few dying gasps for the practice.

There appears to have been a challenge issued in Ottawa about February 1863. A group had raised money to be forwarded to England to help celebrate the 300th anniversary of Shakespeare's birth. Somehow the handling of these funds led to accusations of mismanagement or worse. A challenge was issued, "carried by a gentleman of rank in the Militia," but nothing appears to have come of the affair.[24]

In the spring of 1865 an encounter was reported in Montreal. Two young men in love with the same woman squared off in the presence of seconds and a doctor, exchanged shots without hitting one another and went their separate ways.[25]

A reported 1868 duel in Quebec between a Captain Elmhurst, 53rd Regiment, and a Mr. Lemesurier may have been only a challenge that went no further. That same year a three-act play, *Un Duel à poudre,* was presented in Saint-Hyacinthe which treated a duel as farce, further proof that the practice was now regarded with public contempt. Men quarrelling in the streets might still threaten to "go to the turf," but it would be idle bombast rather than calculated ritual.

Yet another farcical incident took place in St. John's, Newfoundland, on September 23, 1873. A native of Heart's Content, one Din Dooley, had been courting a lady who was also sought by Augustus Healey. The rivals decided to resolve the matter by duelling near Fort Townsend (now the site of a fire station). Their seconds are identified as Fred Burnham and Thomas Allen. Upon firing, Healey stood his ground while Dooley collapsed in a faint. Neither man had been in danger as the seconds had loaded the pistols with blanks. A little later the protagonists resumed the quarrel by more traditional means – bare knuckles. Healey won the fight, but the lady wisely chose to have nothing to do with either man.[26]

A similar incident may have occurred in Windsor, Nova Scotia, in the summer of 1888. Two men, identified only as being from Windsor and Dartmouth, had been courting the same woman. The Windsor resident, feigning outrage, reportedly challenged his rival, and the man from Dartmouth reluctantly agreed. When they met, the Dartmouther fired wide; he was surprised and horrified when his opponent nevertheless collapsed, apparently with blood on his shirt. The "victor" fled, leaving behind both the "victim" and the girl. He had been fooled by an elaborate hoax. The "blood" had been some red flannel, artfully flashed at the right moment.[27]

The story, as recounted in the papers, raises several questions.

How did the Windsor challenger ensure that he would not be harmed? What made him so certain that the Dartmouth man would not rush to his side and immediately recognize the true state of affairs? The melodrama, like others, may be classified as "unsubstantiated," but it does illustrate a certain lingering fascination in society with the practice of duelling.

One further comic drama remained to be performed. On June 8, 1948, Ottawa newspapers were agog with reports of a challenge and refusal between two diplomats. The Consul General of the Dominican Republic, Julio A. Ricart, had formally demanded an explanation of alleged insults or a duel with Dr. Juan Carlos Rodriguez, Argentina's ambassador to Canada. The latter claimed that Ricart had behaved in vulgar fashion at a reception several weeks earlier, and that the Dominican was henceforth *persona non grata* in the embassy. Ricart's offence was not clearly described, and the Ottawa papers gave slightly different accounts of the squabble.

According to the Ottawa *Evening Citizen*, it had begun with Ricart offering "a pleasantry" about dogs; Madame Rodriguez had replied, "You belong to a negro country," and the Consul General had left in a great huff. When he had not been invited to another reception, this one honouring Argentina's national day, Ricart had taken it as both a personal and a national affront. His challenge was issued on either June 6 or 7.

Through statements to reporters the diplomats traded insults. Ambassador Rodriguez having stated that a duel would be against Canadian law, Consul General Ricart had offered to fight in the Argentine embassy itself. The ambassador cited diplomatic rank as preventing him from duelling; the consul retorted that it was an affair "between gentlemen, not between diplomats." Ricart, who boasted of having fought another duel some years before, became more elegantly abusive, and in so doing showed the class-conscious snobbery that lay behind such encounters:

Compare the newspaper headline for a 1948 non-event with the treatment of the 1838 Warde–Sweeney duel (page 131).

One would not duel with a furnace man, but with an equal. We are all gentlemen of the same standing in this affair of honour. He as a man had to answer my challenge; let him show himself to be a gentleman. He must answer as a gentleman and not as an ambassador.

The Ottawa *Journal* was more explicit about the origin of the dispute. In the recent past at least two of Ambassador Rodriguez's dogs had died in mysterious circumstances. The Ottawa Humane Society had attempted to investigate the matter, but had been denied access to the embassy on the grounds of "diplomatic immunity." The quarrel with the Humane Society had been an embarrassing public fracas.

At the May reception, Consul General Ricart (who admitted to being "slightly high" but denied being drunk) asked Madame Rodriguez, "How are the dogs?"

She reportedly replied, "Fine; how is your nigger republic?"

Ricart had left, though not before the lady had offered an apology. However, upon learning that he had been deliberately excluded from the Argentinian National Day reception, Ricart had gone off at half-cock to challenge Rodriguez. He was incensed that the ambassador refused to meet with either swords or pistols, and was further outraged that the matter had become public knowledge. He openly described his enemy as a tattletale and a coward.

The Ottawa *Journal* suggested that the two should meet at Lansdowne Park or in the Civic Auditorium – but with boxing gloves rather than lethal weapons, and External Affairs officials on hand to referee. The humour was heavyhanded, but it was further proof that duelling had gone down to ignominious buffoonery. The "diplomatic duel" never took place, and soon afterwards Ambassador Rodriguez was recalled to Buenos Aires. Undoubtedly the people most relieved were Canada's Minister of External Affairs (Louis St. Laurent) and his Deputy Minister (Lester B. Pearson).

*Appendix*

❦

# The Irish
# Duelling Code

Reputed to have been "adopted at the Clonmel Summer Assizes, 1777, for the government of duellists, by the gentlemen of Tipperary, Galway, Mayo, Sligo, and Roscommon." Also known in Galway as "the twenty-six commandments."

I    The first offence requires the first apology, though the retort may have been more offensive than the insult. Example: A tells B he is impertinent, etc. B retorts that he lies; yet A must make the first apology, because he gave the first offence, and (after one fire) B may explain away the retort by subsequent apology.

II    But if the parties would rather fight on, then, after two shots each (but in no case before), B may explain first and A apologize afterwards.

**N.B. The above rules apply to all cases of offences in retort not of a stronger class than the example.**

III    If a doubt exists who gave the first offence, the decision rests with the seconds. If they will not decide or cannot agree, the matter must proceed to two shots, or to a hit if the challenger requires it.

IV    When the lie direct is the first offence, the aggressor must either beg pardon in express terms, exchange two shots previous to apology, or three shots followed by explanation, or fire on till a severe hit be received by one party or the other.

V     As a blow is strictly prohibited under any circumstances among gentlemen, no verbal apology can be received for such an insult. The alternatives, therefore, are: The offender handing a cane to the injured party to be used on his back, at the same time begging pardon; firing until one or both are disabled; or exchanging three shots and then begging pardon without the proffer of the cane.

      **N.B. If swords are used, the parties engage until one is well blooded, disabled, or disarmed, or until, after receiving a wound and blood being drawn, the aggressor begs pardon.**

VI    If A gives B the lie and B retorts by a blow (being the two greatest offences), no reconciliation can take place till after two discharges each or a severe hit, after which B may beg A's pardon for the blow, and then A may explain simply for the lie, because a blow is never allowable, and the offence of the lie, therefore, merges in it. (See proceeding rule)

      **N.B. Challenges for undivulged causes may be conciliated on the ground after one shot. An explanation or the slightest hit should be sufficient in such cases, because personal offence transpired.**

VII   But no apology can be received in any case after the parties have actually taken their ground without exchange of shots.

VIII  In the above case no challenger is obliged to divulge his cause of challenge (if private) unless required by the challenged so to do before their meeting.

IX    All imputations of cheating at play, races, etc., to be considered equivalent to a blow, but may be reconciled after one shot, on admitting their falsehood and begging pardon publicly.

X     Any insult to a lady under a gentleman's care or protection to be considered as by one degree a greater offence than if given to the gentleman personally, and to be regarded accordingly.

XI    Offences originating or accruing from the support of ladies' reputations to be considered as less unjustifiable than any others of the same class, and as admitting of slighter apologies by the aggressor. This is to be determined by the circumstances of the case, but always favourably to the lady.

XII No dumb firing or firing in the air is admissible in any case. The challenger ought not to have challenged without receiving offence, and the challenged ought, if he gave offence, to have made an apology before he came on the ground; therefore children's play must be dishonourable on one side or the other, and is accordingly prohibited.

XIII Seconds to be of equal rank in society with the principals they attend, inasmuch as a second may either choose or chance to become a principal and equality is indispensable.

XIV Challenges are never to be delivered at night, unless the party to be challenged intends leaving the place of offence before morning; for it is desirable to avoid all hot-headed proceedings.

XV The challenged has the right to choose his own weapons unless the challenger gives his honour he is no swordsman, after which, however, he cannot decline any second species of weapon proposed by the challenged.

XVI The challenged chooses his ground, the challenger chooses his distance, the seconds fix the time and terms of firing.

XVII The seconds load in presence of each other, unless they give their mutual honours that they have charged smooth and single, which shall be held sufficient.

XVIII Firing may be regulated, first, by signal; secondly by word of command; or, thirdly at pleasure, as may be agreeable to the parties. In the latter case, the parties may fire at their reasonable leisure, but second presents and rests are strictly prohibited.

XIX In all cases a misfire is equivalent to a shot, and a snap or a non-cock is to be considered as a misfire.

XX Seconds are bound to attempt a reconciliation before the meeting takes place, or after sufficient firing or hits as specified.

XXI Any wound sufficient to agitate the nerves and necessarily make the hand shake must end the business for that day.

XXII If the cause of meeting be of such a nature that no apology or explanation can or will be received, the challenged takes his ground and calls on the challenger to proceed as he chooses. In such cases firing at pleasure is the usual practice, but may be varied by agreement.

XXIII  In slight cases the second hands his principal but one pistol, but in gross cases two, holding another case ready charged in reserve.

XXIV  When the seconds disagree and resolve to exchange shots themselves, it must be at the same time and at right angles with their principals. If with swords, side by side, with five paces' interval.

XXV  No party can be allowed to bend his knee or cover his side with his left hand, but may present at any level from the hip to the eye.

XXVI  None can either advance or retreat if the ground is measured. If no ground be measured, either party may advance at his pleasure, even to the touch of muzzles, but neither can advance on his adversary after the fire, unless the adversary steps forward on him.

N.B. The seconds on both sides stand responsible for this last rule being strictly observed, bad cases having occurred from neglecting it.

N.B. All matters and doubts not herein mentioned will be explained and cleared up by application to the Committee, who meet alternately at Clonmel and Galway at the quarter sessions for that purpose.

Crow Ryan, President
James Keogh, Amby Bodkin, Secretaries

# End Notes

## Preface

1. *The Last Fatal Duel* by Fred Dixon, produced on *Stompin' Tom and the Hockey Song*, Boot Records (BOS-7112).
2. *The Last Dead Man* by David Jacklin (Perth, 1982).
3. See Ottawa *Citizen* of June 11, 1982, for a letter by Mr. Peter Code, stating Perth's case. See also pp. (LC-II 21-22).
4. Aegidius Fauteux, *Le Duel au Canada* (Montreal, Editions du Zodiaque, 1934). The title is misleading in that Fauteux concentrated on those duels staged in New France, Lower Canada and Canada East; the only Maritime duels he mentioned were those in Louisbourg and the Uniacke-Bowie duel in Halifax; of the many duels in Upper Canada and Canada West, he described only five: Small-White, Dickson-Weekes, Jarvis-Ridout, Wilson-Lyon and Richardson-Rankin. Nevertheless, Fauteux's book was the starting point for this author and cannot be ignored by anyone interested in the subject.

## Chapter 1: The Deadly Ritual

1. V.G. Kiernan, *The Duel in European History: Honour and the Reign of Aristocracy* (Oxford, Oxford University Press, 1988), pp. 53 and 111.
2. *Ibid.*, pp. 25-26.
3. J.D. Millingen, *The History of Duelling, Including Narratives of the Most Remarkable Personal Encounters That Have Taken Place From the Earliest Period to the Present Time* (London, Richard Bentley, 1841), Vol. I, pp. 118-119 and p. 310.
4 *Ibid.*, p. 313; Kiernan, *op. cit.*, p. 71.

## Chapter 2: New France

1. Reuben Gold Thwaites (editor), *The Jesuit Relations and Allied Documents* (New York, Pageant, 1959), Vol. XXVIII, pp. 187-189.
2. The Sovereign Council, established in 1663 and renamed the Superior Council in 1703, was the highest governing body in New France, consisting of the Governor, Bishop, Intendant, Attorney General, Recording Clerk, and councillors who eventually numbered twelve. It had both judicial and legislative functions.
3. P.G. Roy, "Le Duel sous le régime français," *Bulletin des recherches historiques*, Vol. XIII, No. 5 (May 1907), p. 131. See also *Jugements et délibérations du Conseil Soverain de la Nouvelle France* (Legislature of the Province of Quebec), Vol. I (1885), p. 561.
4. E.Z. Massicotte, "Duels et coups d'épée à Montréal sous le régime français," *Bulletin des recherches historiques*, Vol. XXI, No. 12 (December 1915), pp. 353-355.
5. *Ibid.*, pp. 355-356. The death of Ensign Henri de Porteau following a Trois Rivières tavern encounter (August 1687) is counted by Fauteux as a duel (*Le Duel au Canada*, pp. 20-21), but he cites contemporary accounts to the effect that the victim did not have time to defend himself. Clearly that was a case of murder rather than a duel.
6. Fauteux, *op. cit.*, pp. 35-36, gives the name as Maugeant, but Barry M. Moody renders it as Mangeant, sometimes spelled Maugean; *Dictionary of Canadian Biography*, Vol. III (Toronto, University of Toronto Press, 1974), pp. 426-427.
7. *Ibid.*, p. 40.
8. Massicotte, *op. cit.*, p. 357; also mentioned in Fauteux, *op. cit.*, pp. 40-41. Translation by this writer.
9. Fauteux, *op. cit.*, gives her name as Marie, but André Lachance identifies her as Françoise; see *Dictionary of Canadian Biography*, Vol. III, p. 140.
10. C. Hibbert, *Wolfe in Canada* (London, 1959), pp. 93 and 96.

## Chapter 3: The New Régime

1. Fauteux, *Le Duel au Canada*, p. 51; translation by this writer. Fauteux admits, however, that by the 19th century pistols had joined (though not replaced) swords as duelling weapons in France. He dismisses as bombast a claim by Pierre de Sales Laterrière (1747-1815) to have fought (with a sword) against four English naval officers in Quebec in 1772 – an incident which, even if true, would rate as a brawl rather than a duel.

2. See Wilfred Ward, "British Pistol Duelling and its' Weapons," *Men at Arms*, Vol. VI, No. 4 (July/ August 1984).

3. William Blackstone, *Commentaries on the Laws of England* (Oxford, Clarendon Press, 1769), Book IV, p. 199.

4. For the complete code, see Appendix; the text is from Robert Baldick, *The Duel: A History of Duelling* (London, 1965), pp. 34-36.

5. Fauteux, *op. cit.*, pp. 196-200.

6. Carl F. Klinck and James J. Talman, *The Journal of Major John Norton, 1816* (Toronto, The Champlain Society, 1970), pp. xci-xciv.

7. D.O. Luanaigh to the author, December 13, 1983.

8. Sir Jonah Barrington, *Personal Sketches of his Own Times* (Philadelphia, 1827), Vol. II, p. 9.

9. British Military Records, National Archives of Canada, Record Group 8 (I), Vol. 930, on microfilm C.3281.

10. Fauteux, *op. cit.*, pp. 59-64. Of the "Broadstreet" affair it is worth noting that no officer of that name was carried on the British Army List during the period, although there was a Captain Doyle in the 24th Regiment.

11. Fauteux, *op. cit.*, pp. 66-72; E. C. Collard, *Montreal: The Days That Are No More* (Toronto, Totem Books, 1976), pp. 111-112; Lillian C. Grey, "The Legend of Wolfe's Duelling Pistols," *The Atlantic Advocate*, March 1967.

12. Quebec *Mercury*, December 15, 1812; Scottish Record Office, "Guthrie of Guthrie Muniments" (file reference GD 188); Miss E. Talbot Rice, National Army Museum, January 25, 1983. The discrepancy between the year of death and the succeeding Army Lists was not unique; another officer, killed in a British duel in 1801, was carried on the Army List until 1804.

13. Fauteux, *op. cit.*, pp. 72-73.

14. *Ibid.*, pp. 87-93.

15. *Ibid.*, pp. 93-102; Collard, *op. cit.*, pp. 109-111; François-J. Audet, *Les Juges en chef de la province de Québec, 1764-1924* (Quebec, L'Action Sociale, 1927), p. 74-77; Edward Horton Bensley, "William Caldwell," *Dictionary of Canadian Biography*, Vol. VI (Toronto, Univerisity of Toronto Pess, 1987), pp. 104-105; E.H. Bensley and E.R. Tunis, "The Caldwell-O'Sullivan Duel: a Prelude to the Founding of the Montreal General Hospital," Canadian Medical Association *Journal*, Vol. 100 (1969), pp. 1092-95; "Une duel resulta d'une polemique autour de l'Hotel-Dieu et du Montreal General Hospital," *L'Union medicale du Canada* (Montreal), Vol. 100 (1971), pp. 530-535.

16. The Gale-Stuart duel is recorded by A.W. Patrick Buchanan, *The Bench and Bar of Lower Canada down to 1850* (Montreal, Burton's Limited, 1925), p. 134. The story that Gale was injured comes from William Henry Atherton, *Montreal: From 1535 to 1914: Biographical* (Monteal, S.J. Clarke, 1914), Vol. III, p. 57, who mentions that Gale was "forced by the then prevailing customs of society to fight," and describes the encounter as "an event which ... he profoundly regretted, and gladly saw the better day when men ran no risk of forfeiting their position as gentlemen by refusing to shoot, or be shot at, in order to redress real or facied insults." Buchanan mentions many other duels without giving dates or details; most are undocumented elsewhere. Encounters between James Scott (law student) and Campbell Sweeney, Jr. (younger brother of Robert Sweeney) and between Campbell Sweeney, Jr. and William Walker (Walker, a lawyer, losing one finger) are supported by J. Douglas Borthwick, *History and Biographical Gazeteer of Montreal to the Year 1892* (Montreal, John Lovell and Son, 1892), p. 178. There is also independent evidence of a duel between lawyer Murdock Morison and Major John Richardson (see pp. 149-150 and 154). Of the following incidents Buchanan is the only known source: Henry Driscoll vs. Aaron Philip Hart (both lawyers), Francis G. Johnson vs. Aaron Philip Hart, Bartholemew Conrad Gugy and Aaron Philip Hart, Gugy and a lawyer named Grant, plus duels with unnamed opponents by lawyers Lewis T. Drummond, W. H.

Fleet, and Henry Driscoll, Unfortunately for Buchanan's credibility, he describes a duel between James Scott and William Collis Meredith as being fatal to Scott (it was not – see pp. 123-124). He also gives an incorrect date for the Calwell-O'Sullivan duel, and implies that General Sir Henry Warde, father of the last man killed duelling in Canada, had himself shot a man to death while duelling in Montreal; there is no evidence that General Warde was ever in Canada. He probably got no nearer than the Barbados, where he was Governor from 1821 to 1827.

17. Fauteux, *op. cit.*, pp. 105-106. See pp. 137.

18. *Ibid.*, pp. 107-108; *Montreal Gazette*, November 19, 1827.

19. Fauteux, *op. cit.*, p. 107. The Canadian and American newspapers most likely to have reported the incident are incomplete for the appropriate dates.

## Chapter 4: The Duel in Upper Canada

1. Richard Preston, "James Clark," *Dictionary of Canadian Biography*, Vol. V (Toronto, University of Toronto Press, 1983), p. 188; S. R. Mealing, "William Osgoode," *Dictionary of Canadian Biography*, Vol. VI (Toronto, University of Toronto Press, 1987), p. 558; Clarence Alvin Armstrong, *Buckskin to Broadloom: Kingston Grows Up* (Kingston, Whig Standard, 1973), pp. 85-86; William Colgate, "The Diary of John White, First Attorney General of Upper Canada," *Ontario History*, Vol. XLVII, Autumn 1955, pp. 147-170; A. R. M. Lower, "Three Letters of William Osgoode, First Chief Justice of Upper Canada," *Ontario History*, Vol. LVII (Summer 1965), pp. 181-187; Cecelia Morgan, "'In Search of the Phantom Misnamed Honour': Duelling in Upper Canada," *Canadian Historical Review*, Vol. 76, No. 4 (December 1995), pp. 519-562.

2. Robert Joseph Burns, *The First Elite of Toronto: An Examination of the Genesis, Consolidation and Duration of Power in an Emerging Colonial Society*, unpublished doctoral dissertation, University of Western Ontario, London, 1974.

3. Whether White made all these allegations, or whether Smith embellished the Attorney-General's original remarks, is uncertain. William Jarvis, in a letter to his father-in-law dated January 18, 1800, wrote, "This affray was in consequence of the Atty Genl saying that Mrs. Small had been the kept Mistress of Lord Bercley, & that Small had received a sum of money for marrying her that he himself had kept her 'till he was tired of her while in this Province, &c, &c, &c, &c." White's hasty departure from the Small's home following "a little coquetry" does not quite square with this slander; something may have developed later, or the initial tale may have become juicier with retelling.

4. Peter Russell to Sergeant Shepherd, Lincoln's Inn, January 9, 1800, reproduced by Edith G. Firth, *The Town of York, 1793-1815* (Toronto, The Champlain Society, 1962), p. 231.

5. The jurors had less difficulty two days later with convicting Humphrey Sullivan of the capital crime of petty larceny, for which he was sentenced to hang by Chief Justice John Elsmley. Small, of course, was a "gentleman"; Sullivan was merely a transient Irishman.

6. Firth, op. cit., p. 271. See also William Renwick Riddell, *The Life of John Graves Simcoe* (Toronto, McClelland and Stewart, 1926), pp. 428 and 440; Riddell, "The Duel in Upper Canada," *The Canadian Law Times*, Vol. 35 (1915), pp. 726-738; S.R. Mealing, "John Small," *Dictionary of Canadian Biography*, Vol. VI (Toronto, University of Toronto Press, 1987), pp. 721-22.

7. "The Diary of Joseph Willcocks," printed in Jesse Edgar Middleton, *The Province of Ontario – A History* (Toronto, Dominion Publishing Company, 1927), Vol. II, p. 1292. See also Elwood H. Jones, "Joseph Willcocks," *Dictionary of Canadian Biography* (Toronto, University of Toronto Press, 1983), Vol. V, pp. 854-859.

8. Riddell, *op. cit.*, pp. 728-729; Fauteux, *Le Duel au Canada*, pp. 80-81; G.H. Patterson, "William Weekes," *Dictionary of Canadian Biography* (Toronto, University of Toronto Press, 1983), Vol. V, pp. 844-845.

The device of using a national boundary to evade justice worked both ways. Several Canadian Duellists lit out for American territory to fight (see the Rankin-Richardson duel, pp. 70-71; the Vidal-Fournier episode, pp. 169-170; and the Morin-Dessaulles fiasco, pp. 170-172).

Some traffic went the other way. Two American army officers, Captain John Farley and Lieutenant Otis Fisher, quarrelled during court martial proceedings at Fort Detroit, with Farley insulting Fisher in most abusive terms. They met with seconds on Canadian soil near Sandwich (modern Windsor) at 2:00 a. m. of May 3, 1820, and discussed their difference until sunrise. Unable to arrive at a reconciliation, they shook hands, said goodbye to each other, took their places at twelve paces and fired. Lieutenant Fisher was shot through the heart. A Canadian coroner's jury ruled that the young man had been the victim of "Wilful murder," but it was an American court martial, meeting on the 4th, that dealt with Farley. The Captain apparently was let off because the duel had been fought outside the United States; Francis X. Chauvin, *Duelling in Canada* (Windsor, n. d., n. p.).

Another trans-boundary incident occurred on June 20, 1855. Two citizens of New York State, one F. Leavenworth and a J.B. Breckenridge, both members of a social club, had quarrelled, one having accused the other of being unqualified to be in the association. This insult was answered with a glove across the face. They crossed the Niagara River to settle accounts. Placed eight paces apart, they fired with deadly intent. Breckenridge was wounded in one leg; his own bullet wounded Levenworth in both legs. The papers remarked that it was a miracle neither man was killed. See Lambton *Observer and Western Advertiser*, June 28, 1855.

9. Taylor, an officer in the 41st Regiment of Foot, was also training to be a lawyer.

10. William Renwick Riddell, "Another Duel in Early Upper Canada," *The Canadian Law Times*, Vol. 36 (1916), pp. 604-610; Josephine Phalen, "A Duel on the Island," *Ontario History*, Vol. LXIX, December 1977, pp. 235-238; Carol Whitfield and Robert Lochiel Fraser III, "John Macdonnell," *Dictionary of Canadian Biography*, (Toronto, University of Toronto Press, 1983), Vol. V, pp. 520-523.

11. Fauteux, *op. cit.*, pp. 81-82; Riddell, "The Duel in Early Upper Canada," pp. 729-733; Morgan, "'In Search of the Phantom Honour,'" p. 529 and pp. 542-544; Austin Seton Thompson, *Jarvis Street: A Story of Triumph and Tragedy* (Toronto, Personal Library, 1980), pp. 65-92 and 197-199. This last is the most thorough study of the duel.

12. The same may have been true of nearby March Township, settled in the 1820s by former British army officers; see Harry J. Walker, *Carleton Saga* (Ottawa, 1968), pp. 244-245. He reports that two gentlemen in their cups adjourned with seconds to Lighthouse Island in the Ottawa River and attempted to duel; they were frustrated by the seconds who removed the flints from the pistols. However, Walker gives no dates or names; his source is the memory of a grandson of one of the township's pioneers.

13. The incestuous nature of duelling is underlined by the curious interlocking of characters. James Boulton was the brother of Henry John Boulton (second to Samuel Peters Jarvis in 1817); Thomas Radenhurst was married to Edith Ridout (sister of the unfortunate John Ridout). John Wilson and Robert Lyon, the principals in the famous Perth duel, were articled law students under James Boulton and Thomas Radenhurst.

14. In 1904 an account of the duel mentioned that Lyon's bullet had brushed Wilson's temple. This detail was not part of contemporary reports; if true, it would surely have been cited at the time as justification for Wilson's deadly second shot.

15. Riddell, "The Duel in Upper Canada."

16. See Fauteux, *Le Duel au Canada*, p. 137. Most of the duels mentioned by Fauteux are confirmed by other records, but in this instance his original source has not been located, and his book is the only work or document hitherto traced that mentions the incident.

17. Toronto, *The Patriot*, February 27, 1835, and March 3, 1835.

18. Kingston *British Whig*, March 26, 1835; *The Canadian Paper Money Journal*, July 1982, p. 93; see also "George Truscott," *Dictionary of Canadian Biography* (Toronto, University of Toronto Press, 1985), Vol. VIII, pp. 895-898.

19. A.G. McGhie, "Historical Notes on Medical Personalities in the Hamilton Area," *McGregor Clinic Bulletin* (Hamilton, McGregor Clinic, September 1962); see also Charles Godfrey, *Medicine for Ontario* (Belleville, Mika Publishing, 1979), p. 69-70. The author is indebted to Dr. James R. Digby of Hamilton for providing details and references. Godfrey mentions one other duel which he dates at 1813. By his account, one Dr. Shumate lost his life near Newark (Niagara-on-the-Lake) in combat with one Lieutenant Smith, 16th Regiment of Foot. The report is undocumented; furthermore, the 16th Regiment was in the West Indies in 1813, although it moved to Quebec in 1814. At this writing, the author classifies the Shumate-Smith affair as "reported but unconfirmed."

20. David R. Beasley, *The Canadian Don Quixote: The Life and Works of Major John Richardson, Canada's First Novelist* (Erin, The Porcupine's Quill, 1977), p. 122, Footnote 21.

21. This incident was wrongly reported in the London *Times* (April 12, 1839) as having been a

duel in which Baby was killed. In "posting" Baby, Prince put up notices in the three communities describing Baby in these unflattering terms. Contemporary press reports state that Prince had challenged some thirteen individuals to duel with pistols, muskets and swords.

22. Orlo Miller, *A Century of Western Ontario; The Story of London, "The Free Press," and Western Ontario, 1849-1949* (Toronto, Ryerson Press, 1949), pp. 60-67.

23. R. Alan Douglas, *John Prince: A Collection of Documents* (Toronto, The Champlain Society, 1978), pp. 31-33 and 141. See also Douglas, "John Prince," *Dictionary of Canadian Biography* (Toronto, University of Toronto Press, 1976), Vol. IX, pp. 643-647. For other incidents involving duels on the territory of Upper Canada and Canada West, see below, pp. DD2-7, 13-14, 26-28.

24. *The British Whig* was a Kingston newspaper; copies of contemporary Bytown (Ottawa) papers are not extant. See also Howard Morton Brown, *op. cit.*, p. 95, and Richard Reid, "John Egan," *Dictionary of Canadian Biography (Toronto, 1985), Vol. VIII*, pp. 268-269.

25. Charles Godfrey, *op. cit.*, p. 46, *Bathurst Courier*, December 18, 1840, citing *Niagara Chronicle* of December 3, 1840 (original issues no longer extant).

26. Bytown *Gazette*, December 26, 1839 and January 23, 1840; *Bathurst Courier*, January 10, 1840.

27. *Upper Canada Herald* (Kingston) December 8, 1840.

28. Don Akenson, *The Orangeman: The Life and Times of Ogle Gowan* (Toronto, James Lorimer, 1986), p. 224.

## Chapter 5: Duelling in Atlantic Canada

1. *Acadia Recorder*, December 3, 1921; George Mullane, *Duels in Nova Scotia* (unpublished narrative held by the Nova Scotia Archives, MG 100, Vol. 136, No. 22a).

2. Charles B. Fergusson (editor), *The Diary of Simeon Perkins, 1804-1812* (Toronto, The Champlain Society, 1978), pp. 483, 487.

3. "Last Duel in N.S. Caused by Cards," Montreal *Star*, October 30, 1936.

4. Brian Cuthbertson, *The Old Attorney General: A Biography of Richard John Uniacke, 1752-1830* (Halifax, Nimbus Publishing Limited, 1982), pp. 26 and 36. The incident of 1791 is well documented, but that of 1798 was not set down on paper until 1884 and may be much embellished.

5. R. J. Morgan, "William McKinnon," *Dictionary of Canadian Biography* (Toronto, University of Toronto Press, 1983), Vol. V, pp. 545-546.

6. The best study of the Bowie-Uniacke duel is that by George Patterson, "Three Famous Duels," *More Studies in Nova Scotia History* (Halifax, Imperial Publishing Company, 1941), pp. 71-89 and especially pp. 72-82. Patterson relied greatly on contemporary issues of the *Acadian Recorder* which this writer also consulted; Patterson's narrative is an excellent summary of the facts.

7. Mullane, *op. cit.*

8. Patterson, *op. cit.*, pp. 82-85

9. *Ibid.*, pp. 80 and 87; A. A. MacKenzie, "Edmund Murray Dodd," *Dictionary of Canadian Biography* (Toronto, University of Toronto Press, 1972), Vol. X, p. 232. Patterson dates the duel in 1840; MacKenzie puts it in 1838; there is the possibility that Dodd had *two* encounters.

10. John Robert Colombo, *Columbo's Canadian Quotations* (Hurtig, Edmonton, 1974), p. 270, credits Howe with saying, "A live editor is more useful than a dead hero" on declining a duel. He suggests that the incident followed that with Halliburton, but it might just as easily have been related to one of the earlier challenges.

11. Colombo, *Ibid.*, quotes Howe as saying, "Let the creature live" – a bit more racy, but not in agreement with contemporary accounts.

12. Patterson, *op,cit.*, pp. 85-89

13. Originals and microfilms of the *Royal Gazette and New Brunswick Advertiser* for the dates concerned are not available at this time. Material relating to the death of Cobblestone was supplied by Robert Elliot from notes prepared by J. Russell Harper in contemplation of a biography of Christopher Sowers. Harper evidently had, at some earlier date, access to issues which have since been lost.

14. The *Saint John Gazette*, March 3, 1797, gives the date as the 25th, while the Halifax *Royal Gazette* puts the date as the 24th.

15. W.G. Godfrey, "James Glenie," *Dictionary of Canadian Biography* (Toronto, University of Tor-

onto Press, 1983), pp. 347- 358; George F.G. Stanley, "James Glenie: A Study in Early Colonial Radicalism," *Collections of the Nova Scotia Historical Society*, Vol. 25 (1940); Joseph W. Lawrence, "The Judges of New Brunswick and Their Times," *Acadiensis 1906 (Vol. 6)*, p. 150; W.O. Raymond (editor), *Winslow Papers, A. D. 1776-1826* (Boston, Gregg Press, 1972), p. 317.

16. Saint John *Royal Gazette*, August 17, 1803.

17. Phillip Buckner, "Ward Chipman," *Dictionary of Canadian Biography*, Vol. VI (Toronto, University of Toronto Press, 1987), p. 138.

18. Agnew's frustration may have been related to Allan's change of heart during this and another slave trial. A slave owner himself, Allan came to view slavery as illegal; immediately afterwards he set his own blacks free, setting an example for others to follow. See W. A. Spray, "Caleb Jones," *Dictionary of Canadian Biography* (Toronto, University of Toronto Press, 1983), Vol. V, p. 456.

19. Guides in the Legislative Building, Fredericton, tell a charming story of a duel occurring in that structure. No evidence exists of any such encounter in the legislature, but the tale could well be an embellishment on the Bliss-Street duel. The most complete account of that affair was given by Anderson (whose Christian names are not available); his statement did not refer directly to an indoor duel, but he mentioned that during the discussions "the principals were desired to leave the room, and when wanted should be called in." Indeed, considering the date and hour, a duel out of doors would scarcely have been practical.

20. "When Duels Were in Vogue," Saint John *Telegraph Journal*, September 26, 1931; "When John Murray Bliss Fought a Duel With S. Denny Street," Saint John *Telegraph Journal*, September 28, 1931; J.W. Lawrence, *Footprints or Incidents in Early History of New Brunswick* (Saint John, J. A. McMillan, 1883), pp. 57-58; J.W. Lawrence, "The Judges of New Brunswick and Their Times," *Acadiensis 1905 (Vol. 5)* pp. 173-177 and *Acadiensis 1906 (Vol. 6)*, pp. 268-269.

21. Robert Elliot, New Brunswick Museum, to the author, March 6, 1984, citing D.R. Jack, *Biographical Data Relating to New Brunswick Families, Especially of Loyalist Descent* (Unpublished typescript held by the New Brunswick Museum) and Lillian Maxwell, *An Outline of the History of Central New Brunswick* (1937), p. 166.

22. "Linking the Present With the Past," Saint John *Telegraph Journal*,September 24 and 25, 1931; Lillian Maxwell, "History of Central New Brunswick," Fredericton *Gleaner*, February 27, 1934; Theodore Goodridge Roberts, "The Street-Wetmore Duel," *Loyalists* (Toronto, n.p., n.d. ); Connie Shanks, "The Day They Duelled to the Death," Saint John *Telegraph Journal*, August 16, 1980; Joseph W. Lawrence, "The Judges of New Brunswick and Their Times," *Acadiensis 1907 (Vol. 7)*, pp. 406-408 and 414-423; Mary Barker, "The Duel," *Atlantic Advocate*, November 1958, pp. 49-55; Philip Buckner, "George Ludlow Wetmore," *Dictionary of Canadian Biography* (Toronto, University of Toronto Press, 1987), Vol. VI, p. 810.

23. *New Brunswick Courier*, February 22 and March 8, 1834

24. William T. Baird, *Seventy Years of New Brunswick Life: Autobiographical Sketches* (Saint John, George E. Day Printers, 1890), p. 59. "Dr Wilson" was William Wilson.

25. Excerpts from Bishop Medley papers, supplied by Robert Elliot; see also "Plaque is Reminder of Last Duel," Fredericton *Gleaner*, June 20, 1959; additional notes supplied by Robert Elliot.

26. See Paul O'Neill, *The Oldest City: The Story of St. John's, Newfoundland* (Erin, Press Porcepic, 1975), pp. 240-241.

27. The newspaper and legal documents state that the trial was that of the Supreme Court of Newfoundland, presided over by a panel of judges, and that the Chief Judge directed the jury; no names are given. The Supreme Court of Newfoundland had been organized only in January 1826; we may assume that all three judges (Richard Alexander Tucker, John William Molloy and Augustus Wallet DesBarres) were present for this trial, with Chief Justice Tucker delivering this striking address to the jury.

28. St. John's *Mercantile Journal*, April 20 and 27, 1826; Robert Moss, "The Last Duel in Newfoundland," *The Book of Newfoundland* (St. John's, Newfoundland Book Publishers, 1967), Vol. 4, pp. 450-453; O'Neil, *op. cit.*, pp. 233-234; R. B. McCrea, *Lost Amid the Fogs: Sketches of Life in Newfoundland* (London, Sampson, Low, Son and Maston, 1869), pp. 136-160 (this last a colourful but overdrawn description that substitutes detail and drama for verifiable narrative).

29. Charlottetown *Examiner*. March 25, 1872; diary entry of Doctor J. MacKieson for June 25, 1851 (Prince Edward Island Archives, accession 2353, item 343); letter from Mitchell to Palmer, Prince Edward Island Archives.

**Chapter 6: Patriote Days in Lower Canada**

1. Aegidius Fauteux, *Le Duel au Canada*, pp. 173-178.

2. *Ibid.*, pp. 179-182

3. *Ibid.*, pp. 126-133.

4. John Bélestre-McDonnell (1799-1866) was a minor figure in Reform politics; his home was used for the first celebrations by the St. Jean-Baptiste Society in 1834.

5. Fauteux, *op. cit.*, pp. 150-153.

6. *Ibid.*, pp. 117-124.

7. See above, p. 39.

8. Fauteux, *op. cit.*, pp. 143-148.

9. *Rapport de l'Archiviste de la Province de Québec, 1953-55* (Quebec, Queen's Printer, 1955), pp. 368-71; Pierre Dufour, "Pierre-Jean de Sales Laterrière," *Dictionary of Canadian Biography*, Vol. VI (1821-1835), (Toronto, University of Toronto Press, 1987), pp. 680-681.

10. Fauteux, *op. cit.* pp. 154-172

11. *Ibid.*, pp. 172-173. Fauteux points out that an account of this affair, published in 1840, gives a more heroic description of Duvernay's actions, stating that the wounded publisher was ready to go another round but that Bleury departed suddenly. The 1840 version is from an unreliable source; the contemporary version is virtually Duvernay's anyway.

12. *Ibid.*, pp. 189-196.

13. *Ibid.*, pp. 204-206.

14. Douglas Leighton, "Dominique Ducharme," *Dictionary of Canadian Biography* (Toronto, 1985), Vol. VIII, pp. 244-246.

15. Dating the incident is uncertain; the first report of it appeared in an English edition of *Le Liberal*, of which no copies are now extant. An undated translation was published in *La Minerve* on October 23, 1837.

16. *Ibid.*, pp. 219-224; Elinor Kyte Senior, *British Regulars in Montreal: An Imperial Garrison, 1832-1854* (Montreal, McGill-Queen's University Press, 1981), pp. 50-51. The Ormsby-Rodier duel is surprisingly well documented from both sides. Fauteux, however, dismisses a report of a duel reputed to have occurred in the summer of 1837 between *Patriote* Rudolphe Desrivières and a Doctor Jones as being ill-recorded and out of character for both men. Desrivières is alleged not to have removed his hat during a public playing of *God Save the Queen*, Jones knocked his hat off, and the affair ended with two bloodless exchanges of fire on Mount Royal. However, no account of the incident appeared until 1898 – 60 years onwards!

17. See above, p. 25-26.

18. *The Times*, June 23, 1838 and July 14, 1838; Montreal Herald, May 23, 1838; see also Fauteux, *op. cit.* pp. 242-256; Elinor Kyte Senior, *British Regulars in Montreal: An Imperial Garrison, 1832-1854* (McGill–Queen's University Press, Montreal, 1981) pp. 180-181; A.W. Patrick Buchanan, *The Bench and Bar of Lower Canada Down to 1850* (Burton's Limited, Montreal, 1925) p. 135; Edgar Andrew Collard, *Montreal: The Days That Are No More* (Totem Books, Toronto, 1976) pp. 114-118.

19. National Archives of Canada, Manuscript Group 24 B. 2, Vol. 2, pp. 2965 and 2966 (also available on microfilm C-15790).

**Chapter 7: Duels in the West**

1. "John McDonald of Garth: Autobiographical Notes, 1791-1816," printed in L. R. Masson, *Les Bourgeois de la Compagnie du Nord-Ouest* (Quebec, A. Coté et cie, 1890), Vol. II.

2. There is some dispute as to whether Mrs. McVicar was a Scot or Indian; if the latter, the question might be deemed to have been sarcastic. Elliott Coues, *The Manuscript Journals of Alexander Henry and of David Thompson* (Minneapolis, Ross and Haines, 1897), Vol. II, p. 981, identifies McNeil as being from Ireland and having an army background. As a bully in the fur trade he was reported as having fought three duels, although the author knows only of the one described here.

3. Joseph Tassé, *Les Canadiens de l'Ouest* (Montreal, Cie d'imprimerie canadienne, 1878) Vol. II, P. 329, describes the incident, saying that the principals were "lightly wounded" and that they parted as friends. Father A.G. Morice, *Dictionnaire historique des canadiens et des métis français de l'Ouest* (Montreal, Granger Frères, 1908) pp. 203 and 229-230, dates the duel at 1812, and

contradicts himself by writing, under Montour, that the tailor repaired the damage, while of Pillet he writes that he was accidentally shot in the leg and was unable to walk for a month! Fauteux, *op. cit.*, p. 83, records that it was Montour's coat and Pillet's trousers that were damaged, without citing any source other than Cox. The nearest we have to a firsthand account is Cox's terse description.

4. The precise identity of this man is difficult to pinpoint, owing to the numerous McKenzies employed by all parties in the fur trade.

5. It is not clear whether this was over an Indian woman or the right of one or the other to trade with a particular Indian trapper.

6. See Walter N. Sage, *Sir James Douglas and British Columbia*, (Toronto, University of Toronto Press, 1930), pp. 20-21; Elizabeth Arthur, "Duel at Ile-à-la-Crosse," *Saskatchewan History*, Spring 1974.

7. David William Higgins, "The Duel," *Canada West*, Vol. XI, No. 1 (Spring 1981), pp. 49-55. The writer, a gold seeker at the time of these events, later became a prominent British Columbia journalist and politician. His account of the Sloane-Liverpool "duel" was part of some unpublished memoirs. There was no newspaper in Victoria at that time, and thus no contemporary report of the affair appeared.

### Chapter 8: Canadian Duels Abroad

1. See Philippe Aubert de Gaspé, *Memoires* (Grander Frères, Montreal, 1930) Vol. II, pp. 267-68. Aegidius Fauteux, *op. cit.* pp. 73-78 is skeptical of the account; de Gaspé would not likely have met de Salaberry, and was himself notorious for not allowing facts to interfere with a good story. He also points out that the pistol, not the sword, was the preferred duelling weapon. However, the involvement of Desrivières, and the fact that de Salaberry did have a deep scar on his forehead, lend some credence to de Gaspé's melodramatic narrative. De Salaberry himself would not have shrunk from violence; his legendary courage was matched by his ruthlessness as a disciplinarian.

2. W.D. Lighthall, *An Account of the Battle of Châteauguay* (Montreal, Drysdale, 1839), p. 11. See also J. Patrick Wohler, *Charles de Salaberry, Soldier of the Empire, Defender of Quebec* (Toronto, Dundurn Press, 1984), which turns sparse sources into a graphic account.

3. Philippe-Baby Casgrain, *Mémorial des familles Casgrain, Baby et Perrault* (Quebec, C. Darveau, 1899), pp. 131-132.

4. *The Times* (London), November 21, 1835. See also Fauteux, *op. cit.* pp. 179-188.

5. See David R. Beasley, *The Canadian Don Quixote: The Life and Works of Major John Richardson, Canada's First Novelist* (Erin, The Porcupine's Quill, 1977).

6. *Ibid.*, pp. 38, 48-49 and 71 FF.

7. For more of Richardson's duelling escapades, see pp. 154-156.

9. A.H. McLintock (editor), *An Encyclopaedia of New Zealand* (R.E. Owen, Wellington, 1966), Vol. II, p. 501.

### Chapter 9: Duelling in Decline

1. Fauteux, *Le Duel au Canada*, pp. 232-236.

2. W.R. Riddell mentions the duel in a fleeting way through a footnote in "Another Duel in Early Upper Canada," *The Canadian Law Times*, Vol. 36 (1916), p. 609. The newspaper account is cited in *Bathurst Courier* (Perth), July 12, 1839. Other details are in the statute, "An Act for the Relief of John Stuart" (Upper Canada, 3 Victoria, chapter 72).

3. Mary Larratt Smith, *Young Mr. Smith in Upper Canada* (Toronto, University of Toronto Press, 1980), p. 65.

4. Charles Godfrey, *Medicine for Ontario* (Belleville, Mika Publishing, 1979), p. 68.

5. See above, pp. 147-150.

6. Beasley, *op.cit.*, pp. 113-114.

7. *Ibid.* pp. 125-126.

8. *Ibid.*, p. 138.

9. *Ibid.*, pp. 165-66.

10. Bellingham had carried Dr. William Robertson's challenges to Louis-Joseph Papineau in 1834; see above, pp. 113.

11. Fauteux, *op. cit.,* pp. 261-262.

12. *Ibid.,* pp. 262-64.

13. *Ibid.,* pp. 264-268 and 272-278. As melodramatic as these accounts are, they have not been questioned by any serious biographer of Cartier.

14. See above, pp. 124-126.

15. *Bytown Packet and Weekly Gazette,* March 4, 1848; *British Whig,* February 26, 1848. These newspapers reprint items from the Kingston *Argus* and the Prescott *Telegraph,* original copies of which are no longer extant. The relevant *Upper Canada Herald* is also missing, but the tone of its report may be gleaned from the commentary published in the *British Whig.*

16. See endnote 16 or chapter 3, and Fauteux, *op. cit.,* pp. 271-272.

17. Although undocumented in the press, proof of Hervey's insults exists in the form of three of the offensive placards which are held in the Bytown Museum, Ottawa.

18. Fauteux, *op. cit.,* pp. 278-283.

19. The reader may recall similar efforts by the Legislative Assembly of Lower Canada to prevent a duel between C.-C. Sabrevois de Bleury and C.-O. Perrault in 1836 (see pp. 120-122). Accounts of the Blake-Macdonald flare-up are found in Fauteux, *op. cit.,* pp. 283-288, and Donald Creighton, *John A. Macdonald: The Young Politician* (Toronto, Macmillan, 1952), pp. 137-138.

20. Fauteux, *op. cit.,* pp. 289-291.

21. George Irvine, *Correspondence, etc. Concerning a Recent Difficulty Between Messrs Irvine and Pope,*(Quebec, Bureau and Marcotte, 1854).

22. Fauteux, *op. cit.,* pp. 194-303. See also A. W. Patrick Buchanan, *The Bench and Bar of Lower Canada* (Montreal, Burton's Limited, 1925), pp. 137-138, for a slightly different account by which Vidal and Fournier were charged at Sherbrooke, then tried to duel at Island Pond, Montreal, and Caughnawaga before conducting it finally near Plattsburgh, New York.

23. Fauteux, *op. cit.,* pp. 303-306; *Le Pays,* May 16, 1861; *Minerve,* May 18, 1861.

24. Ottawa *Citizen,* March 4, 1863. The paper wrote: "Rumour is rife with the prospect of an *affaire d'honneur* between two gentlemen of respectable standing in this city, arising out of a dispute caused by an accusation made by one of the parties touching the honour of the other in regard to some funds placed in his charge, the proceeds of a recent performance in aid of the 'Shakespearean Fund.' We understand a 'challenge' was sent by the accused to the accuser, and carried by a gentleman of rank in the Militia, but has not yet been accepted. The party who really has held, and still holds the funds, is, we understand, a clerk in a government office here, and the money will be placed in his hands until the arrangements for its transmission to England would be completed."

25. Montreal *Telegraph,* republished in Ottawa *Union* of May 10, 1865: "Notwithstanding the vigilance of the members of the police force of this city, we hear that there took place this morning, within the limits of the city, an occurrence no less rare than a duel. The combatants were an assistant to a respectable druggist store in this city and a young aspirant to the profession of an architect. The principals accompanied by their seconds and an experienced surgeon with surgical instruments were seen wending their way up St. Urban Street between 5 and 6 o'clock. The ground was marked out in the large field behind the Hotel Dieu Hospital and shots were exchanged. Fortunately no blood was shed, but as the combatants seemed satisfied with the result of the attempt, the matter dropped here and the parties retired home, having we hope, learned a lesson. We understand the cause of the difficulty was owing to both parties falling in love with the same young lady, of whom both were too much enamoured for either to think of giving way to the other."

26. Paul O'Neil, *The Oldest City: The Story of St. John's, Newfoundland* (Erin, Press Porcopic, 1975), pp. 234-235.

27. Saint John *Telegraph,* July 28, 1888. There is a persistent legend in Nova Scotia that two officers duelled with pistols loaded by their seconds with strawberries, with one party horrified by the appearance of a pink stain on his opponent's coat. The tale is probably no more than fancy; the blast of powder in a pistol would reduce a berry to pulp in the barrel.

# Bibliography

Armstrong, Clarence Alvin, *Buckskin to Broadloom: Kingston Grows Up*, Kingston Whig Standard, 1973.

Arthur, Elizabeth, "Duel at Ile-à-la Crosse," *Saskatchewan History*, Spring 1970..

Audet, François-J., *Les Juges en chef de la province de Québec*, Quebec, L'Action Sociale, 1927.

Audet, François-J., *Les Députés de Montréal*, Montreal, Editions des Dix, 1943.

Audet, François-J.,"Pierre-Édouard Leclerc (1798-1866)," *Cahiers des dix*, Volume 8 (1943).

Baird, William T., *Seventy Years of New Brunswick Life: Autobiographical Sketches*, Saint John, George E. Day Printers, 1980.

Baldick, Robert, *The Duel: A History of Duelling*, London, Spring Books, 1965.

Barker, Mary, "The Duel," *Atlantic Advocate*, November 1958.

Barrington, Sir Jonah, *Personal Sketches of His Own Times*, Philadelphia, Carey, Lea and Carey, 1827.

Beasley, David R., *The Canadian Don Quixote: The Life and Works of Major John Richardson, Canada's First Novelist*, Erin, The Porcupine Quill, 1977.

Beck, J. Murray, *Joseph Howe: Volume I: The Conservative Reformer*, Kingston, McGill-Queen's Press, 1982.

Bensley, E.H. and Tunis, E.R., "The Caldwell-O'Sullivan Duel: a Prelude to the Founding of the Montreal General Hospital," *Journal* (Canadian Medical Association), Volume 100 (1969), pp. 1092-95.

Blackstone, William, *Commentaries on the Laws of England*, Oxford, Clarendon Press, 1769.

Brown, Howard Morton, *Lanark Legacy: Nineteenth Century Glimpses of an Ontario County*, Perth, author-published, 1984.

Buchanan, A.W., *The Bench and Bar of Lower Canada, Down to 1850*, Montreal, Burton's Limited 1925.

Casgrain, Philippe-Baby, *Mémorial des familles Casgrain, Baby, et Perrault*, Quebec, C. Darveau, 1899.

Chauvin, Francis X., *Duelling in Canada*, Windsor, n.p., n.d..

Colgate, William, "The Diary of John White, First Attorney-General of Upper Canada," *Ontario History*, Autumn 1955.

Collard, Edgar Andrew, *Montreal, The Days That Are No More*, Toronto, Totem Books, 1976.

Colombo, John Robert, *Colombo's Canadian Quotations*, Edmonton, Hurtig, 1974.

Cox, Ross, *The Columbia River*, Norman, University of Oklahoma Press, 1957.

Creighton, Donald G., *John A. Macdonald: The Young Politician*, Toronto, Macmillan, 1952.

Cuthbertson, Brian, *The Old Attorney-General: A Biography of Richard John Uniacke, 1752-1830*, Halifax, Nimbus Publishing 1952.

Desjardins, Édouard, "Un duel resulta d'une polémique autour de l'Hotel-Dieu et du Montreal General Hospital," *L'Union médicale du Canada*, Volume 100 (1971), pp. 530-535.

Douglas, R. Alan, *John Prince: A Collection of Documents*, Toronto, The Champlain Society/University of Toronto Press, 1980.

Fauteux, Aegidius, *Le Duel au Canada*, Montreal, Éditions de Zodiaque, 1934.

Fergusson, Charles B. (editor), *The Diary of Simeon Perkins,1804-1812*, Toronto, The Champlain Society, 1978.

Firth, Edith, G. (editor), *The Town of York, 1792-1815*, Toronto. The Champlain Society/University of Toronto Press, 1962.

Firth, Edith, G. (editor), *The Town of York, 1815-1834*, Toronto, The Champlain Society/University of Toronto Press, 1966.

Gaspé, Philippe Aubert de, *Mémoires*, Montreal, Granger Frères, 1930.

Godfrey, Charles, *Medicine for Ontario*, Belleville, Mika Publishing, 1979.

Gray, Lillian C., "The Legend of Wolfe's Duelling Pistols," *Atlantic Advocate*, March 1977.

Guest, Harry H., "Upper Canada's First Political Party," *Ontario History*, December 1962.

Hannay, James, *History of New Brunswick*, Saint John, John A. Bowes, 1909.

Hibbert, C., *Wolfe in Canada*, London, Longmans, 1959.

Holt, C.A., "Just a Question of Your Honour and How to Regain It," *Atlantic Advocate*, April 1969.

Hunter, A.F., "The Probated Wills of Men Prominent in the Public Affairs of Upper Canada," *Ontario Historical Society Papers and Records*, Volume XXIII (1926).

Irvine, George, *Correspondence, etc. Concerning a Recent Difficulty Between Messrs Irvine and Pope*, Quebec, Bureau and Marcotte, 1854.

Kiernan, V.G., *The Duel in European History: Honour and the Reign of Aristocracy*, Oxford, Oxford University Press, 1988.

Klinck, Carl F., and Talman, James J., *The Journal of Major John Norton*, Toronto, The Champlain Society/University of Toronto Press, 1970.

Lawrence, Joseph W., "The Judges of New Brunswick and Their Times," (Alfred Stockton and William O. Raymond, editors), supplements in *Acadiensis, 1905-1907*.

Lawrence, Joseph W., *Footprints or Incidents in Early History of New Brunswick*, Saint John, J.A. McMillan, 1883.

Lighthall, W.D., *An Account of the Battle of Châteauguay*, Montreal, Drysdale, 1889.

Lower, A.R.M., "Three Letters of William Osgoode, First Chief Justice of Upper Canada," *Ontario History*, Summer 1965.

McLintock, A.H. (editor), *An Encyclopedia of New Zealand*, Wellington, R.E. Owen, 1966.

McNutt, W.S., *New Brunswick, a History, 1784-1867*, Toronto, Macmillan, 1963.

McRae, R.B., *Lost Amid the Fogs: Sketches of Life in Newfoundland*, Sampson, Low, Son and Martin, 1869.

Marshall, Douglas, "You're a Damn Lying Scoundrel," *Macleans*, June 18, 1966.

Massicotte, E.Z., "Duels et coups de l'épée à Montréal sous le régime français," *Bulletin des recherches historiques*, Volume XXI (1915).

Massicotte, E.Z., "Les familles Sabrevois, Sabrevois de Sermonville, et Sabrevois de Bleury," *Bulletin des recherches historiques*, Volume XXXI (1925).

Masson, L.R., *Les Bourgeois de la Compagnie du nord-ouest*, Quebec, A. Côté et cie, 1890.

Middleton, Jesse Edgar (editor), "The Diary of Joseph Willcocks," *The Province of Ontario: A History*, Toronto, Dominion Publishing Company, 1927 (2 volumes).

Millingen, J.D., *The History of Duelling, Including Narratives of the Most Remarkable Personal Encounters That Have Taken Place From the Earliest Period to the Present Time* (2 volumes), London, Richard Bentley, 1841.

Morgan, Cecilia, "'In Search of the Phantom Misnamed Honour': Duelling in Upper Canada," *Canadian Historical Review*, Volume 76, No.4 (December 1995).

Morrice, Father A.G., *Dictionnaire historique des canadiens et des métis français de l'Ouest*, Montreal, Granger Frères, 1908.

Moss, Robert, "The Last Duel in Newfoundland," *The Book of Newfoundland* (Joseph R. Smallwood, editor), Volume IV, St. John's, Newfoundland Book Publishers, 1967.

O'Neil, Paul, *The Oldest City: The Story of St. John's, Newfoundland*, Erin, Press Porcepic, 1975.

Ormsby, William (editor), *Crisis in the Canada, 1838-1839: The Grey Journals and Letters*, Toronto, Macmillan, 1964.

Ouellet, Fernand (editor) "Correspondance de Joseph Papineau, 1793-1840," *Rapport de l'Archiviste de la Province de Québec, 1953-55*, Quebec, Queen's Printer, 1955.

Patterson, George, *More Studies in Nova Scotia History*, Halifax, The Imperial Publishing Company, 1941.

Phalen, Josephine, "A Duel on the Island," *Ontario History*, Volume LXIX, December 1977.

Raymond, William O. (editor), *Winslow Papers, A.D. 1776-1826*, Boston, Gregg Press, 1972.

Riddell, William Renwick, "The Duel in Upper Canada," *The Canadian Times*, Volume 35 (1915).

Riddell, William Renwick, "Another Duel in Early Upper Canada," *The Canadian Law Times*, Volume 36 (1916).

Riddell, William Renwick, "The First Attorney-General of Upper Canada – John White (1792-1800)," *Ontario Historical Society Papers and Records*, Volume XXIII (1926).

Riddell, William Renwick, *The Life of John Graves Simcoe*, Toronto, McClelland and Stewart, 1926.

Roberts, Theodore Goodrich, "The Street-Wetmore Duel," *Loyalists*, (Part One), Toronto, n.p., n.d..

Roy, P.G., "Le duel sous le régime français, *Bulletin des recherches historiques*, Volume XIII (1907).

Sage, Walter N., *Sir James Douglas and British Columbia*, Toronto University of Toronto Press, 1930.

Senior, Elinor Kyte, *British Regulars in Montreal: An Imperial Garrison, 1832-1854*, Montreal, McGill-Queen's University Press, 1981.

Shanks, Connie, "The Day They Duelled to the Death," Saint John *Telegraph-Journal*, August 16, 1980.

Shortt, Edward, *The Memorable Duel at Perth*, Perth, The Perth Museum, 1970.

Smith, Mary Larratt Smith, *Young Mr. Smith in Upper Canada*, Toronto, University of Toronto Press, 1980.

Stanley, George F.G., "James Glenie: A Study of Early Colonial Radicalism," *Collections of the Nova Scotia Historical Society*, Volume 25 (1942).

Sweeney, Alistair, *George-Etienne Cartier: A Biography*, Toronto, McClelland and Stewart, 1976.

Tasse, Joseph, *Les Canadiens de l'Ouest*, Montreal, Cie d'Imprimerie Canadienne, 1878.

Taylor, Rev. W., *A Testimony Against Duelling: A Sermon Preached in the United Session Church, Montreal, August 15, 1838*, Montreal, Campbell and Becket, 1838.

Thompson, Austin Seton, *Jarvis Street: A Story of Triumph and Tragedy*, Toronto, Personal Library Publishers, 1980.

Thwaites, Reuben Gold (editor), *The Jesuit Relations and Allied Documents*, New York, Pageant, 1959.

Truman, Benjamin C., *The Field of Honour: Being a Complete and Comprehensive History of Duelling in All Countries*, New York, Fords, Howard, and Hurlbert, 1884.

Walker, Harry J. and Olive, *Carleton Saga*, Ottawa, Runge Press, 1968.

Wohler, J. Patrick, *Charles de Salaberry, Soldier of the Empire, Defender of Quebec*, Toronto, Dundurn Press, 1984.

# Index